I0549311

Also from Indigo Sea Press
Novels by Paul Stam

The Telephone Killer
Body on the Church Steps

indigoseapress.com

Murder Sets Sail

By

Paul J. Stam

Stiletto Books
Published by Indigo Sea Press
Winston-Salem

Stiletto Books
Indigo Sea Press
302 Ricks Drive
Winston-Salem, NC 27103

This book is a work of fiction. Names, characters, locations and events are either a product of the author's imagination, fictitious or used fictitiously. Any resemblance to any event, locale or person, living or dead, is purely coincidental.

First Stiletto Books edition published
January, 2016
Stiletto Books, Moon Sailor and all production design are trademarks of Indigo Sea Press, used under license.

For information regarding bulk purchases of this book, digital purchase and special discounts, please contact the publisher at
indigoseapress.com

Cover design by Stacy Castanedo

Manufactured in the United States of America
ISBN 978-1-63066-376-6

This is a true story except for the parts that aren't.

To all storytellers everywhere who

deliver us from the mundane.

CHAPTER ONE

It was the kind of day the Hawaii Visitors Bureau wanted every tourist to believe was every day. After three days of wet-season rains, all the lush growth had a new brilliance and sparkle. The skies were the clearest blue with billows of white clouds settled comfortably along the tops of the Ko`olau Mountains. In Waikiki the steadily blowing trade winds rattled the fronds of the towering palms while tugging playfully at towels wrapped around the hips of bikini clad girls.

On Saratoga Road, Chris Jamison stepped out of the air-conditioned coolness of the Waikiki Post office into the brightness of the mid-morning sun. Sorting through all the advertising stuffed in his mailbox he had found two letters. One letter was from his bank. There was no need to open that one. He knew as well as they did how low his bank account was. The second was addressed to Mr. Christian Jamison. He knew without checking the return address it was from his sister. She was the only one who always addressed him by his full first name.

He opened the envelope and read the letter as he walked along the Fort DeRussy side of Saratoga Road. The first line was a quiet but firm reprimand, "We haven't heard from you for several months. Write!" After that there was a lot of family gossip crowded into the two sides of the one page letter, but the main purpose of the letter was to remind Chris April 4, would be his parents thirtieth wedding anniversary and he should, if at all possible, try to be there.

That was out of the question. He had no desire to go back to Seattle, and certainly not for his parents' anniversary. It was not that he disliked them; in fact, he loved them very much, which was one of the reasons he couldn't go back. He had nothing in common with them. He considered their life staid and boring and from their point of view, his life was a total waste. His going home would not make things more pleasant for anyone. The whole time he was there they would be trying to straighten him out and when he left again unchanged, they would just be that much more deeply disappointed in him. Besides, he didn't have enough money to fly to another island, let alone to Seattle.

At Kalia Street Chris cut through Fort DeRussy to the beach. Even walking along with the sand pushing up around his bare feet, he could not get away from the fact that things were pretty desperate. He knew there was enough money in his account to cover the automatic payment for next month's slip fees. Something had to come in soon, or he might lose the slip the *AHWANAH* had been in for more than ten years and have to go to an anchorage. He'd been promised a job installing a new engine for Mel Harrigan, but the engine was sitting somewhere on the coast and no one seemed to know when it would arrive. Bill Whipple had talked to Chris about painting his boat and then decided to do it himself. He could sure use the money from those jobs right now, but more than anything else he wanted to go sailing. What he really wanted was a cruise, a week around the islands, or best of all, someone who was willing to charter his boat for a two or three month cruise to the South Pacific and back.

A week ago Chris thought he had another charter. Some guy for LA named Will Maxwell seemed really interested. Spent the whole afternoon talking about a charter and then the next day he saw the guy getting into a taxi with his luggage in front of the Ilikai Hotel and Chris knew he was headed for the airport.

Along the beach he circled around the Hilton Lagoon to the yacht harbor. Aboard the *AHWANAH* he slid into the booth like table and turned to take down a large volume of ***Shakespeare's Complete Works***. He riffled the pages until he came to King Lear, Act II, Scene 2, where his last remaining bills were hidden. He spread the bills on the table, clamped the book shut and put it back on the shelf right next to ***Ashley's Book of Knots***. He'd had both those books since he was thirteen. Shakespeare was a gift from his father. He bought ***Ashley's*** with money he earned mowing lawns. With what he had in his wallet and the bills on the table he had enough for another month's slip fees with $53.62 left over. He decided to put all but $50.00 in the bank and then at least his slip fee would be covered for the next two months.

He put all the money in his wallet and went up on deck and sat in the shade of the awning over the cockpit. Looking out past the breakwater to the ocean he decided things really weren't so terrible. Being at the anchorage could be very pleasant. He certainly wasn't going to go hungry. He had enough canned and dried food aboard to last three people four months. It wasn't as good as eating fresh food, but he wasn't going to starve. The first thing he would do, starting that evening, was make the rounds of the bars again reminding the bartenders that if any of the tourists asked what there was to do that was different, he had a boat for charter.

CHAPTER TWO

George Costellos was headed toward what his father called the Cottage, though it was larger than most of the other houses along that stretch of the beach. Three miles up the highway was a much larger, more opulent house everyone in the family referred to as the Beach House.

The Cottage was his father's, and now George's, office away from the office. His mother, his wife, his three sisters and his children did not know about the Cottage. Of the four homes his father owned; the house in Palm Springs, the home in Bel-Air, the Beach House and the Cottage, the last was George's favorite.

He rolled up to the security gate of the exclusive community and the guard waved him through. He turned into the driveway of the Cottage. His father's car and Susanne's car were parked in the garage. Larry Anderson's Valiant was parked in the driveway behind his father's car. George was surprised that Larry was already there. George parked his car next to Susanne's car and hit the remote that closed the garage door.

He went through the side door and in the kitchen was met by Susanne, a tall brunette wearing a short, red, mini-skirt and ruffled blouse. She was laying out cold cuts and cheese on a platter. She turned as he came in and smiled at him. "Good morning, Mr. Costellos."

"Hello, Susanne. How's things?" He said on his way through to the living room.

"Fine, sir. A drink?"

"Coke, please."

"Yes, sir," she said knowing that would be his answer. The only thing she had ever known him to drink was Coca-Cola and lime juice. She took down the tall glass, filled it with ice, squeezed the juice of two limes over the ice and poured in the coke. She brought it in setting it on the coffee table in front of him.

"Bring in the food and stuff and then take a walk along the beach or something," Appy said.

"Yes, sir." She brought in the tray of food, plates, napkins and silver and set them on the coffee table. She looked around to see everyone's glasses were sufficiently full and then disappeared into a bedroom. She came out a few minutes later wearing a bikini and carrying a beach bag and towel. The three men watched her as she crossed the living room, went through the sliding glass doors and across the redwood deck to the beach.

"Lovely girl," Appy sighed and then leaned his head of wavy, gray hair back against the top cushion of the high-back chair and closed his eyes. An outsider might have thought Apistolos Costellos was napping, but the other two men knew he was wide-awake and would be concentrating on every word. He closed his eyes to block out any distractions.

“Well, what did you find?” George asked leaning back into the corner of the couch. There was an eager sparkle in his dark eyes as he looked at Larry.

Larry leaned forward, a strand of blond hair falling across his forehead. “There are two possibilities but the best one is a James Harris. He’s a Limey. About thirty, thirty-one I would guess. Couldn’t check for a police record so can’t say about that. He sailed from England to Australia, stopping along the way, picking up crews as he went—”

“How come all his crews leave him?” George asked interrupting him.

“As far as I could find out it’s because they’ve gone as far as they wanted to go. I talked to the two who sailed with him from Down Under who thought he was great, but they just want to go back home to Australia and Harris wants to go to Hawaii. He’s working in a shipyard right now. Getting a little tired of it. He’d quit the job in a minute if anyone would come along willing to pay for stores. The name of the boat is the *ROMSEY*. Says it’s the name of the town in England where he was born.

“What kind of boat is it?”

“Wooden. Thirty-eight foot, double-ended ketch. European built. Looks real good.”

“Were you aboard it?”

“Yeah. He invited me aboard one evening. He’s a real friendly, easy-going type. Trusts everybody.”

“Where is he moored?”

“He’s at an anchorage mixed in with some Hong Kong sampans.”

"Anything more you want to tell me?" George asked.

"You told me to find you a sailboat. You didn't tell me what you wanted it for so I guess there's nothing more to tell."

"OK, Larry, you've done a bit of sailing in your day. Would you be feel good about an extended; twenty, thirty day cruise aboard this *ROMSEY*?"

"Oh, yeah, it's a great boat."

"Glad to hear it. You've done a good job, Larry," George said standing and Larry understood the discussions were over.

"If there's nothing else I'll be on my way. Good bye, Mr. Costellos."

The old man raised one hand, waved a little and Larry headed for the door.

George walked him to the door. "Where are you going to be?" George asked. "I may want to get in touch with you later."

"I'll stop at Tony's for a while. If I'm not there, I'll be at home."

"Fine. I'll want to get ahold of you as soon as Max arrives. Be sure your cell is on," he said and stood in the door watching as Larry walked to his car and drove away.

"Are you sending Larry for the Hong Kong end of it," Appy asked when George returned.

"I was planning on sending Max. He knows the ropes and is one hell of a navigator. Once they leave Hong Kong I don't want anyone using cell phones or GPS. Every cell phone transmission and every use of the Global Positioning Satellite is recorded.

The old man nodded. "Who are you sending with him?"

"I thought I'd let him choose who he wanted to take. They are going to have to spend a lot of time together. It should be someone he gets along well with. My guess is he will choose Larry. They've been friends a long time."

"Where's Max now?"

"He called me from Seattle this morning," George said looking at his watch. "His plane should be landing just about now. He's coming over as soon as he arrives."

"Who's going to Honolulu?"

"I'm going. I'm taking Steve with me." George waited for his father's objections.

Appy was quiet for a moment and then asked, "Why?"

"Because I thought up the plan. I put the whole thing together and I'm the best man for the job. It is bringing it into the States that's going to be tricky and, frankly, I'm the only one I trust with that."

"Why?" the old man said again in exactly the same tone as though his son hadn't said anything.

George took a swallow of Coke and turned toward his father, his hands in front of his chest imploring the old man. "Look, Papa. Ever since your heart attack two years ago certain people have been thinking. They haven't started talking too much yet, but I can see them thinking. They're thinking you may not live much longer. I don't like to talk like this, Papa. I hope you live to be a hundred, but they are wondering if they can take over after you are gone. Mark Heathly is lining people up to take over. Some people, Max for one, told me that Heathly has approached him. Nothing definite, but feeling him out. They're wondering why I should start at the top just giving orders. By the time I'm through with this project not a man out there will be able to say I never made a delivery, or he made a bigger one."

"You think you have to prove something?"

"Not to myself. But I'm going to show them there isn't anything they can do I can't do better. And more than anything else, I'm putting them on notice they had better not try to mess around with me."

The old man nodded slowly. "Be careful, Sonny."

"I will, Papa. Believe me, I will."

They heard a car pull up outside, a door slam and George went to the front door. He opened the door just as Max was reaching for the bell. "Hello, Max. How did it go?"

"Great! Just great! I found a guy with a boat made to order for us."

"Come in and tell us all about it," George said closing the door behind him and leading the way into the living room.

"How are you, Mr. Costellos?" Max asked sitting down at the far end of the couch.

"Just fine, thank you," Appy said and leaned his head back against the cushion.

George sat down at the opposite end of the couch, facing Max. "The guy's name is Chris Jamison," Max said. "He was born in Seattle. Jamison's father is a retired high-school principal. His uncle was a shipwright. After Jamison left school he went to work with his uncle. Jamison has no record at all in either Seattle or Honolulu.

"He's been in Honolulu for ten years or more. Before that he was cruising all over the Pacific. He keeps alive by doing odd jobs on boats and chartering his boat. Not officially, because that would involve all kinds of licenses, Coast Guard certification and taxes. But everybody knows he does it. Mostly around the islands, but he has been chartered for as much as three months at a time so he won't be suspicious of someone wanting to charter him for more than a couple of weeks. There were a couple of others I checked into but they didn't want to leave Hawaiian waters.

"How did you find out about this Jamison?"

"From a bartender. I kept asking around and a bartender in the Chart House, right close to the harbor, told me about Jamison. They're friends, I guess."

"Did you see Jamison himself?"

"Oh, sure. Made like I was interested in chartering his boat. Spent four hours or more with him. Showed me all around his boat. Between him and the bartender I got the impression he's pretty desperate for money right now. And he keeps the boat always ready to go, completely stocked with stores at all times."

"What does he charge?"

"Six hundred a day, Four thousand a week, or ten thousand a month for up to six people."

George pursed his lips and nodded a little.

"Believe me, George, he's the best route to go. Actually it's the only route. They don't have that many boats over there. The amount of boats in the Ala Wai wouldn't even be noticed in Del Rey."

"I believe you, Max. I believe you. What's the boat like?"

"Beautiful, George. You'll love it. Forty-two foot cutter. Clipper bow. Jamison and his uncle built it themselves. Nothing but the best materials and workmanship like you don't see any more. It'll sleep seven if you count the dinette that can be made into two berths. Diesel Volvo engine. Eighty gallons of fuel and a hundred and twenty of water."

Susanne came up the steps, looked through the door, saw they were still talking and went back down. A few minutes later they heard her come through the back door and go into one of the bathrooms. When she came out George called, "Hey, Sue, as long as you're there, bring me another Coke, will you—You want something, Max?"

"Yeah, a beer would be nice."

"Papa?" George asked turning toward his father who raised a hand and waved it a little, "And a beer for Max," he called over his shoulder.

She served them and then left going back down to the beach. "What's the name of the boat?" George asked when she left.

"The *AHWANAH*." Max said and then spelled it. "A, H, W, A, N, A, H."

"*AHWANAH*," George repeated. What is that a Hawaiian word or something?"

"Not as far as I know. I guess when this Jamison guy and his uncle were building the boat people would ask why they were doing it and the old man's answer was, "Cuz ah wan ah."

George leaned forward with his elbows on his knees, his hands clasped in front of him. "Max," he said, "How would you like to go sailing?"

Max smiled. "I was hoping I'd be included in this operation, whatever it is."

"Did you know Larry was in Hong Kong?"

"I knew he was out of town, I didn't know where he was."

"And he didn't know where you were. I didn't want anybody to know any more than was necessary. I still don't. The fewer people know, the less talk there will be. The less talk there is, the less chance of anyone saying anything they shouldn't to someone who shouldn't know anything about it. But I'll tell you this much now that you are in it. We are going to bring in the biggest one-time shipment this organization has ever seen. I'll give you all the details tomorrow."

He got up and went into the den and came back with a large general chart of the Pacific. "Larry located a boat in Hong Kong. An Englishman is looking for a crew to help him sail to Hawaii. I want you to take the Hong Kong boat. I'll take the Jamison boat. You pick up the stuff in Hong Kong and meet me right here." He jabbed his finger down in the middle of the chart and then looked more closely to where his finger had landed. "There isn't anything within seven, eight hundred miles of here," he said pointing to Midway to the east, Wake Island to the south, and Marcus Island to the west. "After you and the stuff transfer to my boat we sink the other one. That way if anyone in Hong Kong is trying to collect an informer's fee, the boat they are looking for won't be anywhere around.

"Now you shouldn't have any trouble with the Englishman. James Harris is his name. He's going to be sailing generally the same direction you want to go. If you have to kill him once you clear Hong Kong, well—" he paused spreading his hands, "but you may want to keep him around until we meet just to stand watches and such."

He paused for a moment counting off the longitudes lines. "You've got about a three thousand-mile-trip. The winds aren't the best going that direction this time of year, so let's give you forty-five days to the rendezvous. Let's say five to seven days to get everything lined-up and we'll aim to meet on March the fifteenth. I don't have as long a trip but I have to make arrangements in Honolulu for getting it ashore. If either one of us gets to the rendezvous ahead of time, sail around up here and then head back down for the meeting. If for any reason either one of us is late, we'll wait until the other one gets there. I'm taking Steve Margolis with me. Who do you want to go with you?"

Max looked at the open beams of the ceiling for a moment and then answered, "Larry, I guess. Since he's already been to Hong Kong."

"Good choice," George said standing up. "Now the first thing you want to do—" he paused, "Is your passport in order?"

"Oh, yes."

"Good. Pick up Larry. He's at Tony's Bar. Get down to the consulate for your visas. Larry tells me they can give it to you while you wait. I don't know if he needs another one or not, but take him along anyway just in case he needs it stamped for reentry or something. Make your flight reservations. Pay for everything from now on in cash," he said holding out an envelope filled with money. "I don't want any kind of trail. Be sure Larry knows that. You're in charge of the Hong Kong end of things. If you need money when you're there, World Trading is authorized to give you whatever you ask for. Take Larry's credit cards away from him if you have to and both of you be here at ten tomorrow morning. Steve will be here then too. We'll go over the final details then."

CHAPTER THREE

Myra Jennings was just straightening up from putting a sheet of cookies in the oven when George let himself in. She was wearing a print dress under her apron and there were little beads of perspiration on her forehead just below the line of blond hair. She pushed a strand of wavy, blond hair away from in front of her blue eyes, "I wasn't expecting you. I look a mess. I was just making a batch of cookies," she said taking off her apron.

He put his arms around her and kissed her playfully on the nose. "You look beautiful," he said and meant it.

"Do you want a drink?"

"Yeah," he said going into the living room while she turned to get the Coke and limes out of the refrigerator. "How would you like to go to Hawaii?" he called from the living room.

"I'd love to."

"Well, that's where we're off to. Call Ricky and tell him I need passports for George and Myra Harris and Steve Harris." He wondered for an instant why he had chosen the name "Harris" and then remembered it was the name of the Limey with the Hong Kong boat. "I'll send the photos over by messenger this afternoon. Tell him I want those passports by tomorrow."

"Do we need passports for Hawaii?" she asked knowing full well they didn't, which meant this was not the holiday she had thought when he asked if she wanted to go to Hawaii. She also knew that having agreed to go and having been told to arrange for the false passports she couldn't back out.

"Well, we might go to Tahiti too. Call some travel agent close by that doesn't know us and have them make first class reservations arriving in Honolulu around noon on Wednesday. The airline doesn't matter."

"You're not taking the company jet?"

"No, I don't want anyone in the company to know I'm gone. Leave the return flight open. If they ask for a credit card number tell them you never give the number out over the phone. Also have them reserve a two-bedroom suite, top floor, for us at the Hawaii Prince.

Tell them to call back when they have it confirmed and you'll be by to pay for everything and pick up the tickets when you hear from them."

He took a sip of his drink and leaned back in his chair while she went to the phone to do as she was instructed. He stood up a moment later and said, "I'll go and get some money, I'll be back in half an hour." He kissed her and left the apartment.

* * *

As he rode along on his way to get the money he thought, not for the first time, that Myra knew more about him than any other living soul, and most unfortunately, did not have the immunity of a wife who could not be forced to testify against her husband. George was married when he was twenty-five to the daughter of a circuit court judge. His three sisters had all married before him and moved into comfortable homes with their husbands all of whom were employed, in one capacity or another, as a vice-president of one of the legitimate enterprises Appy owned. That left George free to control the drug business. When George married he and Margaret moved into one half of the enormous Bel-Air house.

Many times when he was first married he would have liked to have been able to confided in his wife, but that was out of the question. There had been many women at the Cottage before and after his marriage, but Margaret had never been one of them. She knew nothing about the Cottage, or the Organization. George could always talk to his father, but he had always wanted someone he could confide in, who he could use as a sounding board when he was concerned or worried about something.

Eight months after he was married he met Myra. On the first date he took her sailing. He liked her. When, after two months of dating, he told her he was married she had shrugged a shoulder and said, "Who isn't?" They saw a lot of each other and little by little he started confiding in her. A year after they met he established her in a very comfortable apartment in Marina Del Rey. He was faithful to neither his wife nor his mistress, but Myra was the one to whom he could talk, the one to whom he could brag about his successes, the one he trusted for little errands he couldn't trust to anyone else.

On the way to getting the money to finance the biggest operation of his life he thought Myra might someday turn out to be a liability. It was not that he did not trust her, but with enough threats and pressure she might be forced to inform on him. The only way to stay on top in this business was to eliminate possible dangers before they became a reality. He regretted what would have to be done. He genuinely liked the girl, but he had no alternative. He would have it taken care of after he got back. After all, he was going to be at sea for a long time with no other woman around and she certainly couldn't be any danger to him out there. Yes, it could wait until their return.

* * *

Sitting in her apartment after George returned and gave her the money to pay the travel agent, Myra knew any chance of ever having a real acting career had come to an end. Acting was all she had ever really wanted to do. She was twenty-one when she graduated from the University of Minnesota with an impressive list of credits from the University Theater, the Showboat Theater, educational television productions, various community theaters and local television commercials. Upon graduation she auditioned successfully at the prestigious Tyrone Guthrie Theater. Her parents, discovering she was employed in a vocation they considered questionable if not displeasing to God, wrote and called her constantly begging her to do something worthwhile with her life. She let the machine screen all her calls so she never actually talked to them. No matter how often she changed her phone, even getting a number that was unlisted, they somehow managed to find her number and start calling again. They always ended their messages with, "We're praying for you, Darling," which she highly resented. She didn't need, or want, them praying for her. After a year with the Guthrie she left for California hoping to establish herself beyond her parents' reach.

She had been in California a year when she met George Costellos. Before meeting George she'd had hardly enough small parts to keep her fed and clothed. She was on the verge of contacting the Guthrie Theater when George came into her life.

George Costellos was handsome, charming, kind and very rich. He took her sailing on his yacht. He took her to the very best restaurants, concerts, opera and theaters. He had influence. In the first three weeks he got her small parts in four television shows.

After a month of dating two or three times a week he invited her to go to Las Vegas with him and she accepted knowing all that invitation implied. The combination of dating George, the glamour of meeting the show people he knew, and money from her TV work made her forget about returning to Minneapolis.

After the Las Vegas weekend every date ended up at an apartment he had in Marina Del Rey. Three months later he suggested she move in there permanently. She accepted. She was still free to pursue her acting, but now that she had economic security, she hounded her agent less and less, and even turned down jobs she thought would not advance her career.

When George first started telling Myra about his criminal activities, she listened seriously, but privately thought them just fantasies. Everybody had fantasies. The fat person fantasized about being thin. The ugly girl fantasized about being beautiful. The cripple fantasized about being an athlete. Wasn't it possible a respected, secure, community pillar like George Costellos would fantasize about doing dangerous and criminal things? At first she was rather amused that, in a juvenile way, he was trying to impress her with the tales of his activities. The realization his stories were true, came to her slowly, and she adjusted to it slowly. At first she even thought there was something romantic about being a criminal, but she knew crime was not romantic. As she began to know the truth, she kept telling herself she didn't really know anything for certain, even though there were times when she did things that in the light of the law made her an accomplice. After she had gotten the tickets and made all the arrangements he told her what the trip to Hawaii was all about. She couldn't hide the truth from herself any more. Sitting in his apartment now, she knew she had finally been caught up in it. She knew her father would have said, "Whatsoever a man sows, that shall he also reap." There was nothing she could do. She couldn't go to the police. They would laugh at her if she suggested a Costellos was involved in anything criminal. She also knew with his connections he was certain to find out and when he did he would have her "taken care of." She wished she could somehow put a stop to the Hawaii operation, but she had no idea how she could do that.

CHAPTER FOUR

The afternoon flight was right on time. In a window seat in the first class section, Myra Jenkins looked out of the window at her first view of green mountain islands with ribbons of white sand beaches. Looking down she was able to forget temporarily her fears of the past week.

That morning a limousine from a service, rather than one of the company limousines, took the three of them to the airport. They used their new passports, already stamped with Tahiti visas, for identification. George had been a little nervous with all the security checks that someone might recognize him before he got away. Even boarding the plane he paused for a moment to look around the first class compartment to see if there was anyone on board who might know him before going ahead of her to their seats. It was not till they were off the ground that he relaxed.

Now with the runway passing beneath her window Myra could feel his reserve and caution returning. They stayed in their seats after the plane stopped in order to be the last ones off the plane. In the terminal he gave Steve the ticket stubs instructing him to call on the cell phone when the luggage was in the taxi. George had decided to take his chances with a taxi rather than reserving a limousine in advance as Steve had suggested. "Less conspicuous," he had said.

Standing at the rail of the lanai of their sitting room she could see all the way from Diamond Head to Pearl Harbor. Beyond that point details became indistinct because of the distance, but the mountains of the Waianae Range stood out clearly without a trace of smog. Above her puffs of clouds drifted across the clear blue sky. Straight ahead of her was the yacht harbor and a yacht that was destined to be sunk and its owner killed. A couple of sailboats glided across the water in the distance and beyond them there was a tug with two barges in tow.

George came up behind her and said, "Come on, Baby, get us unpacked."

She went into the larger of the two bedrooms and started putting their clothes in the closets and dresser. In the bottom of his suitcase there was a folded, blue canvas duffel bag and under that yellow rain gear that matched exactly what he had given her. Those items reminded her again she was really part of a plan to kill a man.

In the sitting room George looked through the cabinets over the wet bar, opened the refrigerator and then slammed the door shut and called, "Hey Steve, call down and have them send up some limes." He went over and sat down on the couch and opened up the paper he had picked up in the lobby.

The limes arrived just as she finished unpacking and he said, "Fix me a drink, will you, Baby."

She fixed his drink and brought it to him. He took a sip and set the glass on the end table and reached into his jacket pocket for a cigar. He lighted it then set it in the ashtray. He leaned over to pull his money clip from his left-hand pants pocket and peeled off five $100 bills. "I have some calls to make, Baby. Why don't you go to that shopping center we passed just before we got here; just back over the bridge, and get yourself a couple of bikinis, or something. Some island type clothes to put on that luscious bod of yours. And while you're there pick me up a couple of aloha shirts and a wide brimmed straw hat."

"A hat?" she exclaimed. "I've never seen you wear a hat."

"That's just it, Baby, neither has anyone else."

"OK," she said taking the bills he held out to her. "What's your hat size?"

"Seven and an eighth, I think. When you get back we'll take a little walk around the yacht harbor."

She left the hotel walking alongside the boat yard and across the bridge over the Ala Wai Canal to the shopping center. She walked slowly along the mall, pausing to look in store windows and stopping to watch the fish in the mall pools. She sat down on the edge of the lowest pool and watched the gold, silver, black, orange, yellow, and speckled Japanese koi moving lazily through the water, rising to the surface with open, round, wide mouths, sliding their smooth, fat bodies along the immersed hands of children. *What easy, uncomplicated lives you have. You have nothing to do but swim back and forth and be admired. To whom do you owe loyalties? Is it to the mother who laid the eggs and the father who fertilized them? To the beings who keep you confined and safe in clear water pools? To the one who feeds you every day? But you don't have to worry about those kinds of things, do you?*

To whom did she owe loyalty; to her parents who had done what they could to keep her from following her dream of an acting career? George had stopped her acting. He had never said she should give up acting; he had just made it so easy to give up trying. He had given her everything she had asked for and a lot more. He was a generous provider, and had even arranged for some minor TV appearance. However, from something her agent had once said, she had the feeling George had also made sure she had not gotten any major breaks. He was a charming companion and because of him she was now financially secure. She should have been content and satisfied, but she wasn't.

She thought it was her parents and her upbringing that made her discontented with her situation. There was always inside of her something that made her uncomfortable with George's lack of morals and scruples. She blamed her parents for that. She wished in a way she could be as lacking in principle as George was, and yet at the same time she was glad she wasn't like him. She didn't owe anything to the poor slob whose boat they were going to use. What had he ever done for her? Nothing! That was just it. He had not done anything for her, but nor had he ever done anything against her. He was an innocent. He didn't have any idea of what was happening. He was a poor fish about to bite on the lure that would raise him out of his water to his death. She had to warn him not to take the bait. If she could do that he would be saved and maybe the whole operation would fail. Then she would not be part of what she knew was going to end in at least one death, maybe more. If only George had not insisted she come along. Could she have gone on pretending she didn't know anything?

She walked the length of the mall and back, and then knowing George would not want her back too soon, she stopped in the Mariposa Restaurant in Neiman Marcus for a cup of coffee and a piece of pie. An hour later she went to the men's department. There was a wide variety of hats to choose from; straw safari hats with leopard skin bands, straw hats with one side of the brim pinned up like Australian campaign hats, straw hats from Tonga and Taiwan, and white Panamas with the edge of the brim rolled back all the way around. That would be more his style. She bought three shirts and the hat and went back to their rooms. When she walked in George was standing at the open glass door scanning the yacht harbor with binoculars. “Hi, Baby, What did you get yourself?” he asked handing Steve the binoculars.

“I didn’t see anything I really liked, but I got you some things,” she said taking the packages into their bedroom. “Why don’t you try them on so I can take back anything you don’t like?”

He followed her into the bedroom trying on each shirt as she handed it to him. “That’ll do,” he said after each one and she took it from him taking the tags off and hanging each in the closet. He kept the last one and put on the hat and a pair of dark glasses and said, “Well, how does it look?”

“It’s not the George Costellos I’m used to seeing.”

“That’s just the point. I’m not George Costellos anymore. Don’t use that name again. From now on until we get back to L.A. I’m George Harris. Don’t you forget it!”

“I won’t. Here let me take the tags off that shirt and hat.” She smiled, trying to mitigate the threat underlying his last words.

He turned and examined himself in the mirror. He thought anyone passing him on the street who knew him might think he looked familiar, but they would be a couple of blocks away before they would say to themselves, “Gee, that guy looks a little like George Costellos.” He turned back to Myra, clapped his hands together and held them that way for a moment. “Tell you what, Baby. Let’s take a walk around the yacht harbor and take a look at that boat of ours. Want to come along, Steve?”

“No thank you, Sir.”

“Better drop that ‘sir’ stuff, Steve. We’re supposed to be brothers. George is what you call me. Remember that. George!”

“Yesss—George,” Steve said catching himself just in time.

They left the hotel walking along the first row of boats, looking at them, but not paying any attention to them. At the end of the row they cut straight across, behind the harbormaster’s office, skipping all the rows in between until they came to the last mole. They started down the second to last row of boats. They paused occasionally looking across to the other side, past the cars parked in the middle of the mole, trying to locate the *AHWANAH*. “There it is,” George said nodding his head toward the other side. They walked a little farther toward the end of the mole and then crossed over heading back to where the *AHWANAH* was tied up. There didn’t seem to be anyone on board and George stopped in front of it, looking critically, holding onto his hat when he leaned back to look up the mast.

He was pleased to see it looked as well maintained as any boat in the place. The hull was white with a royal blue boot top at the water line. The deck was oiled teak and the varnish of the mast, bowsprit, toerail and cabin trim gleamed in the afternoon sun. The cabin top was painted a light blue. The only thing not varnished or painted was the weather-beaten wood figurehead, the head of an old man with long hair and beard that flowed back from the face to separate and flow around the name plaque. The face showed an angry defiance and reminded Myra of pictures she had seen of Moses on Mount Sinai about to throw down the stone tablets, his face angry, his head and beard blown by the storm raging about him.

George started away and Myra fell in beside him. Three slips away he turned and looked back over his shoulder and said, “It’s a beautiful boat all right. Too bad we’ll have to sink it.”

Her heart sank. What really frightened her was that he regretted having to destroy the boat, but not at all the man who owned it. And when she was no longer useful to him, he would get rid of her with no regrets either. She made up her mind in that moment she would have to warn the man who owned that boat. What was the guy’s name; Chris something? She glanced at George fearful he might have read her mind, but he seemed unaware of her. She smiled a little as she reached over and took his hand. The worst thing she could do was give him any reason to be suspicious of her. He turned and looked at her, smiling down at her, and asked, “Do you want to go back to the hotel, or do you want to walk a little more.”

“Oh, let’s walk a little more,” she said afraid sitting around the hotel room she might start worrying again and her face would betray her turmoil. “You promised to show me Waikiki.”

Riding back to the hotel loaded down with the packages of things he had insisted on buying for her she found it hard to reconcile the generous pleasant man she had always known with the emotionless killer. Back at the hotel they found Steve lying on his bed reading a magazine. George waved to him as he walked by on the way to their bedroom. He waited by the door until Myra entered and then closed it behind her. “Come on, Baby, we’ve got two hours till dinner.”

“Not now, George. Steve’ll hear us.”

“Who cares? He’ll hear a lot more when we’re on that little

boat," he said sitting on the edge of the bed slipping off his shoes and unbuttoning his shirt. She turned toward him and raised her arms around her neck to untie the yarn that held up her bikini top knowing how much he enjoyed watching her undress. Up until that day she had enjoyed being watched, as a model in an art class or in private by George. Now she was ashamed of her association with him, but whether she enjoyed it or not, she was an actress and she could act as though she still did. She would do all the things she knew he liked rather than give him any reason to be suspicious.

CHAPTER FIVE

George Costellos moved away from the room service breakfast cart taking his cup of coffee with him. He sat down on the couch setting the coffee cup on the end table next to him and took out one of his cigars. "Hey, Baby, get my wallet for me, will you? It's in the left hand top drawer."

He took time lighting his cigar, took a drag, blew out the smoke and said, "Steve, I want you to make a phone call to Lester Kalama. K, A, L, A, M, A. You got that?" he asked reaching for the wallet Myra held out to him.

"Kalama," Steve repeated.

George took a card out of his wallet and handed it to Steve. This is the phone number. Don't use your cell or a hotel phone. Find a public phone somewhere. Identify yourself as Steve Harris. He should have been notified by now either Steve or George Harris would be contacting him this morning. He'll probably play dumb, and then you say something like, 'John said when I got to town I should look you up and shake your hand.' 'Shake your hand is the code.' Use it anyway that seems right, just work it into a sentence somehow. You got all that?"

"Yeah. Shake your hand."

"Right. Set up a time and place for us to meet him. My guess is he'll send a car around for us."

"OK, George. Any particular time you want to see him?"

"Whatever is convenient for him."

"OK, George," Steve said standing up.

"Give me your cell phone, Steve. You too, Myra," George said holding out a hand toward each of them.

"What do you want them for," Myra asked going to her purse to get her phone.

"So neither of you will use them. From now on no cell phones and no credit cards."

* * *

Steve Margolis gave George his cell and left the room and

headed for the elevators. He was sick and tired of being ordered around by George Costellos, had been tired of it for years. Taking orders from the old man in the old days was one thing, but the old man wasn't giving them anymore, and taking orders from his punk kid was something else. For almost six years he had kept his feelings to himself, supporting George because of the old man, until he was considered one of George's trusted ones. But it was hard to tell just how far George trusted anyone. George never told anyone everything. Like this meeting with Kalama, not telling him anything about it until the last minute. That was like George. Probably the only person George trusted completely was his father.

He knew he wasn't going to go any higher in the organization with the kid taking over. But why should George take over? Up to now he was there because his father was behind him. He hadn't really proved himself yet and Appy was getting old. He'd had one heart attack already. He could go at any time. The top place would go to whoever could take it. Maybe George could hold it, maybe not. Steve didn't owe Appy, or George, anything. If anything, they owed him. If it weren't for him Appy wouldn't be where he was now. Maybe now was the time to make his move, one jump ahead of everybody else.

Walking to the pay phone he had seen in a convenience store the night before, Steve wondered who Kalama was. It was like George not to tell him anything. Well he'd know soon enough. Maybe Kalama was his man, maybe not. He'd know within a few minutes after meeting him how committed Kalama was to George and Appy. He dropped the money in the slot and dialed the number. It rang three times before a woman's voice answered. "Hello."

"This is Steve Harris. I'd like to speak to Mr. Kalama please. I believe he's expecting my call."

"One moment please." He heard the click of the hold button being pushed. He was beginning to think she had hung up on him when she said, "Mr. Harris?"

"Yes."

"Mr. Kalama isn't here right now. You can reach him at 923-9972."

"Thank you," he said repeating the number over and over to himself while he dug in his pocket for more change. He dialed the number. A man's voice answered. "Mr. Kalama?" Steve asked.

"Who calls, please?"

"Mr. Harris. Mr. Kalama is expecting my call."

The phone went dead again and a moment later there was a click and a voice said, "Kalama."

"Mr. Kalama, my name is Steve Harris—"

"Do I know you, Mr. Harris?" Kalama said interrupting him.

"No, sir, but I've heard so much about you I decided if I ever go to Honolulu I wanted to meet you and shake your hand."

"I see. Where are you staying?"

"The Hawaii Prince."

"Very well, I'll send a car for you. It will be there in half an hour," he said and hung up. Steve stood there for a moment longer not believing there was nothing more to be said. Walking back to the hotel he decided Lester Kalama either didn't know who they were, or didn't give a damn about the Costellos. If it was the latter maybe he and Kalama could work out a deal. But one thing was obvious. Kalama was a big man and used to giving orders.

"Well?" George asked when Steve walked in.

"He's sending a car around. It'll be here about quarter of eleven."

"Fine," George said looking at his watch. "Hey, Baby, what are you going to do while we are gone?"

She wondered how long they were going to be gone. She was sure she had enough time to get to the boat and back before they returned. The only problem was they could see the boat from their room. "I don't know. Maybe go to the beach."

"Fine," he said reaching for his wallet and taking out some money. "And if you get bored you can go shopping. Here's some money."

"I don't need any money."

"Take it. We may be gone quite a while. Don't stay at the beach too long. You don't want to get burned. Afterward you may want to do some shopping."

"O.K. Thank you, George," she said kissing him and taking the money.

Suddenly she was very frightened. "I think I'll go get ready," she said wanting to leave the room the same time they did so she could know for sure they got in the car and left.

They rode down in the elevator together, George carrying her beach bag. At the car he kissed her and handed her the bag. She stood watching the car pull away, waved and then headed for the harbor toward his boat wondering just what she would say to him. More than wondering what she would say she was worried he might not believe her. What if, on a whim, maybe even jokingly, he told George she had been to see him and told him what George intended to do?

She walked along the sidewalk toward the boat, looking over her shoulder from time to time to check the black Cadillac was not driving down the other side of the mole. At the dock-box in front of the *AHWANAH*, she turned around to have one last look. She was going to call his name when she saw the gate had not closed completely and she pushed through the open gate and started down the narrow, concrete dock alongside the boat. She was relieved to see the main hatch was open. She leaned over trying to see down the hatch. "Chris?" she called tentatively. *Was that his name? Had she remembered it correctly?* "Chris? Chris, are you there?"

She jumped when a voice behind her said, "He isn't here. Went ashore about ten minutes ago."

"Oh—Do you know when he'll be back?"

"Can't say for sure. He usually goes to the post office about this time. If that's the only place he's going he should be back in half an hour or so, but he might be stopping off some other places. You can wait aboard my boat till he gets back if you want to," he said smiling.

"No. No. Thank you. Maybe I'll stop back later." She said wondering how long she could be gone without raising suspicion. *I can spend a half hour in the sun. Then couple of hours shopping and I can probably claim another half hour for lunch. Three hours at the most.* "Does Chris have a phone?" she asked turning back.

"No, but I do. You can call him here. I'll write the number down for you," he said starting down the hatch.

"No. No. That's all right. I wouldn't want to be any bother."

"Hey. It's no bother. Believe me. Besides, it's half his phone. I take all his calls for him. We split the cost that way."

"Well, all right," she said thinking she could call later and see if he was back. She didn't know when she would have the chance to get away again. He disappeared down the hatch and returned a moment later with a slip of paper. "My name's Charlie. It's there with the phone number," he said holding the paper out to her.

"Thank you, Charlie," she said and turned to go.

"Hey, who should I tell Chris was looking for him?"

"Just an old friend," she said and walked away quickly, aware he was standing in the cockpit watching her.

* * *

At the beginning of a high stonewall on Diamond Head Road the driver flicked on his turn signals, slowed down, and turned in between two open iron gates. There was a gatehouse on one side of the drive and a garage of the same architectural style on the other. The car proceeded slowly down the incline between the two buildings and then circled around a large Banyan tree and stopped in front of a high wall. George got out of the car without waiting for the driver to come around and open the door for him. As soon as George stepped out of the car, one of the carved doors set in the wall was opened by a short Asian man in a steward's jacket who bowed a little as they entered. He closed the door behind them and then reached for George's hat setting it on a table.

"Follow me please, Gentlemen," he said walking across the polished hardwood floor of the vestibule, down three steps and through the center of the courtyard. A narrow path led between lush tropical ferns and flowers. A footbridge spanned connecting pools that held lazily swimming koi.

On the opposite side from which they had entered they climbed two steps, through the living room, and down three steps to a large stone terrace with a kidney shaped swimming pool. At the far end of the terrace was a pool house of yellow brick with its own blue tile roof, half of which was the dressing rooms and the rest was just a roof supported by pillars. Under the open roof area were some deep cushioned, redwood armchairs.

"Please be seated, Gentlemen. Mr. Kalama will be here shortly," the steward said and left.

A short time later Lester Kalama came through the living room and around the pool toward them. He was of medium height with a stocky build. His smooth, dark, skin was the result of Chinese, Hawaiian, Korean and Portuguese ancestry. His wavy hair, with alternating streaks of deep black and gray, was combed back and around his ears. George stood up as he approached and Steve followed his example. Kalama shook hands with each of them, nodding seriously at their greeting, but saying nothing.

They sat down and he spoke for the first time. "I was led to believe the request to meet with you came from Appy Costellos himself. I assume therefore it is important." He spoke with a slight British accent and the back of his index finger rubbed underneath his jaw as he talked. The implication was he would not have bothered with them if Appy had not requested it, and if that were not the truth he would find that out in time.

"I sent the message asking you to meet with us," George said and a frown started to form on Kalama's face. "I am George Costellos. Apistolos is my father. He knows about this meeting.

The frown changed to a wide grin. Kalama leaned over, suddenly emotional, and grabbed George by the shoulders shaking him a little. "I thought you looked a little familiar," Kalama exclaimed. "We met fifteen, sixteen years ago at your father's beach house. You had short hair then, cut flat top," he said running his open palm back and forth above his own graying hair. "How is your father?"

"Very well, thank you. He sends you his regards."

"Ah—Fine man, your father," he said waving to the steward, who was standing just inside the living room, out of hearing range. "Maybe you would like something to drink."

"A coke with the juice of a couple of limes, if you have it," George said. Steve would have liked a gin and tonic, but ordered ginger ale instead. Kalama ordered tea. They made small talk until the drinks were served and the steward was back at his station in the living room. Then Kalama said, "Now—What can I do for you?"

"We need a boat."

"What kind of a boat you want? You want a boat, any kind, I'll get it for you."

"First of all it has to be a boat that can be trusted completely and isn't suspected by anyone. Possibly a fishing boat that goes out for two or three days at a time so no one will think anything of it when it goes out to get us. As you've probably already figured out, we're bringing in a shipment. A big one. The biggest our organization has ever brought in at one time. I'm here setting it up. The boat should be fast enough to run and hide if it has to. Should have a range of maybe three hundred miles. It probably won't have to go that far, but—" He spread his hands and shrugged a little. "And it should have somebody on board who knows every little inlet and bay in these islands. My own thinking is this island is a little too populated, but your people would know about that better than I do."

"I'll take care of it," Kalama said.

"Thank you. We greatly appreciate anything you can do."

Appreciate anything you can do. Steve knew what that meant. It meant Kalama would get a big slice of the pie. That was the way it was. They talked about appreciating something when they meant a big pay-off. It worked the other way too. *I'm a little worried about the trouble Joe Hart is giving us in the fifth district.* Anybody who heard that would say to someone under them that Appy was pretty upset about Joe Hart. It would keep going down the line. "Appy thinks Joe Hart has gone too far." "The boss wants Joe Hart straightened out." Finally someone who had never met Appy or George would say, "Stop Joe Hart." Maybe all it took was a warning, like a bomb going off in Joe's empty car. Or, Joe Hart might be stopped permanently. That's the way it was. They appreciated something or were worried about something.

"Don't mention it. Being associated with you and your father for the past fifteen years has been nothing but good for me. It's the least I can do. I'll go make a few phone calls and get things started. It may take fifteen minutes or maybe two hours. Who knows? But either way will you stay and have lunch with me?"

"Thank you. We'd be delighted to stay."

"Good. Good." He stood. "If you would like to go swimming there's plenty of towels and clean swimming attire in the dressing rooms here. Or, Jimmy there can show you the billiard room. Now if you'll excuse me I'll go make those phone calls. If you want anything, just ask Jimmy there," he said starting for the house.

* * *

At one thirty Myra went to a pay phone in the Hilton Hawaiian Village and called Charlie's number. The phone was answered on the third ring. "Yeah?"

"Is Chris back yet?"

"No, he ain't back yet. Don't know where he went. Is there some place he can call you when he comes back."

"No, not really—and I wish you wouldn't tell him I was there or that I called. I want it to be a surprise."

"O.K., but all can say is Jamison has all the luck."

That was his name. Chris Jamison. "Oh, you're probably much luckier." She laughed and hung up. She stood there for a moment wondering what to do. She called their hotel and asked for their room. The operator let it ring for almost a minute before coming back on. "There doesn't seem to be any answer."

"Thank you." They weren't back yet. That gave her a little more time. She would wait an hour and then call Charlie again. She walked along the beach to the Moana Hotel and sat on the verandah wondering if George and Steve had gotten back yet. *Did it really matter? Probably not. What if she got back an hour after they did? It would just be better not to give George anything to be upset about.* She called the hotel again and there was still no answer, which was a relief. She was in luck. She had never expected them to be gone that long. She dialed Charlie's number, certain Chris would be there by now, relieved she would be able to warn him and the whole thing would be over soon. The phone rang once, twice, three times and she began to be anxious. *Answer it. Please! Answer it!* She let it ring eighteen times becoming more discouraged with each ring. She hung the receiver up slowly. She would try again later, but her chance, maybe her only chance was gone. She told herself she would try again in half an hour, but she didn't think it would do any good.

* * *

At a little after two Jimmy leaned over to tell Kalama there was a telephone call for him. Kalama excused himself and returned in ten minutes saying, "Well, I think I have just the man for you. Should have thought of him myself. Johnny Bigelow. He's one of our distributors on Maui." Kalama sat down and lit a cigarette. He's got a forty-two foot Hatteras and his two passions are fishing and whoring. No drinking or gambling, just women and fishing. He goes out fishing for as long as a week at a time so nobody will think anything of it. He's in right now so I told him to stick around and I took the liberty of having someone make reservations for you on the ten o'clock flight, Hawaiian Airlines, to Maui tomorrow. Bigelow will meet you at the plane. I could have had Bigelow come here, but I thought you might like to look over both him and his boat.

"Fine. Sounds good."

"I didn't tell him who you are, you're just 'George and Steve

Harris,' but he has orders to answer any questions and do whatever you ask. After you see him, if you don't think he's the right man—" he shrugged. "He won't know anything unless you tell him. We have a couple of alternatives. I still have my people looking."

"I'm sure he'll be fine," George said standing up. Jimmy left to order the car around. "When we get back I'll come see you again and let you know exactly what the set-up is with Johnny."

"Oh, there's no need for that."

"Well, he's your man and there may be some other business I want to discuss with you."

"Any time," Kalama said. He walked them to the front door, his hand resting on George's shoulder. "Anything you need just let me know. You want a car and driver?"

"No. No. It's less conspicuous if we stick with taxis."

"Of course," Kalama said and shook hands with them at the car and then went back in as the car pulled away.

On Paki Avenue George Idly looked out the window as the car moved along Kapiolani Park and the back of the zoo. A third of the way along the Ala Wai Canal he suddenly leaned forward and said, "Hey, slow down," and a moment later added, "Stop by that girl up there at the intersection. Hey, Myra," he called through the open window.

Myra stopped, stood frozen for a moment when she heard George call her name, and then remembered she had an explanation for being there. Regaining her composure she stepped off the curb and smiled.

"Hey, Baby, jump in," he said swinging open the door. She crawled by him to sit in the middle between them. The door closed and the car pulled away from the curb. "Did you walk all the way down here?"

"Yeah," she said sighing. "I'm beat. I was just going back to the International Market Place to find a cab." She started tell him about her day and that she had called the hotel a couple of times to see if they were back yet.

"I'm sorry about that, Baby. I really didn't think we'd be gone that long. And I'm afraid Steve and I will be gone all day tomorrow too."

"Oh?" she hoped she sounded disappointed.

"Yeah. We have to meet a man on Maui. But I'll tell you what.

Monday and Tuesday we'll go to a couple of the other islands. Fly over in the morning, look around a little and come back in the evening."

She nodded and smiled, exited at the thought she would have another chance to warn Chris.

CHAPTER SIX

At 9:10 Sunday morning George kissed Myra on the cheek and then opened the back door on his side to let her out of the taxi. When he had asked what she was going to do while they were gone she had said, "Oh, I'll probably go to the shopping center, then maybe to the beach."

"Good, we'll drop you off at the shopping center on the way to the airport."

She had tried to protest but he had insisted. All morning she had wanted to pick up the binoculars to see if there were signs Chris was at his boat, but thought it was better if George didn't see her scanning the yacht harbor. As soon as the taxi was out of sight she found a phone and dialed Charlie's number. She let it ring more than a dozen times and when there was no answer hung up and headed for the yacht harbor.

She was at the end of the mole when she saw a mast moving away from among the other masts. From that distance she couldn't see which boat it was, but she started walking faster, almost running, afraid it might be the *AHWANAH.* From four boats away she saw his slip was empty. She looked quickly, further down the line, hoping she had made a mistake. No, it was his slip. She remembered the potted plant growing next to the dock box. The gate was a little ajar. She pushed through, the gate clanging behind her, and ran to the end of his dock. Down the waterway she saw the oval transom and the name *AHWANAH* on the curved name board and under it, Seattle. She tried to call once, but knew it was no use. He was too far away to hear above the sound of the engine pushing the boat away from her.

* * *

Johnny Bigelow was waiting for them at the arrival gate at Kahului Airport. He was a big man with long, black, styled hair, dark smiling eyes and mahogany skin. He was wearing a striped Polo shirt, wine slacks and white, crepe-soled shoes. He started talking pleasantly, happily, almost the moment they were away from the gate. "You from California, yeah? Not been mainland yet. All time like go, but auwe, no got time. Haole friends say fishin' real good Baja. All time want go Baja. You like da kine fishin', Mr. George?"

"A little, but my father's the one who really likes it."

"Aye, Man, you bring father. I take eem wit me," Johnny said throwing an arm around George's shoulder. "We catch mahi-mahi, aku, marlin. You' father like eet heah," he said dropping his arm and nodding his head. "You want top up?" he asked opening the door for them when they got to the convertible.

"No. No. Top down is fine."

George held onto his hat as Johnny drove from the airport to Kahului Harbor, pointing out places of interest along the way. "My Tutu live dat road. You like learn 'bout old Hawaii, you talk her. She almos' huntred now. My bruddah live dere too. He good man, but he no like fishin'."

George, who normally didn't like people who talked all the time, found he could not dislike Johnny Bigelow, though he continued to wonder if Johnny was the right man. As they walked along the docks to the boat people called to Johnny as they passed, "Howzit Bruddah?" "Catch-um, Johnny," And Johnny waved to them, answered and bantered with them in Hawaiian.

At the boat he let them board first and then climbed aboard himself, unlocked the cabin door, and went right over and started the engines. When they were running smoothly at warm-up speed he took three fishing poles down from their brackets along the cabin top, handed one each to George and Steve, and waving his hand to indicate the rest of the harbor said, "You just two friends go fishin' with Johnny. Everybody know I not go out and not fish." He headed for the open after-deck and they followed, attached lures to their lines and set the rods in their holders, and stood around watching while Johnny checked the storage wells, the live bait wells and readied the outrigger lines. Everything ready for trolling.

Out in deep water he set the course to parallel the shore, set her on auto-pilot, adjusted to trolling speed and streamed all the lines. Back in the cabin he put on a pot of coffee and sat down at the table opposite George. He took out a cigarette, lit it, and slid the box of matches toward George who was unwrapping a cigar. He waited until George was through lighting his cigar and then said, "Biggy Kalama say maybe you got beeg job for me."

George looked at him a moment before answering. The pleasantness was not really gone from around Johnny's eyes, but he was completely serious now, and George realized the former geniality, although natural, had also been an act so others watching them would think of them only as tourists. "Yes," George said. "We're bringing in a shipment by boat and we want it off that boat before it pulls into Honolulu."

"When you want me meet dis boat?"

"About the first of April. It's coming in by sailboat so we can't say exactly when they will get here. You'll have to be out there every night after that until it arrives."

Johnny nodded. "No problem. Where I meet dis boat?"

"Got some charts?"

"I tink so. Nevah use 'em," he said getting up to look though some drawers and finally came back with charts. One was of the Hawaiian chain, one of Oahu, and one showed the western end of Molokai and the head shaped section of Maui.

"Where would be the best place to land for you? Anywhere on Oahu?"

"No way. No got family on Oahu. No place to land somebody not see you. Molokai mo bettah."

"Can you land anywhere along here?" George asked running his finger along the north shore of the island.

"Auwe! No way! Da kind leper colony dere. Kapu. Must have permission land dere. Every boat checked. All else no good. Surge too much. Cannot land. Down here is mo bettah," he said pointing to the south shore. "Kalaeloa O.K. Pukoo O.K. Have cousin live Pukoo. Not much people dere. All know Johnny Bigelow. Go dere plenty time have dinner with Auntie. Always bring presents. Nobody think nothin' I carry boxes ashore. Pauwalu O.K. Nobody dere, but have to go ovah reef to get to shore. Not so good like Pukoo. Can store stuff at cousin's place."

"Can your cousin be trusted?"

"He my cousin. If I not trust eem, I keel eem."

"There will be four people coming aboard your boat with the shipment. Can they stay at your cousin's until they catch a plane to Honolulu?"

"Ah sure. No sweat. Sometimes I take mainland Haole dere so can see where poor Hawaiian live." He grinned broadly and George couldn't help but smile a little himself. "Is mo bettah bring others 'cuz always dey come wit suitcases on way to catch plane to Honolulu."

"O.K. Where do you want to meet?"

"Any place O.K."

"Is around here all right?"

"Ah, surah. All da boat go down dis place."

"Fine, let's say we'll meet—" he paused to look at the chart "ten miles due north of Molokai Light," he said looking up. Johnny nodded. "Now we won't be showing any lights," George went on. "When we see you we'll flash a light - one long, two short, one long. You answer with one short, two long, one short. We won't make the change during daylight. Too easy for a passing plane to wonder what you're doing. But every night after April first you'll have to be out there."

"I be dere."

"Good. I guess that takes care of everything."

"Now we fish for surah, yeah? We come back with couple fish, everyone know all we do is fish, yeah?"

George nodded, smiled a little, and Johnny went up to the flying bridge.

* * *

On Monday evening after spending the day on Kauai with Myra, George again arrived at Kalama's house in one of his host's limousines. The steward opened the door for him, led him to one of the side rooms, knocked on the door and opened it without waiting for an answer. Holding the door while George walked in, he closed the door behind him and stood silently by. Kalama was sitting behind a large, ornate, Chinese table covered with papers. He got up as George entered, came around the table-desk to shake hands, and then motioned to the two deep armchairs. "Will you have a drink?"

"If you're going to have one I'll join you. Make it a light scotch and water."

Kalama waved the steward away and got up to get the drinks himself. He brought them over, handed one to George and sat down. He took a sip of his drink and asked, "Were you satisfied with Johnny Bigelow?"

"Completely."

"I'm very glad to hear that," Kalama said levelly, and George knew there was more to the remark than just the fact Kalama had recommended him.

"Yes, from what I saw of him I think he is a very good man," George said and then went on to tell Kalama the details of the pick-up. "Now what I would like, if it is not too much of an inconvenience, is for you to have someone in reserve, someone who could rush in at the last minute if anything should happen to Johnny Bigelow. I'm sure nothing is going to happen to Johnny, but you never can tell. At the last minute he might get an appendicitis attack, or some drunk might run him down. It would be good to have a backup plan just in case. Where he decides to land is of course between you and him. Only he will know what he thinks is safest for him."

"That can be arranged with no problem at all," Kalama said. He looked across the room for a moment, hesitated, and then said, "Excuse me for asking this, Mr. Costellos—"

"Call me George. Please," George interrupted.

"Very well, George, how much do you trust your associate?"

"Steve Margolis? Why I don't trust him in the least."

"May I ask, then, why you have him with you?"

"He is still with the organization because several years ago, when he was just a hit man, he saved my father's life. My father has a sense of gratitude. The reason he is with me now is because my two best men are handling the Hong Kong end of the operation. I have him with me because he is a reasonably good sailor and too dumb to cause any real trouble."

"Then I think you should know he went to Maui today and tried to convince Johnny the two of them should make off with the shipment."

George smiled and shook his head. "One of Steve's great failings is he is no judge of character. Did Johnny refuse him?"

"No, he left Steve with the idea he would go along with it and then called me as soon as Steve left."

"Good! Good! He feels smug now. A dumb triggerman trying to be big. Well, he will have to be dealt with."

"Would you like us to handle it for you?"

"No. I'll deal with it personally. And tell Johnny I'm grateful. He'll be hearing from me."

CHAPTER SEVEN

In the shade of a tin-roofed shed, Jimmy Harris folded the blueprints and offset sheets in anticipation of the end of the working day. Below and in front of him, on the strip of land that separated the shed from the water's edge, were several fiberglass-hulled boats in various stages of completion. Around those boats large crews of Chinese laborers worked diligently and quickly, polishing hulls, laying teak decks, framing cabins and inserting portholes. They would continue working until the moment the gong sounded signaling the end of the working day. Only then would they slow down, put the tools away and clean up.

To one side of the yard were several junks and sampans hauled out for repairs, their bottoms being cleaned in the time-honored manner of being burned with straw fires. The sampan's blunt bows, charred hulls, and ornately carved deckhouses, contrasted sharply with the smooth lines, white hulls of the yachts that would soon be shipped to be sold in countries as far away as Europe and North America. The gong sounded and Jimmy walked through the yard as tools and supplies were put away. He did not leave until every tool was checked in and the last workman had left.

Closer to town the narrow streets became more and more crowded as throngs of people were released from factories, shops and mills. A car trying to proceed along the street did so only by constantly blowing its horn and actually nudging aside the flood of people surrounding it. In an ocean of black-haired, gray-garbed Chinese, Jimmy Harris, with curly, light brown hair hanging long around his ears and wearing a skin tight, orange T-shirt stood out like a channel buoy in a stream. He pushed his way along the street, feeling the relief, as did everyone else, at the end of a working day.

From the industrial street at the end of which the yard was located, he turned into a more commercial street. In all the pushing and rushing crowds the only stationary people were the curbside vendors holding samples above their heads for all to see. Filling the street with cries and chants they described their wares. Soapstone, ivory and jade jewelry, good luck charms, potions and medicines were the familiar items. Fortunes also were told and letters written. Foods of all kinds were available. A seller of ducks from whom Jimmy had bought before saw Jimmy coming and yelled, "Me, Jim. Me, Jim. Buy from me, Jim," while waving his right arm and pointing to the duck in his left hand. Jimmy pushed his way through the crowd and stood in front of the rack of ducks which had been cooked right there on a charcoal brazier.

Lai Luk smiled and bowed. He hung the duck on the rack and picked out another one. With a lot of hand waving and head shaking the two of them haggled over the price of the duck. When Jimmy left he was sure Lai Luk had gotten a little more from him than he would have gotten from a native, but he couldn't resent it.

The street ended at the waterfront. In the harbor the dark-hulled sampans were clustered in floating islands with little alleys of water between them. In the greens, tans, browns and reds of the sampans, the white hull and mast of the *ROMSEY* stood out as obviously as its owner did on land.

Liu Lau was waiting for him at the usual place and he jumped aboard the little fourteen-foot sampan that was a water taxi and a home for her, her two children and her husband who worked as a dyer in one of the fabric mills. She nodded a greeting, smiled at him, and started sculling through the alleys of water toward his boat. He had become a regular customer whom she could count on for a trip from his boat in the morning and back to it in the evening. She was always at his boat in the morning and waiting for him at the wharf in the evening. In the past five months they had become friends of sorts, in much the same way a passenger who catches the same bus to work every day might become a friend of the driver. He knew that as she moved about the harbor during the day she kept an eye on his boat for him.

After his dinner, half a duck, steamed rice and some broccoli left over from the night before, Jimmy Harris sat in the small cockpit feeling content and full. It was the hour of dusk when everything is softened by the shadows of beginning night. From one of the intersections of the water alleyways he saw one of the many water taxis turn down the alley at the end of which he was anchored. The single prow lantern reflected in the still water. Behind the light was the silhouette of a man, his legs spread across the square platform of the stern, his body rocking back and forth, both hands holding onto the long oar with which he skillfully sculled the taxi forward. Watching its slow approach Jimmy wished he had film in his camera fast enough to capture the night picture. He had lots of daytime pictures of the world of the water people, but almost every night he wished he could capture the changing shapes and glows of the night harbor.

The taxi's lantern was even with his bow when he saw the head and shoulders of two men appear above the arched top of the sampan. Even in the dimness he knew they were not Chinese. One of them called out, "Aye, Harris, are you aboard?"

He stood up, leaning over the side, trying to see more clearly. "Who is it?"

"Larry. Larry Anderson. We met last week."

"Ah, yes," The sampan came skillfully to a stop alongside with six inches of water separating the two boats. "Come aboard if you like."

Before stepping aboard, Larry indicated to the sampan to wait for them and then said, "This is a friend of mine. Will Maxwell. Most people call him Max."

They shook hands in the darkness. "Hold on a minute while I get a light," Jim said and went below. He came up a few minutes later with an oil anchor light that he set on the cabin top. He sat down and said, "We can go below if you like, but it is much nicer up here. You chaps want a beer?"

"No, thank you. Maybe later. Are you still thinking of going to Hawaii?" Larry asked.

"Sure, if I can find a crew."

"Well, I was telling Max about it, and the more we talked the more we thought it might be fun to do something like that."

In the dim light of the lantern Jimmy looked from one to the other wondering why someone who could jet wherever they wanted to go would want to subject themselves to the discomfort of an ocean crossing on a small boat. "I think most people would consider a trip like this more work than fun," he said cautiously.

"I suppose your right," Max said. "But look at all the people who go camping, sleeping out in the rain, eating burned food, getting bitten by bugs. Or the guy who has to have the air conditioner on in his office all the time and then on vacation goes tracking across some desert. I guess we're kind of like that. We've both done a little sailing off the California and Oregon coasts. I've been out for as much as a week at a time and every time I'm out I keep telling myself I'm going to make an ocean crossing. It is something I've always wanted to do."

Jimmy nodded. "Just as long as you blokes know what you're letting yourselves in for. It won't be an easy crossing. Beating into the wind most of the way I imagine. Fortunately the *ROMSEY* sails pretty close to the wind."

"When do you think you would be leaving?" Max asked.

"You understand you buy all the supplies?"

"Yes, just give us a list of what we need and we'll get it."

"Well, I'm pretty much ready to go. Should give them a couple of days' notice where I work, which should be all right because it will probably take you two a couple of days to get the stores on board. Why don't we plan on leaving right after New Year's? Next Saturday. I think New Year's Day is on Friday. I want to stay around and see Chinese New Year, you know the lion dances and fireworks and all that."

"That's fine with us."

"I'll probably work through Wednesday so I won't be able to help you much with supplies before Thursday."

"But we can start bringing some things aboard before then, can't we?"

"Don't see why not. I'll make the list out now and show you where to put things. Or better yet, just stack them in the main cabin and we can store them away together then we will all know where things are."

They went below where he showed them the storage areas and then he sat down at the dinette and started making out the list of what they needed while the other two looked around, asking questions and making comments. "Heavy boat, isn't she?" "When was she built?" "No radio, huh?"

He finished the list and handed it to Larry. "Those are the bare essentials. Anything you want to add to it, well, and as the vicar said, 'All donations gratefully accepted.'" He hoped they would notice there was no beer or liquor on the list and would do something about it.

"Will the boat be open so we can put things on board?" Larry asked starting up the ladder.

"I'll give you a key to the main hatch. There is also a woman who runs a taxi who kind of watches it for me. Her name is Liu Lau. She doesn't speak much English, but I think I can make her understand you might be bringing things out to the boat. In fact if one of you could meet me at the dock where the taxis hang out about 7:00 tomorrow morning, I can introduce you to her. I'd like you to use her if you could. She can use the business."

"Fine. In fact we may hire her by the day and then she will always be there when any of us need her." They got into the sampan and Jimmy stood for a moment watching it pull away and wondered if he should have asked for some money in addition to the supplies. If they were just going this way for fun instead of using him as a cheap way to get to Hawaii, they could probably afford it. But the deal was made. It was too late now to make any additions. He never was much of a businessman, never been able to drive a bargain. That was onc of the reason Mary had left him. He couldn't blame her really. Working on the farm from before sunup till after sunset might have been acceptable to her if she had believed eventually there would be something to show for it. But each year they were just a little more in debt. The farm he had inherited was free and clear of any debts, but unlike his father he just couldn't make a go of it. At the market he couldn't haggle over the price of his produce. He would accept the first offer some wholesaler made for fear of not getting another offer at all.

He was twenty-two and Mary nineteen when they got married. She was too young to be confined to a farm and all the work of it with none of the pleasures in life except for an occasional beer at the local pub. After three years of trying, and he had to admit she had really tried; she simply couldn't take it anymore and left him. He couldn't blame her. He wasn't bitter. The truth was, he had also become discouraged with the farm.

When she left he put the farm up for sale. With what money there was left after the bills and taxes he was able to buy the boat and give Mary enough to pay for her nurses training. He went to work for a year in a boatyard, and when he finally did take off he knew more about how boats were built than how to sail them. But with a lot of reading on the subject and even more trial and error he learned most of what the he needed to know by the time he reached the Canary Islands.

He picked up the lantern from the cabin top and went forward to tie it to a stay and then went back to sit in the cockpit. He was excited. In a few days he would be on his way again. It didn't bother him he didn't really know anything about his passengers. He wanted to go to Hawaii and now he had a way to do it. Things always seemed to work out for him after he left the farm. There had been times when he had been lonely, even times when he was hungry, but all in all, he was happy with his life.

CHAPTER EIGHT

Monday evening Max and Larry sat in their hotel room waiting for the phone call. A little more than twenty-four hours before they had settled things with Jimmy Harris. At nine that morning they had met with Fred McGuire, president of World Trading Company Ltd, a Costellos-owned enterprise. McGuire had phoned in the afternoon to assure them everything was arranged and they would be contacted that evening.

It was just after eight when the phone rang. Larry answered the phone and a voice that spoke perfect English with a slight Chinese lilt asked, "Is this Mr. Maxwell?"

"No, this is Mr. Anderson."

"May I speak with Mr. Maxwell please?"

Larry handed Max the phone. "Maxwell," he said into the mouthpiece.

"I understand you are interested in acquiring some jewelry, Mr. Maxwell."

"Yes. Antique pieces if you have any."

"We have some very fine old jade that might interest you."

"Actually, I'm interested in fine quality carved ivory."

With the exchange of the four key words—jewelry, antique, jade and ivory—the voice on the other end became less businesslike and more congenial. "I'm in the lobby of your hotel right now, Mr. Maxwell. If you are free possibly you would like to go to our showrooms now and see what we have to offer."

"Good. We'll be down in five minutes. How will I recognize you?"

"I will recognize you, Mr. Maxwell," the voice said and hung up.

He put on his jacket and from an attaché case took two sealed envelopes, one blue, one white, which George had given him before they left. He had no intention of handing over the blue one, but he took it along just in case Pakash wanted to see it.

When they got to the lobby a man approached them, his hand extended, smiling politely. "Hello, Mr. Maxwell. So good to see you again." He was short and thin. His black hair was cut short, parted on the right, and combed straight to the side both directions from the part. With his steel framed glasses, black suit, black tie and black shoes he looked like a graduate student or a young instructor and Max knew he had never seen the man before in his life. "I'm sure you will be pleased with our jewelry this time. Did you have a pleasant trip?"

"Oh, yes. Very pleasant, thank you," Max said. They walked along with him to the front doors and went outside. A doorman whistled for a taxi. A black car pulled up sliding in ahead of the taxi that had answered the doorman's whistle. It was not until they had pulled away from the hotel the man dropped his pretenses and introduced himself. "I am Choi Kwok, assistant to Mr. Pakash," he said and then settled into the corner of the seat without saying another word.

They drove for a short distance along a main street where taxis, private cars and double-decker buses fought for ownership of the lanes. On either side of them towered high-rise office buildings with double neon signs in both western and Chinese characters proclaiming their businesses, Fiat and Zanussi of Italy, Sony and Hitachi from Japan, Winston Cigarettes from the United States, watches from Switzerland, perfumes from France, all of them gathered together in Hong Kong.

They turned on to a less brightly lit side street, drove through a warehouse district till they came out at the waterfront. They stopped in front of the Red Dragon Bar. From the car they passed under a large neon sign, made their way through the dancers and past the tables, and went out again through a back door to a dimly lighted hallway with doors on each side. They followed Kwok up a set of stairs, all the time feeling they should look back over their shoulder. Kwok knocked on a shabby door that had no doorknob. The man who opened the door was dressed like Kwok. He was taller and did not wear glasses. In no way did he fit the Western concept of a big, burly bouncer, or bodyguard. He closed the door after they entered and faded into the corner. The instant the door closed behind him, Max forgot the man was there.

Max had expected the room would be elaborately decorated with golden dragons, carved wooden screens, and Chinese statuary. Instead the room was ultra-modern, even futuristic. Underfoot was a deep, plush carpet of the same deep red as the ceiling and drapes covering the opposite wall. Tiny recessed lights in the ceiling cast an even glow over the whole room. The wall through which they had entered was done in smooth white. In it were oval recessions of various sizes, each with a single glass shelf across its center supporting one art object, a jade vase, a glass bird, or a gold statue of Shiva. Each piece glowed warmly under invisible spotlights beaming down from the ceiling.

The only furniture in the room was a large, solid, oval, white desk with not a single thing on it and some white, leather chairs alongside the desk. The man who rose from behind the desk was not Chinese, but Indian. He had wavy black hair with a streak of gray in the middle, heavy black eyebrows and he was wearing a brown suit, tan shirt, and a brown and tan checkered tie that exactly matched the colors of the suit and shirt. Choi Kwok bowed a little and said, "Mr. Pakash, may I present Mr. Maxwell and Mr. Anderson."

"Won't you be seated, gentlemen," he said waving toward the two white, leather chairs without any gesture toward shaking hands.

"Thank you," they said sitting. Pakash settled back into his chair, his elbows on the arms of it, his hands folded under his chin, exposing jade and gold cuff links. "Would you care for a cup of tea?"

"Not just now, thank you. Possibly later," Max said.

"Fine. To business then. You have a letter for me."

"Yes," Max said reaching into the inside pocket of his jacket. He took out the white envelope and handed it to Pakash who opened it and quickly read the single sheet of paper enclosed. He laid the paper on the desk in front of him without saying anything and opened the right top desk drawer that contained a telephone. He dialed a number and turned on the speaker. When someone answered he said, "This is Mr. Pakash. I would like to speak to Mr. Reynolds."

A voice answered, "Reynolds."

"Hello, Park. I understand I have a new account with your house."

"Yes. I signed the certificate of deposit myself."

"And what is the amount in that account," Pakash asked.

"Two million dollars... American."

"Any conditions?"

"Same as always. Present the certificate of deposit in person."

"Very well. Thank you, Park," he said turning off the phone. He closed the desk drawer, "Your order is ready. Do you wish to take delivery now?"

"No, thank you. Day after tomorrow. Mid-morning would be preferable if that's convenient for you."

"Perfectly. Ten o'clock all right?"

"Ten is fine."

"See you then," Pakash said raising. "Kwok will pick you up at your hotel at ten. There's a car waiting below to take you back to your hotel." Business was over.

Max and Larry stood up saying their thanks. The man who let them in opened a door across from the one by which they had entered. Both doors were so well fitted as to be almost indiscernible. Max and Larry had not noticed the second door until it was opened for them. They followed Kwok through it to a room on the other side, a typical Western business office with overhead fluorescent lighting and six gray steel desks with computers on them. They walked between the desks, down a stairway, and through a steel fire door that opened onto an alley. A car was waiting. Kwok held the door for them, gave the driver the name of their hotel and went back inside as the car pulled away.

* * *

Pakash Sin Sze sat at his desk wondering just who the financial power behind Fred McGuire was. He had been doing business with World Trading Company for many years, usually in small amounts, five to ten kilos twice a month. There had never been anything like this. He knew World Trading Company was a well-managed, profitable little import-export firm that did well exclusive of its operation as a front for smuggling heroin. In all respects, except for the size of the purchase the transaction had been exactly the same as the others. The money was deposited in an account and the certificate of deposit handed over to him upon delivery. Usually two Chinese picked up the order. He had always assumed they took the heroin to some World Trading Company warehouse where it was probably sealed in the plastic bodies of dolls or hollowed out statues of elephants before being shipped to America. These two couriers were obviously from America and he couldn't help but wonder how they planned to smuggle such a big shipment into the United States.

His interest was more than idle curiosity. Mr. Pakash was a good businessman who delivered what he promised. But part of being successful in business was being in the right place at the right time, anticipating when someone else might make a costly mistake, and being on hand to capitalize on that mistake. He had no intention of informing anyone about the two Americans. That would not be to his advantage and might even jeopardize his own business. The authorities might, for example, wonder how he knew about the two Americans. Being an informer was for the unscrupulous kind. But if these two Americans were to be careless, such as setting one of the cases down while making a phone call, or be so unfortunate as to have a flat tire, it would be highly advantageous to him to have someone on hand to step in and walk off with one or more of the cases.

* * *

"We have most of the stores aboard," Max said when Jimmy arrived at Liu Lau's sampan after work. "We have some more to get, but we were wondering if it would be all right for us to move aboard tomorrow."

"Don't see why not if you want to. We won't be leaving for a couple of days and these bunks aren't nearly as comfortable as the beds in your hotel, but go ahead if you want to."

"Well, if it's all right with you we'd kind of like to get used to things a little bit before we get underway."

"Sure. Move aboard any time you want. Are you coming out now?"

"No. We have some things to clear up at the hotel."

"Right-oh. Tomorrow then," he waved and stepped aboard Liu Lau's sampan.

CHAPTER NINE

Kwok showed a certain reserved degree of surprise when he picked them up to find Larry and Max had two other men with them; Asians that, from the bulges in their jackets, obviously were carrying handguns in shoulder holsters. Larry and the two men got in back and Max got in front with Kwok.

It was 10:18 by Larry's watch when Kwok stopped the car by the steel door at the back of the Red Dragon. He led them through the steel door, up the steps, and through the office. Men in shirtsleeves looking intently at their computer screens while their fingers moved swiftly over the keyboard occupied every desk. Not one of the men looked up as they passed through. Kwok knocked once and the door swung open and he went into Mr. Pakash's office ahead of them.

The red and white room was exactly the same as it was the last time they were there except that next to the white oval desk there was a chrome and glass serving cart holding a silver coffee service with red and gold china. The silent man who had opened the door for them stood behind the serving cart. The top of the white desk was bare except for a cup half filled with black coffee. Pakash stood up, coming around the desk to shake hands with Max and Larry, while the two men who had come with Max and Larry stood along the wall. Pakash motioned for them to sit and went back around the desk.

"Your order will be here shortly, Gentlemen. In the meantime may I offer you a cup of coffee?" He paused for just an instant and then added, "Or would you prefer something else? Scotch, or whiskey, or something of that nature?" making it sound as though he had just that instant considered offering them a drink.

"Coffee will be fine," Max said sitting down.

"Is this your first trip to Hong Kong," he asked pouring the coffee.

"Yes," Max answered while Larry said, "I've been here before."

"Ah, yes," Pakash said. "Were those business or pleasure trips, Mr. Anderson?"

"A little bit of both I guess."

"Yes. Hong Kong is a fine place for both business and pleasure.

It is the financial center of the East. As far as pleasure is concerned—well," he spread his hands and raised one dark bushy eyebrow, "if it exists anywhere in the world it is duplicated in Hong Kong. I suppose our transaction concludes your stay in Hong Kong for this trip."

"Yes. We'll be leaving shortly," Max said thinking Pakash was fishing for something. He was doing it subtlety, but he was trying to find out something. All this socializing was not because Pakash was a hospitable man. He could just as easily have had the delivery waiting for them when they arrived, but he had arranged to have a little time to talk to them.

"Ah, too bad. I was hoping I might introduce you to some of the sights and pleasures of our city. Possibly next time."

"Possibly."

"Of course, if there is any way I can be of assistance while you are still here, please don't hesitate to call on me."

"Thank you. The best assistance right now would be for us to take delivery. We do have somewhat of a tight schedule to maintain," Max said.

"Of course. I understand. I'll find out what is holding things up," he said nodding to the butler who went over to open the door. Kwok walked in followed by two men each carrying two cases. The cases had brass rivets along the seams and brass plates at the corners. "Ah. Here we are," Pakash said standing. He stood by as the cases were lifted one by one to the desktop. Kwok stepped forward with keys in his hand, unlocked each of the cases, opened the lids and stepped back handing Max the key. Max stepped forward closing and locking each of the cases without picking up a single one of the large, clear plastic packages inside. "We have facilities near by for both testing and weighing if you wish to do so," Pakash said.

"There's no need for that," Max said. "We were made to understand any discrepancies in either weight or quality would be corrected."

"Of course! I always deliver what I promise," Pakash answered, but he wasn't sure whether Max's statement was an acknowledgment of his honesty, or a threat.

From an inside jacket pocket Max took the blue envelope and handed it to Pakash. He opened it while Max, Larry and the two men each took one of the cases, carrying it in their left hands leaving their right hands free to reach for the guns in the shoulder holsters if they had to. Pakash smiled, put the certificate of deposit in his pocket and said, "Where can we take you gentlemen now, back to the hotel?"

"If you could have someone take us to World Trading Company, that would be very kind. Thank you."

"Certainly," Pakash said nodding to Kwok who headed for the door followed by Max, Larry and the two others. There was no shaking hands or saying good-byes. As soon as the door closed behind them, Pakash waved to his butler who left by the other door, running down the old stairway and hall, through the bar and into the street. He got behind the wheel of an empty taxi. He waited until Kwok and his passengers went by him then pulled away from the curb, following. He pulled over to the curb half a block behind Kwok when he saw him stop in front of the main entrance to the World Trading Company. The four men got out carrying the cases and the butler continued to wait after Kwok had pulled away. A few minutes later Kwok came back and parked his car across the street and down from the World Trading Company. The two of them sat, each in his own car, watching the front and driveway alongside the World Trading Company. They had been instructed to watch. If Max and Larry came out without the cases they were to return to Pakash. If there was unusual traffic leaving World Trading Company, they were to follow those vehicles.

Half an hour later three vans, one right after the other pulled out of the driveway. The first two turned left and Kwok followed them. At the corner one went either direction and Kwok chose to follow the older of the two vans. The taxi followed the other van. From a third floor window Max and Larry watched Kwok and the taxi take off after the vans. They waited looking out the window until none of the cars in the street had been there when they arrived and then Max and Larry and the two men went down and got in a mini-van.

Neither McGuire, nor the driver, knew where they were headed. For the first few blocks Max just told the driver to turn right or left, indiscriminately, while he and Larry watched from the back window making sure they were not being followed. Then he gave the driver the names of an intersection where he was sure they would be able to catch a taxi. At the intersection they waited a few moments, each of them holding two cases until the van was out of sight and then caught a taxi. At first Max had trouble making the driver understand where they wanted to go, but finally he nodded and started through the crowded streets toward the waterfront.

Liu Lau was in her usual place when they got there. She smiled at them sitting on their black cases as she sculled toward the boat. On board they put the cases in the bottom of the storage area under the forward bunks, piling cans of food on top of them. They put down the lids and lowered the mattresses. “Well, that’s it,” Max said. “Now we just take it easy until we pull out of here.”

Larry went back to the galley to get himself a beer and Max, fully clothed in suit and tie, lay down on the port bunk feeling satisfied and confident. Within arm’s reach below him was two million dollars’ worth of uncut heroin. By the time it had been cut, and split, and divided, and distributed it would have multiplied its value five, ten, maybe twenty times. That kind of return on one’s investment was worth talking about.

CHAPTER TEN

It was late Sunday afternoon. The sun, caught between the horizon and the bank of clouds off Barber's Point, created an umbrella of pink and orange clouds. Headed for his boat, Chris was aware of the setting sun as both awesomely beautiful and as a weather forecaster. He unlocked the gate and started down the narrow dock between his and Charlie's boat. Halfway along the dock he saw a man who had been sitting in the cockpit stand to his feet. He was wearing a wide brimmed Panama hat, a flowered aloha shirt and white slacks. "Are you Chris Jamison," the man asked.

"Yeah, and just what are you doing on my boat?"

"My name is George Harris. I was told your boat is for charter. I was standing around waiting for you and got talking to Charlie and he let me in. I got tired of standing and I hoped you wouldn't mind it I went aboard and sat down."

"Well, I do mind," Chris said stepping aboard.

"I apologize, Mr. Jamison, I didn't mean to upset you," he said taking off his hat and Chris saw his face clearly. He had heavy, dark eyebrows and deep-set brown eyes over strong cheekbones. His was the kind of face usually called ruggedly handsome, but there was something about the face Chris didn't like. He set the hat on the cockpit seat and reached for a cigar and unwrapped it. He crumpled the wrapper with one hand and stuck it in his pocket and Chris was relieved he hadn't just thrown the paper on deck or into the water. He lit the cigar with a gold lighter and Chris stood up-wind of him thinking if they did charter his boat to the man he would have to make it clear there was no smoking below decks.

"Who told you my boat was for charter?"

"A friend of mine. Will Maxwell. He said he talked to you. Do you remember him?"

Chris nodded and sat down. "And what did you say your name was?"

"Harris. George Harris. Bill knew I was thinking of coming to Hawaii and hoping to charter a boat for extended cruising. He gave me your name, slip number and told me how you built this boat yourself. Beautiful job," he said looking up at the mast and rigging admiringly. "There is nothing like a well-built wooden boat. There is nothing like wood."

"I see," Chris said hesitantly.

"Bill told me your rate is $10,000 a month. Is that correct?" Chris nodded and the man went on. "I want to charter your boat for a minimum of two months, maybe longer. There will be three of us. My wife and I and my brother." He paused for a moment and reached into his pocket and brought out a money clip. "We'll pay for two months in advance. I'll pay you $20,000 in advance. Cash." He started peeling off some bills. "Here's a thousand up front to make sure no one else comes along and charters it out from under us. If we want the boat for longer than that I'll pay you $10,000 the first of every month and if we get bored with the whole thing before the two months is up, well, you still keep the money," he said holding out the money. "We'd like to get underway as soon as possible. I'll bring the rest of the money around in the morning."

Chris looked at the money. God, how he could use it, but he didn't reach for it. "And just where were you thinking of going in two months?" Chris asked.

"We were thinking of sailing to Tahiti."

"Yeah, we could do that. I could take as long as 22 to 30 days to get there, the same amount of time to get back pretty much chews up two months. That doesn't give you much time to enjoy French Polynesia. Why don't you just fly there?"

"Because we like sailing. I particularly like sailing with a destination in mind, not just going out for a day or two," he said stuffing the ten $100 bills in Chris' shirt pocket. "And you are right, of course, we'll have to charter it for at least three months."

"You've done deep water sailing before then, have you?"

"Well, yes. I crewed on one of the boats in the Transpac race four years ago and I've been sailing ever since I was a kid. We chartered a boat in Virgin Islands last year and liked it so much we decided we'd try the South Pacific this year."

Chris took the money out of his pocket and looked at it. "Before you charter a boat don't you want to look below, see what the accommodations are like?"

"Well, Bill told me about it and I'm kind of in a hurry. We'll come by tomorrow and look it over. From what Bill told me, I'm sure it will be fine, but I want my wife to see it. I'll bring another $19,000 tomorrow for the first two months. And like I said, if we get bored with the whole thing by the time we get to Tahiti and fly back, well you keep the whole amount."

"That'll be fine," Chris said wondering why he felt uncomfortable about it. This was what he had been wanting. With the money from this charter he could live for a year.

"Shake on it," George said holding out his hand and Chris took it. "I'll bring my wife and my brother by tomorrow when I bring the rest of the money. Is ten in the morning all right?"

"Sure. That'll be fine."

"See you then," He said stepping to the dock.

Chris went below and struck a match and lit the oil lamp above the dinette table. He could have turned on electric lights, but there was something soothing about the soft glow of the oil lamp. He turned on the flame under that morning's coffee and sat down at the table. He reached for the volume of Shakespeare and the bills fanning them out on the table in front of him; $1,000 down and $19,000 more to go with it in the morning. There was no question he needed the money, and everything seemed to be working out perfectly, then why did he have the little, painful, tightness right above his stomach. It was the same feeling he got when he was entering into a bay, or harbor, for which he had no charts. It was a feeling he got when he was approaching a reef or a rock. It was the signal to back off and investigate what was in the waters ahead. He had the same knot in his stomach now. *What is it makes me think I should get out the dinghy and go ahead and see what is there before I try to take the boat in? Why am I uncomfortable? Was it the irritation of finding the guy aboard my boat? Could it be I just don't like the looks of the guy?*

There was something in the guy's attitude that had irritated him, and yet he couldn't say exactly what it was. He told himself he should be grateful for his good luck. He really didn't have any choice. He needed this charter. He pushed the bills together and put them in the volume of Shakespeare. Maybe tomorrow he would see things clearly and the knot in his stomach would come undone.

* * *

At 11:10 at night there was a timid knock on the door and when

Myra opened it a bellboy handed her an envelope with the hotel logo in the corner. “Tip the man,” George said to Steve as Myra took the envelope. It was a fax from Max. “Sorry I can’t make the party on February 8. Got delayed here, but congratulations and best wishes.” From the fax George knew they had the heroin on board and they would be leaving on February eighth. Everything was shaping up beautifully. They both had plenty of time to get to the rendezvous. It might even be they would both get there ahead of time. He wished now they had thought of some way to signal each other if they were there early.

CHAPTER ELEVEN

It was 8:30 when Chris stood up in four feet of water in front of the Hilton Hawaiian Village and took off his goggles. The sun, well up over Diamond Head, felt good on his back and shoulders. He walked out of the water and headed the short distance to the yacht harbor. He had just completed a three-mile swim to the Natatorium and back. It was something he did at least three or four mornings a week. He did it more because he liked to swim than for any health reasons. He liked the water, to sail over it, or swim through, it always made him feel better. He usually swam along the beach in water that was three to four feet deep. He swam at that depth for two reasons: first, if he ever got a cramp it would be shallow enough for him to stand up and get out of the water, and second, that was about the depth at which most of the beach goers stopped. At that time of the day there were not many people in the water and the bottom was undisturbed. With his goggles on he could see the bottom clearly and it was not uncommon for him to find things people had lost in the water: coins, car keys, rings and other things. If it was of any real value he turned it over to the police at the Waikiki station and when they didn't find the owner in thirty days it was his. Once he had found a $10,000 diamond ring that had been lost three months before. Unfortunately the owners had reported the loss to the police, describing it exactly and so Chris didn't get anything for that find. He had hoped to find something this morning, just because he had the superstition that finding something first thing in the morning, even if it was only a dime, was a sign of good luck.

Chris was painting the anchor winch when he saw them approaching slowly along the mold. He kept painting but looked up from time to time to watch them. George was still wearing his Panama, dark glasses and flowered shirt, but had white shorts on instead of slacks. The man with him, who Chris guessed must be the brother, was dressed the same way without the hat. But it was the woman walking between them who really attracted his attention. She was wearing a bikini with a matching hip wrap-around, which was not unusual. Lots of girls walked around the yacht harbor wearing bikinis, some of them skimpier than this one, but it was the way she filled it, or rather over filled it that was unusual. It was not just that she was strikingly attractive, but there was something about her, a look he couldn't exactly define that just didn't fit. He didn't know if it was something in the face, or the body language in the way she walked and carried herself that made him feel concern for her for some reason.

"Good morning, Captain," George called when they were even with the boat moored in the slip next to him.

Chris looked up pretending he was just seeing them, stood up, waved a little and went along the dock to let them in the gate. He didn't like being called "captain." He had always felt there was something phony about it, and he was certain George was saying it to flatter him rather than sincerely.

"This is my brother, Steve," George said as Chris turned the key in the gate to let them in, "and this is my wife, Myra."

"Hi," Chris said and walked along ahead of them down the dock. He held out his hand to help Myra step over the one-foot open space between the dock and the boat. She held his hand for just an instant after she was on board, squeezing it a little and looking him in the eye. It puzzled him, because the look she gave him was not at all flirtatious, but worried. He stood there while George and Steve came aboard and then excused himself to put the paint and brushes out of the sun. "May we go below?" George asked.

"Sure. Go ahead," Chris said and walked to the dock box with the paint things. When he came back on board they were all below sitting around the table. Myra was seated in the corner on the same side of the table with George. They sat facing the ladder. Steve sat across from them.

"Well, there's the rest of your money, just like I promised," George said holding out a thick, white envelope when Chris came down the ladder to stand at the end of the table.

Christ took the envelope, looked inside and laid it on the table. There wasn't time to count it now. "Well, before I take your money, maybe we should get a few details straightened out." He slid into the seat beside Steve. "Yesterday you mentioned Tahiti. But I think we should have a definite understanding of which islands you want to go to, how long you want to stay in each place and so forth." He looked around at each of them. Myra was frowning a little and he thought he saw her shake her head slowly, a very little from side to side, or was it just his imagination?

"Tahiti, of course. But we could stop at the Marquesas on the way down couldn't we? They are practically on the way. I think that'll probably be all we can do this trip. If we run out of time, well, we can always fly back from Tahiti. I would, of course, pay you for the time it would take to get back, even if we weren't on board. How many days do you think it would take to get to the Marquesas?"

"Eighteen to twenty-two days depending on the winds. You'll have to have passports and Visas."

"We took care of all that along with immunization in Los Angeles. Everything's been taken care of. When can we leave?"

"In a couple of days, I guess. Take on fresh stores, top off water and fuel, and of course I'll have to see your passports and visas," he said standing up at the end of the table. George had done all the talking since they came aboard. Steve sat looking bored by it all. Myra was leaning back now, looking down at her hands folded in her lap. He had the distinct impression she didn't want to make this trip and no matter how beautiful she was he didn't want someone along who was going to be complaining all the time. "Do you like to sail, Mrs. Harris?" he asked.

She looked up a little surprised and then smiled when George turned to look at her. "Oh, yes! I love to sail," she said.

"Have you ever done any extended sailing? I mean more than just for a day or two or a weekend? Being cooped up on a little boat for two or three weeks at a time can get pretty trying if you aren't enjoying it."

"Oh, yes. We chartered a boat in the Bahamas last year for a couple of months and I loved it."

The knot that had almost come undone just pulled a little tighter. He was sure George had said the Virgins. Nobody who had been to either place would get them confused. Maybe he had heard George incorrectly, but he doubted that.

"Well, I guess that takes care of it," George said. "Oh, by the way, I don't see any global positioning system."

"No, I still use a sextant and azimuth tables."

"I don't blame you. I like the feel of the sextant in my hand. Well, when can we get underway?"

Chris continued to stand at the end of the table blocking them from getting up. "Do you want me to find a cook, or will we take turns cooking."

"Myra will do the cooking," George said.

Chris looked at her. She nodded and smiled looking relieved for the first time since they'd come on board. "Oh, yes. I love to cook."

There just was no excuse for not leaving except he didn't feel good about it. He couldn't just pass up a charter that had absolutely nothing wrong with it except he wasn't totally comfortable. "Then I guess we can get underway any time after we get the stores aboard. Day after tomorrow if you like."

"Fine. Fine," George said getting up and clapping him on the shoulders. "Oh, I almost forgot. You'll need money for fresh stores, won't you? How much do you need?"

"I don't know exactly. It's covered in the charter fee."

Chris followed them up the ladder and off the boat. They shook hands all around outside the gate and Chris stood leaning against the dock box watching them walk away. When they were out of sight he turned back to the dock box to get the brush and paint to finish painting the anchor winch. Walking back along his dock he called, "Hey, Charlie. I need the keys to the truck."

Charlie emerged from the hatch holding out the keys to the pickup they jointly owned. "That's the one, Chris. Some looker, huh?"

"What are you talking about?"

"That's the bird who was around here looking for you. That's the same one."

"Are you sure?"

"Swear to God."

"Huh. Never saw her before in my life." He stood for a moment, a puzzled frown on his face, shook his head once and then went to finish the painting. He had things to do, deposit the money in the bank, go downtown to the French consulate to get a visa for French Polynesia and then out to Costco's to pick up the fresh stores. He felt good. He had money again and he was going sailing. Everything was right with his world.

* * *

"You dumb bitch," George said when they were well out of

earshot of the *AHWANAH.* "You could have ruined everything with your remark about the Bahamas. I told the two of you last night it was the Virgin Islands. Can't you remember anything? Fortunately for you, he didn't seem to notice."

"I'm sorry," Myra said contritely and wondered what had come over George. He had never talked to her like that before.

"I can sense this guy is hesitant about something. When we go to see him tomorrow I want both of you to be friendly, I mean really friendly. Steve, you were acting like you didn't want any part of this trip. If he's doing something when we come by tomorrow, Steve, offer to help him with it."

"Sure, George. Sure," he said and thought, *Go ahead and give orders while you can. You won't be doing it much longer*.

"And you, Myra. Play up to the guy. You were as cold as a fish today. What the hell is wrong with you anyway?'

"I don't know."

"Well snap out of it. I don't care if you give him the idea he can make it with you. He has to want us on board so bad he can taste it."

"Yes, George," she said meekly and wondered what would happen if sometime during the afternoon she suggested to George she go visit Chris. She could warn Chris about what was really happening when she was supposed to be seducing him. But that wouldn't work. As soon as she told Chris and the trip fell through George would blame her. She would have to run. But there was no place to which she could run and hide right now. She had to have a head start and get far enough away that one of George's fingers couldn't find her and pick her off.

But she also knew George would probably agree to her going to visit Chris. He had as much as suggested it himself and she realized suddenly that to George, she was just something to be used, like a car, that he liked and might even be proud of, but he was willing to loan to someone else if it would help whatever it was he was doing.

* * *

Charlie had let them in again and they were sitting around the cockpit waiting for him when he returned at noon with a load of fresh stores. George waved a cigar-holding hand as Chris started down the dock with a carton full of cabbage and carrots. "Aye, how is it going?" George said putting the cigar in his mouth and reaching for the box.

"Pretty good. I have a few more things to get, but we can get underway tonight or tomorrow morning if you want."

"Fine. Fine. Tomorrow morning will be just fine."

"You got more stuff to be brought aboard?" Steve asked.

"A whole truck full."

"I'll help you with it," he said stepping ashore.

"Hi," Myra said softly. If the tone of her voice and the way she looked at him wasn't a come on, he'd never seen one. She was wearing very skimpy, very tight blue shorts, and a white blouse that wasn't much more than a film. It was obvious she had no bra on. If she didn't want to be stared at she shouldn't dress like that, he thought, nodding in answer to her greeting and looking away. He turned to unlock and open the hatch.

"You folks want to stay aboard tonight, or are you going to get one last good night's sleep ashore?"

"Oh, we'll probably stay at the hotel tonight. I have some calls to make. But we'll bring most of our gear aboard today," George said as Steve arrived with two net sacks of onions.

"O.K. Well, as long as you are all here I'll show you where you can stow your gear. I'll leave her unlocked so you can get in if I'm not here when you get back," he said starting down the ladder. "I have the quarter berth there next to the chart table. You decide which of the other berths you want. The dinette table here pushes down into a double berth, the settee here opens up into above and below bunks and there's the double V-berth in the forepeak." He showed them the wet locker right next to the ladder where they could stow their foul-weather gear and narrow hanging lockers, one for each of them with drawers below. He explained the peculiarities of pumping out the toilet. "And while I'm at it, I might as well show you how to work the stove so you can fix a pot of coffee whenever you want it," he said as they started aft.

"Show Myra. If I want anything I'll ask her to fix it for me," George said starting up the ladder. "Steve and I will go and bring the rest of the food on board."

He stood looking through the hatch as they stepped over the cockpit combing to the deck. When he turned around she was leaning back against the reefer, her elbows behind her resting on its top. Her chest was thrust forward against the thin material of her blouse. He looked away quickly. She smiled a little and then stood up straight. "Show me the stove," she said coming over to squeeze in next to him in front of the stove.

"This is a propane gas stove just like the ones in any kitchen except it is a lot smaller and doesn't have a pilot light. You have to light it with a match or with this flint lighter here. Lots of people don't like gas stoves on a boat because propane is heavier than air and can settle and build up in the bilge and then one little spark and BOOM"—he threw his arms in the air—"ALL GONE. But if you're careful, a gas stove isn't any more dangerous than alcohol or kerosene. The only thing to remember is to close this outside valve first when you are done," he said pointing to a bronze valve in the overhead. "This is the way you do it." He started though the procedure. "Open the outside valve first. Then turn on your burner. Light it. When you're finished cooking turn the outside valve off first so the gas in the line bleeds out. When the flame goes off, turn off the burner. She had stood next to him nodding all the time he had been talking and he had been very much aware of her perfume and the warmth of her body. "If I see you've forgotten to turn off that outside valve you'll hear me holler like you've never heard before."

"I'll remember! I'll remember. I promise," she said shaking her head and raising both hands in a gesture of surrender. The action separated the front of her blouse giving him an even clearer view of the firm rounded breasts, their pink nipples reaching out to him. She lowered her arms and smiled at him knowingly and said, "Do you find me attractive?"

"Lady, you are dangerously attractive. I think it would be best right now if I go help them get the rest of the stores. I can show you where the food stores are later," he said going up the ladder.

George and Steve helped finish bringing the stores from the truck piling the boxes on deck while Chris took them below. She helped put some of the things away and when the last of the boxes were on board the three of them left, George in front, Myra behind the others. At the gate she looked back and in that moment Chris knew she was not being sexy, or flirting, but that she looked scared.

CHAPTER TWELVE

In his sleep Chris heard the ship's bell strike three bells and knew it was five-thirty. He had reached the point where he could sleep through the sound of the striking bell and still be aware of what time it was. Waking now, he lay in the bunk luxuriating in the idea of staying in the bed another hour with the bunk level and unmoving beneath him. The next time he came to lie down the bunk would be tilted to one side with the heel of the boat and rocking back and forth with the movement of the waves. That too could be pleasant. Whether asleep or awake he liked the motion of the boat underway.

The clock struck four bells and he jumped quickly out of the bunk deciding the thing to do was have a big shore side breakfast before getting underway. He dressed and washed quickly and went to the Chart House restaurant for papaya, a double order of eggs and sausage, and waffles. When he came out of the restaurant the sun had climbed over Diamond Head sending long steaks of sunshine through the shadows of the high-rise hotels. He walked back to the boat feeling full and satisfied. It was a perfect day for getting underway with high, light clouds and normal tradewinds.

Chris was sitting in the cockpit with a cup of coffee, the sail covers off and the outboard mooring lines in; ready for getting underway when the Harrises arrived a few minutes after eight. They came through the gate he had propped open, each carrying a backpack with overnight things. They had brought the rest of their things aboard the day before.

"Well, here we are, raring to go," George called walking down the dock. He stepped aboard then turned around for Myra's bag and said, "Are we ready?"

"Oh, yeah. Why don't you get yourself one last steady cup of coffee and then we'll go around to the fuel dock and top off the tanks and be on our way."

"Great! Great!" George smiled starting down the ladder with their bags. "Hey Myra, fix me a drink, will you," he said over his shoulder.

"O.K.," she said stepping over the combing into the cockpit. "Do you want your cup refilled, Chris?"

"No. I still have enough, thank you. Well, are you ready to go sailing?" He asked while leaning over and starting the engine.

"I guess so."

"Huh, that doesn't sound too enthusiastic."

"Oh, don't worry. It's not the sailing."

"Do you get seasick?"

"I have once or twice when it was really rough, but not usually."

"I have lots of Dramamine aboard. Do you want some?"

"I don't think I'll need any today," she said and went below to fix George's limes and Coke.

Steve mumbled something in answer to Chris' greeting, took his bag below and returned almost immediately with a cup of coffee. He sat down across from Chris, sipping his coffee and looking glum. Chris had the feeling he was trying to avoid getting into a conversation. George was the only one who seemed eager about starting out. Maybe the other two didn't like getting up early when they were supposed to be on vacation, or maybe they'd had a big night and were just hung over. Maybe Steve was one of those slow starters who couldn't stand anyone until he'd had a cup of coffee. If so then Steve would probably always be fifteen minutes late to relieve the watch. Fine. Then let Steve relieve George. Steve was obviously the older of the two brothers, but George was the one who made the decisions. Let him be the one to complain if Steve was continually late.

George and Myra came back on deck, Myra with a cup of coffee and George with his drink. George was still wearing his hat, but had changed into shorts and a T-shirt. Myra had changed into one of her skimpy bikinis. "Well, I guess we're ready, huh?" George said unwrapping the cigar he had brought with him.

Chris had talked to them about not smoking below decks and he was pleased to see George had waited until he was on deck before lighting up. "Yeah, just let the engine warm up a few more minutes. There are three of us to stand watches so we'll stand a regular four on and eight off. George, you'll have the first one until noon. Steve will relieve you and I'll have the first dogwatch. As soon as we're underway, Myra, I'll show you all the different places food is stored. Any questions?"

"I don't think so," George said and Chris stepped ashore to throw off the lines.

Charlie stepped off his boat. “I’ll get those for you,” he said walking along behind Chris along the narrow dock. “Sure wish I were coming with you.” He stood at the end of the dock as the *AHWANAH* slowly backed out. “Hey, when you get there tell Harry to write sometime,” he called across the widening water separating them.

“Have you written him?” Chris called back.

“What does that have to do with it?”

Chris waved in reply and George asked, “Who is Harry?”

“A friend or ours in Papeete. Married a Tahitian and lives there now.”

“Do you know a lot of people in Tahiti?”

“A few,” Chris said shrugging a little.

“I suppose you wrote to tell them to expect you.”

“Oh, I sent off a couple of cards. They’ll tell the others.”

“Well, there should be quite a welcoming committee on hand when we get there then.”

“They may not be waiting on the dock, but they’ll be looking for me.”

It was nine-thirty when they passed the channel entrance buoy, raised the sails and set a southeasterly course. It was comfortable sailing with the trades blowing steadily out of the northeast. George took the helm and Chris was relieved and a little surprised at what a good helmsman he was. Chris put out the taffrail log, streamed a fishing line and then went around putting things away, mooring lines and fenders stowed under the dinghy and checked there was no chafing on any of the sheets. When he was satisfied everything was as it should be, he and Myra went below to check through the stores.

He showed her where all the fresh fruits and vegetables were. “You should check through these every couple of days and pick out any that are starting to get soft.” He showed her the dry foods; flour, rice, beans, dried milk, sugar under the seats in the main cabin and the canned goods under the V-bunk in the forward cabin. She was attentive and pleasant, but she seemed distracted by something.

He closed the bunk covers, put the mattresses back in place and sat down on the bunk. She sat on the one across from him, their knees touching in the confines of the V-shaped area between the two bunks. She was looking at him attentively and he knew she was expecting him to say something more about the stores, or about cooking. "Tell me. Did you come around looking for me before I met you with George a couple of days ago?"

"What makes you think that?" she said indignantly.

"Charlie told me."

"Oh." She said nodding slowly. "Yeah, I was looking for you, but it was nothing."

"I don't think it was nothing when you go looking for a man you have never met before. It seems to me when a woman goes looking for a stranger she must have a good reason for it."

"It doesn't matter now. Just forget it."

"If it mattered then, it matters now."

"Look, just forget the whole thing. Please!

"O.K. O.K.," he said. She obviously wasn't going to talk about it. He wondered if maybe she didn't want to make this trip and wanted to talk him out of it before her husband made the arrangements. He didn't like not understanding what was going on. "Look! If you don't want to make this trip it's not too late to turn back. I'd rather do that and refund the money than have an unpleasant trip."

"Oh, no. You can't do that," she said desperately. More calmly she added, "It's really nothing at all. Please. Can we just forget the whole thing? Please!" She stood up and he watched her as she walked aft through the main cabin.

* * *

George Costellos sat comfortably, a little to the left of the wheel, His right leg extended across the cockpit and braced on the other side. He was relaxed, confident and content. They were on their way. Everything had gone smoothly. For the next three weeks he had nothing to think about but sailing and getting to the rendezvous on time, which should be no problem at all. Steve would have to be dealt with eventually, but not until Max and Larry were on board. He wanted them to witness Steve's execution. Furthermore it was convenient to have Steve aboard to stand watches. Without Steve, Chris and he would have to relieve each other every four hours and that could begin to get tiring. Steve couldn't do any damage out here, and if Chris did not cooperate, then he would certainly need Steve until Max and Larry came aboard.

Chris presented a problem he had not thought of. He had not expected Chris to know people in Tahiti. For some reason it had never occurred to him. He had planned all along to get rid of Chris when Max and Larry came aboard. Now if they were not in Tahiti in twenty or thirty days those people might start getting concerned and writing letters and informing the authorities the *AHWANAH* was overdue. If for some reason the Coast Guard were notified to be on the lookout for the *AHWANAH*, they would have to find it with the owner on board. Nor would it do for them to find the boat with the owner on board who might expose them. He had to find a way to make Chris go along with him whether he wanted to or not.

Myra came up from below and suddenly George had his answer. George had no doubt in his mind Chris was one of those noble kinds who would not sacrifice someone else for his own safety. Sometime between now and when he took over the boat Chris and Myra would have to become, if not lovers, at least friends who trusted and confided in each other. Chris wouldn't dare try anything if he thought it would cause her harm. From now on he would give them every chance to be alone together. He would start ignoring Myra and being mean to her; not real mean, not physically mean, but mean enough that she would want to talk to someone about it. If he worked it right, Chris would be the one she talked to. Chris would sympathize with her and feel protective. They could get rid of Chris when they sank the boat. He laughed a little within himself, the captain going down with his boat.

CHAPTER THIRTEEN

The first week the sailing was everything Chris, or anyone else, could have hoped for with clear skies and steady, northeasterly winds. Steve was the only one who seemed unhappy with the trip. He never really complained. He just didn't seem to enjoy anything. When everyone else was up on deck watching a herd of passing whales, or flying fish, or porpoises jumping alongside the boat, he stayed down below sacked out, or reading something from the stack of magazines he had brought with him. If he was on watch, he never called the others to see a new sight. Chris often wondered why the other two had brought him along.

Myra was undoubtedly the best cook he'd ever had aboard. She was comfortable in the galley, able to substitute for things she didn't have and she never complained. She was always smiling and cheerful when the others were around, but sometimes when she thought no one was watching her, Chris would see a worried frown on her face, or a fearful look in her eyes.

On deck he would see her lying on her back on the cabin top, holding a book in front of her, and he knew she was not reading it. She was staring past it to the clouds above and the expression on her face was not one of tranquil daydreaming, but concern and worry. He studied her, noting the biting of her lips, the blinking of her eyes as though fighting back tears, the tormented shaking of her head, the rising of her chest with a resigned sigh. He studied her the same way he observed the changes in the sky, or the surface of the sea as indications of something, but whereas he could tell what might be troubling the sky and the sea, he could not tell what was troubling her. More than once when they were alone he had an impulse to ask her what was bothering her.

Chris got his answer the eighth day out, just after he had taken and plotted the noon sight. He was sitting relaxed in the forward end of the cockpit, aware of Steve sitting sullenly at the wheel, but he was really mostly looking down through the hatch to where Myra was doing the lunch dishes in the galley. Looking through the hatch he could see her with her legs spread a little bracing against the motion of the boat. He was looking at her now wishing he could console her somehow. George had said something to her that had made her physically shudder and then he had seen her wipe her cheek more than once as though she were wiping tears away. He tried to keep looking at the sea, the sky and the sails, but he couldn't keep from glancing at her.

He saw George pass behind her and was aware there was something different about him, but did not realize what it was until George started up the ladder toward him and he recognized what he had thought was a strangely striped shirt was a shoulder holster. His first reaction was surprised curiosity because George had not mentioned having a gun. His next thought was that George was going to throw some cans over the side for target practice. George stepped over the lip of the hatchway and sat down opposite Chris. He nonchalantly pulled the thirty-eight out of the holster, pointed it at Chris and said, "O.K. Steve, bring her about and steady up on three zero zero."

"What the hell's going on here?" Chris asked starting to get up as Steve turned the wheel.

"Stay right there, Jamison," George said waving the point of the pistol a little. There was something in the tone of voice and the look on his face that made Chris back down. He had an impulse to grab the gun out of George's hand. George wasn't sitting that far away, but he knew somehow that before he could grab the gun George would pull the trigger. *The guy must be mad to pull something like this.* He looked through the hatch hoping Myra might give him some clue as to what was going on, but she was busy scouring a frying pan.

The boat came around into the wind. The sails shifted to the other side. The boat heeled over on the starboard tack and settled into the new course. Chris sat there with the gun still pointed at him until Steve had the sails trimmed and then he asked, "Now will someone please tell me what's going on here."

"Why, it should be obvious," George said smiling. "We've pirated your boat."

Chris looked at each of them, unable to believe what he had heard. Steve, sullen and indifferent as always, sat behind the wheel looking at the compass. George was sitting comfortably across from Chris, his left arm resting on the cockpit combing, his right hand holding the gun. Chris looked below to where Myra was standing to one side facing him, out of George's line of sight. In her right hand she was still holding the sponge. She shook her head emphatically and her lips formed the word "don't." *Who does she think she is telling me not to do anything?*

"A little warning, Jamison," George said. "When we started out we needed both you and the boat. Now we no longer need you. You can still be convenient to stand watches and so on, but we don't have to have you. So behave yourself. Don't cause any trouble, or ask any questions, and you'll be all right. Believe me, the minute you try anything that will in any way cause me the slightest trouble, you go over the side. And when we don't need your boat any more we'll send it down to meet you."

"You're still going to need me to do the navigating."

George burst out laughing. "Shit, Jamison, I can navigate circles around you. And don't get any ideas about using the radio. I've ripped it out." He stood up and walked back to give the gun to Steve, who took it, keeping it pointed at Chris while George went below. He returned a minute later with the transmitter box in his hand, went to the rail and dropped it over the side. He went back and got his gun, put his hand on the wheel and said. "I'll take her for a minute, Steve, while you go below and get your gun."

Steve went below and came back with a gun stuck in his belt. It looked bigger than the one George had. Steve took the wheel again, adjusting the revolver in his belt as he sat down. George slipped his pistol back in the holster. "We're both going to be watching you all the time, Jamison. You may be able to jump one of us before we blow a hole through you, but you sure ain't going to get both of us," George said sitting down and propping his foot against the other side of the cockpit. "And don't try anything cute when you're on watch. Like I said, don't give me any trouble and you'll be all right. Foul up and you're dead."

"Do you still want me to do the navigating?"

"I'll take care of that. All you have to do is stand your watches and keep this thing sailing."

Chris started to get up and George automatically reached for his gun pointing it at him. If Chris hadn't been so angry he would have been amused that George jumped whenever he moved. He went forward and lay down on the bowsprit catwalk. He had to get away from them for a while and suspended above the water on the narrow platform at the front of the boat was as far away as he could get. He wondered what they wanted the boat for. He had chartered it to them. If they wanted to go someplace why didn't they just tell him? He'd have taken them wherever they wanted to go, but on this course they weren't going anywhere. They would probably change direction later, but if they stayed on this course they would go right down the middle between the Hawaiian chain of islands and the Christmas Island - Palmyra chain. Maybe it was some kind of bizarre, practical joke, but if it was, it was about as funny as a hole in the hull.

But it wasn't a joke. These bastards had stolen his ship. Threatened to kill him and stolen his boat. The more he thought about it, the angrier he became with them and with himself. He had let himself be taken. He'd known all along, felt it in his gut, that there was something wrong with this charter. He'd never been uncomfortable with any other group he'd taken out, but this one had made him uneasy before he had even started and he had ignored his instincts. He had let himself be conned.

If he only had a gun he'd make them pay for what they had done. But he didn't have a gun. He thought for a while that maybe one night when he had the midnight watch and they were all asleep he might be able to sneak down and turn on the gas. With the hatches closed he would be up on deck in the fresh air while down below the gas would asphyxiate them.

For a while he fantasized about going below as the sun came up and finding them all lying peacefully dead in their bunks. But then what would he do? Take the bodies back and try and explain what had happened? No, he couldn't take the bodies back. By the time he got to any port they would have been stinking rotten. Maybe he could throw them over the side and claim they had been washed overboard in a storm or something. But it wouldn't be hard for the authorities to find out if they had gone through any storms.

There was bound to be an investigation and he had visions of standing trial and being sent to prison. The idea of being cooped up behind walls for the rest of his life, not being able to smell the salt water, not being able to take his boat out any time he wanted to, was worse than the idea of being killed. It was just too much to understand. One minute he was convinced George was capable of killing him, and the next minute the thing was just too absurd.

He faintly heard the ship's bell strike eight bells and went aft to take the watch. Steve stood up when he saw Chris coming, keeping his left hand on a spoke of the wheel, his right hand close to the butt of the pistol protruding from his waistband. Chris sat down behind the wheel and Steve went below. Half an hour later Myra stuck her head out the hatchway and said, "Want a cup of coffee, Chris?"

He glared at her. "Does what I want make any difference anymore?"

She disappeared below without answering and a few minutes later reappeared with his coffee mug in her hand. She worked her way toward him, legs spread to steady herself against the rolling of the boat, careful not to spill any of the coffee. He sat there watching her, not standing up to help her by reaching for the cup. She stopped in front of him, holding out the mug. "I'm sorry, Chris."

"Are you?" he asked reaching for the cup.

"Yes, I really am. I'm sorry I had anything to do with this. Believe me, I had no choice. There's nothing I could do."

"Is that so?" He asked sarcastically.

She glanced over her shoulder quickly. "Look, I tried to warn you. Twice when I could get away I came by to warn you not to take this charter." She looked over her shoulder again to make sure neither of the other two was within hearing.

So that's why she had come around the boat. "There were times after that when you could have warned me."

"Once you had agreed to take us there was nothing I could do. If you had changed your mind, George would have started wondering why. He had Max check you out before we came over here. He knew you were nearly broke, that you need the money." She turned to look down the hatchway again. "He would have figured someone had tipped you off, and if he had found out it was me, he would have had me killed."

"That's absurd," he said, but he knew it was the truth.

"It's the truth. If you want to stay alive, do exactly what he says," she said and started to leave.

"Hey, wait a minute," he said grabbing her arm. "At least tell me what this is all about. What's this about investigating me? What does he want with me?"

"It wasn't you he wanted, it was your boat."

"O.K. why did he want my boat?"

She looked toward the hatch again. “To pick up a shipment of heroin.”

“What?”

“They’re meeting a boat from Hong Kong out here somewhere and they are going to transfer the stuff from that boat to this one. George figured someone might possibly know about the other boat and be watching for it, but they will never suspect this one.”

“Oh, Christ, why me?” He wasn’t asking her the question, but she answered it for him.

“Because you’ve never been in trouble of any kind. You don’t even have traffic violations.” He let go of her arm and sat there looking at her shaking his head. “I’m sorry, Chris. I really am. If I could have prevented it, I would have,” she said and went below to continue preparing the evening meal.

Chris sat there trying to sort it all out. Now that he knew what they were doing he had no doubt George meant what he said. He appreciated the fact Myra had tried to warn him before they left and she regretted the situation now. Although he was not quite as angry with her as he had been, he still considered her one of them. She was after all, George’s wife.

He wondered for a while if he would be able to escape in the dinghy, but gave up the idea almost immediately. Even if he could provision it with a little food and water and get it over the side without them knowing about it, it would be almost impossible to get to any land in an eight-foot dinghy. The important thing was to stay alive, to wait until he could get the upper hand. Maybe when they were asleep at night he could jump one of them, get the gun away from him, and then at least things would be a little more even, except he knew he couldn’t shoot a man. But they didn’t know that. Steve was the one to go for. He would be sleeping in the main cabin while George and Myra would be forward with the door closed. That was the way to do it. He would be on watch again from midnight till four in the morning. Sometime during that watch he would tie off the wheel and sneak down and get Steve. Then just wait there with the gun in his hand until George, unsuspectingly, came out of the forward compartment.

For the next hour he kept going over the scheme in his mind, refining it, thinking of things that might go wrong and how to deal with them if not prevent them. After he got the gun he would have to gag and tie Steve somehow. But all Steve would have to do was kick the bulkhead or something and that could wake up George and Myra. The thing to do would be to get the gun and then bring Steve up on deck and tie him up so tightly he couldn't make any noise. He would have to convince Steve he was desperate enough to shoot him. He thought he could do that.

He might not be able to do anything tonight, though. This was just the first day and they would probably all be extra cautious. He would cooperate with them, let them get confident and careless, and then some night when they were both asleep he would make his move.

At almost exactly six o'clock George came up on deck with an after-dinner cup of coffee in one hand and a fresh cigar in his mouth. The cigar was already lit which meant his policy of no smoking below deck was no longer in effect. The only indication of the holster and its pistol was a six-inch length of leather strap showing through the front opening of his light jacket. Neither of them said anything as George set his coffee on the seat next to him and moved behind the wheel relieving Chris at the helm. Chris walked around the deck once, a morning and evening habit of his, feeling the tension on the shrouds as he passed, looking up at the mast and the stays to make sure none of the sail hanks had broken or pulled loose, checking there was no chafing on any of the lines.

When he went below Myra was dishing up his dinner, a chunk of ham, boiled potatoes, cabbage and carrots. He took the plate of food and started to sit down at the place set for him. Across the table from him Steve lounged in the corner with a cup of coffee on the table in front of him and a cigarette burning in a makeshift ashtray. "I guess I'll eat topside," he said picking up his fork and paper napkin and starting up the ladder. In the cockpit he wasn't much farther away from George than he would have been from Steve at the table, but at least the air was clear up here and he didn't have to sit facing any of them.

Chris was halfway through his dinner when he saw Myra and Steve walking back and forth between the forward compartment and the main salon. He leaned forward wondering what they were doing, watching while Steve carried his personal gear forward and Myra brought hers back, dumping her things on the bunk opposite the dinette. "What's going on?" Chris asked when Myra came back to the galley to finish the dishes.

She shrugged a little. “George said Steve and I had to change places. Are you finished?” she asked coming halfway up the ladder to get his empty dish and fork.

Chris took a sip of his coffee, hesitated a moment wondering if this was one of the questions he wasn’t supposed to ask, but went ahead anyway. “How come you’re having Myra and Steve change places?”

George smiled around the cigar that was stuck in his mouth, took a drag on it before taking it out and said, “Just cautious, Jamison. I got to thinking that one night when you were on watch Steve and I might both be too tired to stay awake and watch you. I put a lock on the forward door. You can’t get through there without making enough noise to wake us. Now we can both sleep peacefully and not have to worry about you.” He raised his eyebrow while waving his cigar holding hand. “Of course, having Steve bunk in with me won’t be as pleasant as having Myra there, but business before pleasure.”

That son-of-a-bitch seemed to think of everything. It was almost as though he had been able to read Chris’ thoughts. “Why don’t you just kill me and get it over with, then you won’t have to worry about me at all,” he said angrily.

George laughed. “I’m not a murderer, Jamison. You haven’t given me any reason to kill you yet. Besides, I need you a little longer. If you were gone and something were to happen to Steve, I would have to sail this thing all by myself and that might get to be like work.” He was laughing all the time he was talking.

Chris sat looking across the water to the setting sun and felt truly discouraged for the first time that day. Up to then he had been angry, or frustrated, or feeling he had been made a fool of, but he had not been discouraged. Now he knew how powerless he really was.

Myra came on deck carrying her cup of coffee. She was wearing a long-sleeved, blue sweatshirt to protect against the evening chill. She sat down opposite him, facing a little forward; looking into the wind so her blond hair blew straight back and it seemed to Chris she was making a point of not looking at him. He went below without saying anything, rinsed out his cup, and went to bed. A few minutes later Myra came down and he could hear her moving around in the darkness, spreading out her bedding on the bunk just forward of his. He heard her get into bed and quietly say, “Good night, Chris,” but he didn't answer her.

Chris Jamison fell asleep almost immediately. He was not the kind to be kept awake by worry. Some people eat to take their minds off their worries, others drink, but Chris used sleep as an escape. There was no sense worrying about something that could not be changed. When he found himself starting to worry about something he would lie down and most often fall asleep thinking about the things that would have kept others awake. Sleep gave situations time to change, and when he woke up, he was able to think, which was entirely different from worrying. He slept lightly, as he always did when he was underway, aware, even in his sleep, of what was happening around him. At seven bells he was aware George went through the cabin on his way forward to make sure Steve was up to take the watch. He was aware of the smell of Steve lighting a cigarette in the forward compartment and that irritated him almost enough to wake him up completely. Half an hour later Steve went on deck and George came below going right to his bunk without stopping at the chart table to fill out the log. When Chris was in control he had required everyone fill out the log when they came off watch and that omission now both angered him and gave him hope. If George was getting sloppy about filling out the log, he might also get sloppy about other things.

CHAPTER FOURTEEN

In her bunk, separated from Chris by only the four-foot space occupied by the chart table, Myra lay sleepless. She had known all along her association with George would have to end someday. She had also known she could not be the one to end it, not in the usual sense. His pride would not let her be the one to end the affair. He would have to be the one who said he was finished with her. But she had expected, when the time came for her to disappear, that she would be safely on land with her plans made and her bank accounts in order. She would leave him sometime when George was off on one of his many trips. When he came back she would be gone to England, or France, or maybe Australia. It had never occurred to her they would be on a little boat in the middle of the Pacific when he decided to dump her. Nor was there anyone who would miss her.

For the past several years the only associates she had were George and his friends. They would not wonder or care she was gone, and if they did they most certainly would not ask what had happened to her. Even her parents would not know she was gone. She wished now she had at least sent them a card from time to time. She wouldn't have had to let them know where she was, just that she was still alive. She thought now her parents had been right about one having to account for the way one lived their life.

She had known, though she refused to admit it, that George was through with her. Nor did she have any illusions about the finality of it. Since they left Honolulu George had not had anything to do with her. Not once had he crossed over to her bunk or ordered her into his. Not once since they came aboard the boat had he run his hands over her body, fondling her, or even hugging her. He had always been a toucher, a hugger, but not once during the past week had he touched her. She had known when he was through with her sexually, he was through with her completely. She had expected, though in her heart she knew otherwise, she would be able to keep him interested indefinitely. Even after leaving Honolulu she had told herself he was ignoring her because he was preoccupied, he was tired, the irregular hours of standing watch and the fresh air made him sleepy. She knew now she had told herself those things because she needed something to hold on to.

When he told her to change places with Steve she had said, "I don't have anything to protect myself with. What if he tries to use me as a hostage or something?" It was a test question. If George had answered he didn't think Chris would try anything, or that they could rescue her from anything Chris tried, she would have made herself believe there was still some hope. Instead he had answered, "I couldn't care less what he tries to do to you."

She wondered now why he had brought her along. She had never really minded being considered a sexual toy. As long as he was still interested in his toy she was safe. The problem was she had not been just his toy, but she knew too much about too many things. She had suspected all along he intended to kill Chris and sink the boat. He couldn't leave that kind of witness alive. Back in a safe-deposit box in L.A. there were computer disks with her life with George. She had thought of it as protection. But that protection couldn't do her any good out here. Now she was in the same situation as Chris. She was alive now because it was convenient for him to have her as a cook. But the day would come when he no longer needed her as a cook. When that day came she would be as expendable as Chris.

She heard Chris get up and move around in the darkness, dressing to go on watch, even before being called. For a brief moment there was the light from the flaring match when he lit the stove to warm up the left over coffee, then just a slight blue glow. The glow diminished as the pot was put over the flame and then a short time later the smell of warming coffee. She saw the silhouette of him reach up to turn off the overhead valve and then the blue glow was extinguished completely. He took his coffee up on deck with him. A few minutes later Steve came through, knocked on the door to the forward compartment saying, "Hey, George, it's me." She waited until she thought they were both probably asleep and then got up, put on a jacket, and went on deck.

He was sitting in the corner of the cockpit, his arms resting on the combing on either side of him, his left leg stretched out on the seat in front of him, his right leg bent at the knee with the bare foot resting against one of the spokes of the wheel. His right knee kept rising and lowering a little as he kept the boat on course with his foot. She sat down next to him and he moved the arm that would have been around her if he had left it on the combing. “I couldn’t sleep,” she said. He didn’t answer, but she thought she saw him nod his head a little.

She sat there silently for a while feeling the awkwardness of his silence. She stared at the stream of phosphorescence left by the passing of the hull, at the stars above, each standing out clear and stark. She almost made a comment about the night but stopped herself. She had not come up here to make idle chatter. He absent-mindedly reached for his cup, tipped it toward him, and then set it down again when he saw it was empty. “Want me to put on a pot of coffee?” she asked.

“If you want to.”

She went below, taking his cup with her. She worked in the darkness, rinsing the pot and cup cautiously, making sure they didn’t clang against the side of the steel sink, pumping the water slowly so there would be no gurgling sound from the sucking of the pump. She suddenly realized her actions were not out of consideration, but out of fear. Fear George might consider her making coffee for Chris as disloyalty and get angry. For the past several years she had been living in a state of continual fear, afraid of doing something that might displease him.

She turned on the small overhead light and did the rest of the job, measuring out the grounds, lighting the stove, and putting the pot on. She didn’t intentionally make any noise, but she didn’t any longer care if she angered George.

She turned off the light and climbed the ladder, sitting down on the top step where she could see over the cabin top, but still know what the coffee pot was doing. She sat there thinking of the number of times she had dreamed about getting away, thinking of places she could go to where he was not likely to find her, changing her name, dying her hair, and creating a whole new identity for herself. But she had never done it because she had been afraid it might not work. Also, it had always been easier to hope something would happen to free her without having to do anything herself. Now it was too late.

She heard the first perk of the pot and went below to turn the flame down so it would continue to perk at a slow and steady rate. She stood leaning back against the sink staring at the blue glow underneath the pot. If only something would happen to George. If only he would fall over the side or something, but those were the kinds of thoughts she always had when she was desperate, and she had never been more desperate.

She turned the flame off, poured them each a mug, and went on deck. She handed his to him, sat down, started to raise the cup to her mouth and then realized it was still too hot to drink, and set it down to cool. "I can understand why you didn't believe me when I said I was sorry this morning, but I really did mean it, you know."

"I suppose."

"You don't really believe me now either, do you?"

"Yeah, I believe you. I guess a wife has to go along with her husband even if she doesn't like some of the things he does, especially if he's that kind of a guy."

She hesitated for a moment and then said quietly, "He's not my husband."

She saw him turn to stare at her. "Then why in the world do you stay with him?"

"I was always too scared to leave." She started telling him about her life with George. She talked for almost an hour and he didn't interrupt her except occasionally when he was confused about something. "I was too weak to do anything about it myself. I kept hoping for some miracle, for something to happen to him that would set me free. Even now I'm hoping for something to happen. When I was down in the galley making coffee, I was hoping he would fall over the side, but I'm too weak and scared to push him over the side myself. Lots of times, until today, it would have been so easy to give him a little push, but I never could do it."

"And if we..." He paused for just an instant and she knew it was because he had inadvertently used the word we, "did push him over the side, what difference would it make? Wouldn't Steve just take over?"

"He'd probably try to, but he's just a peon. I doubt he knows where we are supposed to meet the other boat. George's father is probably the only other person, except Max who knows the meeting place."

"Well, there's no question George is going to be on guard now, so we're not going to get a chance to do it anyway."

"If you did get the chance, could you do it?"

"No."

"That's where he has the advantage. He wouldn't bat an eyelash before he pushed one of us over the side, but we would hesitate. We don't stand much of a chance do we?"

"Oh, we'll get out of this some way," he said, but he wasn't nearly as confident as he tried to sound. All he had learned made the situation seem worse. He thought he had just been caught up with three insane people. Instead he was confronted with the Costellos Organization. Nor was there much consolation in the fact he now had an ally. He believed all she had told him about George, and his father, and how she had come to be associated with them. He understood her position and sympathized with her, but from a very practical point of view having her as an ally was more a liability than an asset. There might come a time when she might be able to help him with whatever plan he came up with, but at the moment all he knew was that now he had two people to worry about. It would be hard enough for him to try and escape by himself. Having to take her along would only make it that much harder.

"Well, I guess I'll go down and see if I can get some sleep," she said, hoping he would ask her to stay on deck with him a little longer. When he didn't say anything she asked, "Want me to bring you some more coffee?"

"No, thanks. What I've had will hold me."

She went below and stalled for time by taking the stem and the basket out of the coffeepot, coming back on deck to throw the grounds over the side, and finally forced herself to go to bed more frightened than she had been before. She had been disloyal. She had talked of things she wasn't supposed to talk about. She had done the unforgivable and George was sure to find out about it. She tried to tell herself the end result would have been the same whether she talked to Chris or not, but she couldn't really be sure of that. She lay in the bunk, perfectly still, afraid the slightest movement would alert George and bring him out of the forward compartment knowing she had talked.

At three-thirty she heard Chris come down the ladder and lift the pot to see if there was anything left in it. In the dimness she saw he was looking at her as he walked by her bunk, and then he stopped suddenly and bent over, peering into her face. "How come you're still awake?" he whispered.

She moved her shoulder, shrugging a little. "I can't sleep."

"Get some sleep," he said, brushing the hairs away from her

cheeks with his fingertips. "Everything's going to be all right." He sat down on the edge of her bunk, bent over and kissed her lightly on the forehead. It was a comforting, protective, fatherly gesture. It was the assurance she had wanted when she was on deck.

He got up and walked forward to the closed door. "Hey, George. Time to go on watch," he called knocking on the door.

"O.K., O.K., I'm awake."

"There's some left over coffee in the pot. You want me to put the light under it? Warm it up?"

"Yeah."

He came back toward her with his hand held out to keep his balance. She reached for it and he squeezed her hand as he passed. She turned over facing the bulkhead and started crying silently. She didn't know why she was crying exactly, but it was a relief. She was asleep fifteen minutes later when George walked through.

* * *

During the next several days life aboard the *AHWANAH* appeared placid, even cordial. The men stood their watches as they had before and Myra cooked and served the meals. She brought George his Coke and cigar when he asked for it, Steve his beer, and Chris his cup of coffee. A stranger would not have know anything was wrong, though he might have wondered why two of them always had guns with them.

The most irritating thing for Chris was seeing George using his sextant to do the navigating. A sextant is, to a navigator, what a good set of tools is to a highly skilled craftsman. It is a precious thing the owner has grown to depend on and cares for. A sextant, like good tools, is not something one loans to another unless the other person is a trusted friend. When George first came aboard he had looked around the chart table area and said, "I see you don't have any satellite navigation equipment."

"No, I still do it the old fashioned way with sextant and tables." Now seeing George using his sextant everyday was a personal daily insult. Once when Chris took out the sextant, George said, "Put it back, Jamison. I told you I would do all the navigating. There's no need for you to know where we are."

Another constant reminder was the plastic, gallon jug of water sitting in the sink. George had filled it up at breakfast the first day after the takeover and said, "From now on we get one gallon of water a day. No more brushing your teeth or washing in fresh water. We're each allowed one quart of water a day. If you get thirsty, then have a can of pop. Maybe we'll run into some rain and can fill up the tanks, but until then, one gallon a day for all of us. That's a quart each. Do you hear that, Jamison?"

"I hear you," he said, but he didn't pay any attention to the edict. He continued to brush his teeth and wash his face with fresh water and took a drink directly from the pump whenever he felt like it. He wasn't openly flagrant about it, but he did not see any need for the restriction. They still had almost a hundred gallons of water aboard. He didn't know how long George thought they might be at sea, but if running out of water would cause any hardship for George and Steve, he was going to contribute what he could to that hardship, and there was the minor satisfaction of defying George even if it was only by drinking water.

Aside from that, Chris appeared cooperative. He acted as though nothing had changed, but he was always alert and watching, while underneath he was seething and sometimes even discouraged. It seemed everything was going George's way. The winds continued to be steady, blowing them toward George's destination, wherever that was. George had confiscated the large flare gun the day he took over, but hidden among the emergency stores was a small flare tube George didn't know about. Nor did Chris tell Myra about it. It was not that he didn't trust her, but he believed the only real secret was one known only by one person. There were times when she joined him on deck during the night watch when he wanted to tell her about it just to encourage her, to demonstrate he had not given up hope of their escaping.

On the fifth day after the takeover, Chris saw the thin, high clouds that indicated a change in the weather. He hoped for gale winds and high seas. He studied the waves all that day and night hoping to see some indication of a real storm. He wanted a hurricane, something to make them so seasick and weak they wouldn't be able to lift a finger to prevent him from taking their guns away from them. But all that developed during the night were clouds. At breakfast George said, "Aye, Jamison, where have you got the awning stored?"

"In the lazarette."

"Well, break it out. Looks like we might be getting some rain."

They spread the awning, its edges tied to the lifelines to catch the rain that would run off the sails. At noon the first squall hit them. For the next three days there were heavy squalls. Sometimes the winds gusted hard and at other times the sails flapped, empty of wind, until the next squall came along. They had enough water dumped on them to fill the tanks with buckets of rainwater left over to bathe in. And although it was a little uncomfortable with all the rain and dampness, the sea never did get really rough. Everything still seemed to be running George's way.

At ten in the evening, sixteen days after leaving Honolulu, they passed south of Johnston Island. George had not told them that was where they were, but Chris guessed it. For two days George sailed without running lights at night so as not to attract any attention. During that time Chris hoped to see a ship or a plane in the vicinity. There was a big missile-tracking station on Johnston. Throughout the afternoon and evening when he wasn't on watch, Chris sat on the foredeck with the flare tube hidden close by looking the direction of the island, but nothing showed. He went below late at night discouraged, certain his last chance to signal for help had been missed. In the morning George ordered the jib lowered and from then on they averaged two-and-a-half, three knots under staysail and reefed main.

CHAPTER FIFTEEN

At three-thirty in the afternoon the burning heat had gone out of the sun. Within another hour the sun would be easing down behind the horizon clouds at the start of a spectacular sunset and the beginning of the evening chill. But for the present it was still pleasantly warm. On the foredeck of the *ROMSEY*, Jimmy Harris, clothed only in streaks of soap lather, sat on the deck next to the rail and dropped a bucket over the side. The line jerked taut as the bucket splashed and filled with water and then dragged alongside, bouncing heavily until it was pulled up. He emptied the bucket over his head. The water ran down his body in shocking coolness, carrying away some of the lather with it. The second bucket was less of a shock, and by the third bucket he was used to the temperature. He poured seven buckets of water over himself and then pulling up one last bucket full, set it on deck, and kneeling over it, immersed his head in it up to his neck. With his head under water he ran his fingers through his floating hair to make sure all the soap was out of it, and then jerked his head from the water in one fast movement causing the flying hair to spray a line of water drops along the deck. He emptied the bucket along the deck to wash away any soap bubbles, tied the bucket to a cleat and dried himself.

Back in the cockpit with his wet hair combed straight back in a ponytail, and wearing clean shorts, Jimmy Harris felt relaxed and unworried for the first time since leaving Hong Kong. It had not been a rough trip, just a tense two weeks of having to be continually alert. First there had been the continual parade of ships heading to or from Hong Kong. They had to be on the lookout all the time. It was easy for large ships crossing the Formosa Straits and through the Bashi Channel not to notice a small sailboat. He was delighted to find his passengers were as alert and conscientious as he was. After that there had been the islands, rocks and reefs between the tip of Taiwan and the Philippines. There was plenty of safe water, but still there were dangers to be aware of and he was continually checking and rechecking his navigation to be sure he was where he thought he was. After that there had been almost a week of open, easy water, except he had been constantly aware the Marianas were ahead of him. Now he was through that chain of islands and the only thing between him and Midway Island at the western end of the Hawaiian Chain was Marcus Island.

Larry came on deck with a pot of potatoes and onions for peeling. It would probably be some kind of stew again for supper. Whenever Larry cooked it was stew and with Max it was almost always spaghetti. At least they each cooked a different thing and if they were not the best cooks in the world they had certainly not been stingy. They had brought all kinds of food on board which neither of them seemed to know how to prepare. But, all in all, he had to rate them one of the best crews he'd had.

He went below to get himself a beer before going on watch. "Either of you chaps want a beer while I'm down here?" he called while snapping open a large can of Australian beer.

"Yeah," they both answered and he handed up two of the quart-size cans. He came on deck and took a long drink of the warm beer, savoring the full, rich malt flavor. "Now if this were just ice cold," Larry said, "it would be the best beer I ever tasted. If I had a boat like this I'd sure as hell have a refrigerator on it."

"Ugh. You Yanks always want everything cold. Ain't you learned yet icing a beer deadens the flavor?" He stood for a moment looking over the endless, unobstructed horizon and then went back and relieved Max at the tiller a few minutes early. Max went forward to take his saltwater bath while there was still some warmth left in the day. A few minutes later Larry threw the potato peels over the side and went below to start cooking.

Alone in the cockpit Jimmy started thinking about Mary. He'd thought of her a lot since leaving Hong Kong. They had corresponded since he left, exchanging three or four letters a year. But it was not until this trip that he started wondering if she would like to join him. He knew she hadn't remarried. They were still close enough he was sure she would have mentioned if she was involved. They'd had a lot once. It had been the situation that had driven them apart, not their feelings for each other. That she had not remarried gave him hope. It would be nice to have Mary always alongside him, to share things with. She had always been one he could depend on. When he got to Honolulu he would write her and ask if she wanted to join him for a while. She might like this kind of life and decide to stay on indefinitely. The more he thought about it, the more pleasant the idea became, and the more possible it seemed. He thought of what he would say in his letter, phrasing and rephrasing the wording.

With the words forming in his mind he envisioned her reading it and reacting to it, and it suddenly became a desperate necessity to write and mail the letter as soon as possible. Why wait till he got to Honolulu? Write it now, tonight when he got off watch. Marcus Island was just ahead of them. Only a day or two away. He could mail the letter there and maybe there would be an answer waiting for him when he got to Honolulu.

He didn't know anything about Marcus Island except the chart showed it had a radio beacon on it. If it had a radio facility it might have people there to man it, and if it had people then it probably had mail and supply service. He decided to stop in there. If there were no people there, he hadn't lost anything except a little time.

He didn't say anything when the other two came on deck for dinner. He was too engrossed in his dreams of Mary. He saw her running toward him at the airport in Honolulu, her blond hair shining in the sunlight, though he had no idea what the airport looked like. He had visions of the two of them walking along deserted, palm-lined beaches. They would sail together to some of the nicer places he had been to, and together they would explore new places.

Larry relieved him at the tiller and he went below and sat down at the drop leaf table. He started the letter several times. *Dear Mary, I know it has been several years since we've seen each other and I suppose we have both changed a bit.* No. No. That wouldn't do at all. He would have to tell her about the sailing before he asked her to join him. *Dear Mary, It is after supper now and I am sitting in the cabin writing this. I'm on my way to Honolulu with two chaps I picked up in Hong Kong. They're rather nice chaps, really. They're Yanks in some kind of telly advertising business I think.* No, that wasn't it either. He wasn't writing to tell her about them. He made several more attempts and finally gave up. Maybe the things he wanted to say would go on to the sheet of paper easier in the morning. There was no hurry really. He had two days before they got to Marcus Island.

He went to the chart table and spread out the charts. They were headed in generally the right direction. He decided he would not change course until he had taken the sights the next day and knew exactly where he was. He went to bed certain that when he got to Honolulu there would be a letter waiting for him saying she was on her way.

After plotting the noon sight he came on deck to take the noon watch and changed course ten degrees to the north. Neither of the other two paid any attention to him as he trimmed the sails for the new course. It was not till Larry came to relieve him at four o'clock and he said, "The course is zero-five-zero," that they discovered the change.

The two of them stared at him. "You changed course?"

"Yes. Thought we might stop at Marcus Island. Maybe take on some water. Look around a bit."

"Marcus Island," Max exclaimed. "There's nothing there. We'd just be wasting our time." Max didn't know if there was anyone on Marcus Island, but he didn't want to take any chances on stopping there.

"It wouldn't be wasting any time. It's right on our way."

"You don't even have a chart for it. It is nothing but an atoll. If there is a harbor, how are you going to find your way in? You'll probably put the boat on a reef."

"Ah. No. There's a radio station on the island. They must have some kind of harbor there."

"And if they don't, what do we do, spend half a day sailing around the thing looking for a harbor that isn't there?" Max taunted. He saw Larry reach to the bottom of the cockpit for the short stubby club they always used to kill the fish they caught. Max knew what Larry was thinking and at the same time wondered if it was necessary yet. "I still think it just be a waste of time," he said to keep Jimmy's attention.

Larry hit Jimmy from behind, just above the right ear.

Jimmy Harris twisted a little as he went down, his knees folding so for just an instant he was sitting on the edge of the cockpit before his body fell backward across the deck, his head catching on the lower life line. He lay there, arms spread out to the side, his head turned to the left, his eyes wide open, staring straight ahead. Keeping the club poised in his right hand Larry felt for a pulse at the wrist of the outstretched arm.

"Dead?" Max asked.

"Think so. At least he's close enough to it not to give us any more arguments." Larry said and laid down the club and lifted the legs out of the cockpit.

"Better weigh him down before you throw him over," Max said moving back to take the tiller while Larry finished stretching the body along the deck.

"Why bother. He ain't going anywhere."

"I'd just as soon not have him floating around. You can never tell when some other boat might come along and find him, or he might get washed up on some beach somewhere on that island he was so anxious to get to. No sense giving anyone any reason to wonder where he came from."

"I suppose," Larry said. "I just figured the sharks would get him before anyone found him."

He went below to get the spare anchor. He started up the ladder with a fifteen-pound Danforth and the first thing he saw was a bare foot moving slowly back and forth. For an instant he had the startling fright the body had come back to life, then he realized the rolling of the boat caused the motion of the foot. He came on deck and quickly tied the two legs together stopping the motion of the foot. He attached the anchor with a length of line to the feet. He pushed the anchor over the side between the toe-rail and the lower lifeline, and it clanked against the side of the boat. He picked the body up at the shoulders, turning it athwart ships, the weight of the anchor pulling at the feet. The knees bent suddenly when they got to the rail and then the body passed through, the back of the head thudding against the toe-rail before it went over the side. What little disturbance the entry of James Harris caused in the water was lost in the bubbles of the wake.

"Wish this thing had a self-steering vane," Max said thinking now he and Larry would be standing four on and four off. It was the only expression of regret at the passing of Jimmy Harris.

CHAPTER SIXTEEN

Fifteen days after passing Johnston Island, thirty days out of Honolulu, the *AHWANAH* arrived at the rendezvous point. From then on they sailed in a square around the rendezvous point, changing course every watch, four hours north, four hours west, four south, then east and back to north again. They sailed in the little twelve to fifteen mile square for almost a week, and every morning and evening George took star sights and plotted their position. Sometimes they had to go a little longer on one leg or another to compensate for the drift, but they were always in the same general spot.

On the third night it rained heavily from midnight to nine in the morning and they spread the awning again to catch water. Otherwise the sailing was slow and easy, but everyone was becoming irritable with boredom and monotony of the food. "Why don't we take the sails down and just wait for them. Why do we have to sail all the time?" Steve complained.

"Because, Stupid, if something passed by and saw a sail boat without the sail up they might wonder if something was wrong and send someone to help us."

"Well, how long are we going to wait for them, anyway?"

"Until they get here."

George's eyes narrowed angrily and he said, "You know, Steve, you bitch too much to be worth keeping around."

Steve glared at him for a moment; a look filled with hate but also with fear and then went below.

Chris was the first one to see the other boat, a little white spot on the horizon. He didn't say anything to the others, but for the next half hour he occasionally glanced in that direction to see if it was still there. Twice during that time George looked around the horizon and Chris wondered how he could have missed it. Then he suddenly jumped up and went below for the binoculars, looked through them for a minute and then said, "I think that's it. Head for it, Jamison."

It took almost three hours for the two boats to close the twenty miles separating them. Most of the time George sat on the cabin top staring at the boat through the binoculars. When they were about a hundred yards apart he took the wheel and said, "OK, Jamison, take down the sails." He took the wheel and reached down and started the engine while Steve helped Chris with the sails. When they were through he got up from the wheel and said, "O.K., Jamison, take her in close. Steve, get the dinghy ready in case we need it."

Chris eased the *AHWANAH* toward the other boat that had the sails down and was dead in the water. On board it he could see two men bringing cases up from below and as he watched them he recognized Will Maxwell who had come by the *AHWANAH* in Honolulu. "We'll use our dinghy," Bill shouted across the short distance separating them.

"You can stand off for a while, Jamison." George said and sat down on the cabin top to watch as Bill and the other man took turns pumping up the small Avon dinghy. When it was full they threw it over the side. It landed upside down the first time and they had to pull it up again. The second time it landed correctly slapping loudly as it hit the water. They let down a rope ladder and Max stood for a moment on the rubber bottom of the wobbling dinghy and then sat down quickly to avoid losing his balance. A Seagull outboard motor was handed down to him and he attached it to the stern. He started the engine letting it idle while black cases were handed down to him. He came to the *AHWANAH* and handed the cases up to George and Steve. "Have you pulled the plug on her?" George asked.

"Not yet. A few more personal things to bring over."

"Do you have any decent stores on board?" Myra asked.

"I don't know. Why, are you running low?"

"Bring everything you can and then send her down," George said turning to carry the black cases down below.

Max went back to the *ROMSEY* and the two of them brought things up from below, their personal gear and two of Jimmy's duffel bags filled with canned goods. When that was done Max went below one last time. He removed the panel in front of the engine compartment and down on his hands and knees, reached in to turn off the water intake valve. With a screwdriver he loosened the clamps that held the hose in place. He tried to pull the hose off, but it had been on there so long it was rusted in place. He sat down on the floor and tried to kick it off, and when it still wouldn't budge he went to the toolbox for a hacksaw and cut through the heavy rubber hose.

He walked forward to the head, turned off the valve to the flushing system, and without even trying to loosen the hose clamps, cut through that hose also. He stood to one side so as not to get hit by the stream of water and slowly opened the valve. The water trickled in as he turned the lever handle, then flowed, and then shot in a steam across the companionway, hitting the bulkhead on the other side and spraying back on him before he could get out of the way. He ran back to the engine compartment and this time hooked what was left of the hose under the engine bed so the stream of water would go into the bilge instead of the overhead. He opened the valve and when he started up the ladder the water was already sloshing against the bottom of the floorboard.

They took the dinghy over to the *AHWANAH* and handed up the bags and then with George and Steve giving them a hand were aboard the *AHWANAH.* "Good having you aboard, Max. For a couple of days now I was beginning to worry something had gone wrong."

"Things went pretty well, really. She's just not very good to windward."

George nodded and then stepped around Max to shake hands with Larry. "Welcome aboard, Larry."

"Thank you. It's good to be here finally."

Max and Larry both said "Hi' to Steve, looked appraisingly at Chris without saying anything. "Things already over there?" George asked.

"All taken care of," Max answered and George pulled out his gun and put three shots into the dinghy. The air hissed out of the air-tubes, the rubber folding in on itself and twisted, still hissing and bubbling as the weight of the outboard motor started to pull her under. The pointed bow, with air trapped in it bobbed for a few moments until George put another shot into it. The trapped air hissed and then bubbled as it sank slowly under the water. The floating bowline snaked along the surface of the water until it too was pulled out of sight.

With all the activity, Chris had not been paying any attention to the other boat. He looked over at the *ROMSEY* and realized the water was halfway up to the gunwales. "That boat's sinking," he shouted reflexively and jumped up from where he was sitting behind the wheel. As soon as he said it, he knew he should have expected it.

"That's right, Sailor Boy," George said calmly without looking at him.

Chris sat down again slowly and looked around at the people on his boat. Max and Larry were standing forward, holding onto the main shrouds and looking over at the other boat. George was sitting on the cabin top just forward of the main hatch, replacing the spend bullets in the magazine of his pistol. Steve who was closest to Chris, standing in the forward part of the cockpit, was looking over his shoulder at Chris, grinning as though amused by Chris' shock. Looking through the hatchway he saw Myra sitting at the table, her elbows on the table, her head supported by a hand on each side of her face, staring dully at the table in front of her.

When he looked back at the *ROMSEY* it was wallowing heavily, the water sloshing over her deck. A long swell came by and she was too heavy to rise with it. The water flowed across the deck, foaming around the deckhouse, and rushed through the hatchway and open portholes. She just kept going straight down after that, disappearing slowly, the cabin top, the boom, the spreaders, and finally the tip of the mast vanishing below the water. All that remained was a blue and white floatation pillow and an orange life ring bobbing on the surface.

"Well, no one is ever going to find her," Max said looking back toward George.

"That's for sure, "George answered and then said, "Hey, Steve, come up here a minute."

Steve walked forward, his legs spread to balance himself against the rolling of the boat, his left hand holding onto the lifeline. He stopped three feet away and said, "Yeah, George?"

George reached over and yanked the gun from his waist. "Is this thing loaded?" he asked.

"Of course, it's loaded."

"Good! Because I know all about the deal you tried to set up with Johnny Bigelow."

"No, George. No! You have it all wrong. I..."

The blast was much louder than the blasts that sank the dinghy. Simultaneous with the blast was the suddenly look of wide-eyed fear and astonishment on Steve's face. Then his arms flew out to the side and he fell backward over the lifelines as though someone had pushed him. He lay on his back in the water for an instant, his eyes wide open, and then slowly rolled over on his stomach leaving a floating brown stain on the water as he turned. The circle, as big as a basketball, of torn flesh, bones and clothing in the middle of Steve's back almost made Chris throw up. He looked away quickly and heard George saying, "That'll teach you to try and double-cross me." When he looked at George he was just in time to see him throw the gun into the water next to the body. George was headed toward him, stepping down into the cockpit. "OK, Jamison, get the sails up," he said reaching for the wheel.

Chris moved forward quickly, unsteady and unsure, but propelled by fear. He raised the sails, the main, the jib, the staysail, without thinking about what he was doing. When the sails were up he looked up automatically to the top of the mast and clear blue sky spotted with white, good-weather clouds eased his fears and softened a little what he had just seen.

Walking aft, aware now of what he was doing, of George trimming the sheets and the slight difference in the feel of the boat as each sail was trimmed to pull its maximum. "You can take her now, Jamison. Your course is zero-five-zero," George said standing up and moving from behind the wheel.

Chris sat down behind the wheel and George motioned for Max and Larry to follow him below. Myra came on deck as soon as the others were below. She sat down at the far end of the cockpit. Their eyes met for an instant and then they both looked away.

CHAPTER SEVENTEEN

It is one thing to know about an avalanche, to see pictures of the destruction and the dead, and quite a different thing to be there. It is one thing to hear of a car crash and quite another to be in one. Chris understood now what Myra had tried to tell him about George. He understood the fear that kept Myra obedient. And more than anything else he understood that as surely as he had seen Steve killed, he and Myra were scheduled to be killed. He was certain that even before they left Honolulu, George had known exactly when he would get rid of Steve. As soon as the other two came aboard, Steve was no longer needed to stand watches. Even now, George probably knew exactly when he would no longer need Myra and him. He guessed Myra would be kept to the end of the trip to do the cooking. But him? He consoled himself with the fact that since he was still alive George must have some further use for him.

"Do you have any idea what his reason for killing Steve was?" he asked.

She shook her head a little while sliding along the cockpit seat toward him and then said, "You heard him. He thought Steve had tried to two-time him. I don't know any more than that."

"Do you think the owner of the other boat was aboard when it went down?"

She shrugged her shoulders still not looking at him.

"But he was aboard when they left Hong Kong, or wherever it was they came from?"

She nodded with tiny little jerks of her head and bit her lower lip."

"I wonder when he plans to get rid of me?" Chris said.

Her head jerked around suddenly. She stared at him for a moment with a shocked expression on her face, and he realized that although they might both be thinking of the same thing, she didn't want to confront it out loud yet. "Chris, I'm scared," she said finally.

He reached over and took her hand, squeezing it a little, and then let go of it when he saw Larry start up the ladder from below. He was wearing a shoulder holster and a gun he hadn't had when he came aboard. He was carrying Steve's duffel bag and overnight bag that he threw over the side and then came back and said, "George says I'm supposed to take your watches."

Chris got up slowly, letting Larry have the wheel, and then saw George come on deck and was absolutely certain they were going to kill him. If they didn't need him to stand watches then they didn't need him for anything. He was surprised to realize how calm he was. He had some regrets about dying right now. He would have liked to have established good relations with his parents and sister. There were places he'd always wanted to sail to that he hadn't been to yet. He had always thought he would like to try hang-gliding, but he hadn't done that either. There were certain regrets, but strangely enough, there was no fear. Even as he was thinking these things he was wondering if there was a way he could take control of things and save his own life and Myra's. He looked back over his shoulder at Larry who glanced up at him from the compass looking unconcerned and a little bored.

George sat down in the cockpit, unwrapped a cigar and lit it. So it was not going to be right now. They were going to wait a while. He suddenly had a desperate need to know when it was going to be. "I suppose now that you no longer need me to stand watches you're going to do the same thing to me you did to Steve."

George glanced at him, took the cigar out of his mouth, rolled it back and forth between his fingers and thumb and said, "You haven't given me any reason to kill you yet." The way he said yet made it obvious that when the time came he would find a reason. "Besides, I may still have need of you."

"Need of me? What for?"

George smiled, self-satisfied, and said, "Well, I don't really need you, and the chances I might are so small as to be almost nonexistent, but on the very slim chance some Coast Guard boat might pull alongside and wonder why we didn't make it to Tahiti, it would be good to have the owner on board who is just overjoyed with his charter and has a good story ready about how we changed our minds and went somewhere else."

"What makes you think I'd go along with that? The minute they were close enough I might jump over the side. You could shoot me, but that would kind of blow your cover, wouldn't it?"

"She's the reason you'll go along with it," he said pointing the glowing end of his cigar toward Myra. "The minute you goof up she's dead. Now you might have tried to be hero all by yourself, but she's going to be down below with a knife to her throat, and you try anything like jumping over the side, or signaling them in any way, and she'll probably be dead before you are."

"Why should I care what happens to her? She's your wife."

"First of all because that's the kind of jerk you are. Secondly, she's not my wife, and you know it. Don't try to play games with me, Jamison. Now, where have we been since we didn't go to Tahiti?"

"I don't know," he said hesitating, thinking from now on he would pretend to be cooperating with George. "The Fijis maybe, except it's unlikely anyone would go there without stopping at the Samoas. America Samoa is out and Western Samoa is too close to American Samoa. Maybe Gilbert or Ellis Island. No one would know whether we had been there or not."

"I'm sure when the time comes you'll be able to think of something," George said and went below.

Chris felt both relieved and desperate. At least he was not going to be killed right away, but there was no doubt that was what George had in mind. The possibility George would need him to provide an alibi where they had been would become more likely the closer they got to Hawaii. It was in those waters the Coast Guard might be looking for him and his boat. If George was telling the truth, then he would keep Chris alive until he no longer needed the boat. How long would that be? With good weather it might take twenty days to get to Hawaii. With bad weather it would take longer. He had twenty to thirty days in which to find a way to save himself and Myra.

He went down the ladder over to where George was standing by the chart table. "George, I'd like to make a deal with you."

George looked around slowly. "I doubt very much you have anything to deal with, Sailor Boy."

"How do you know until you've heard it?"

George stared at him, shrugged a little and then said, "O.K. Go on."

"You probably have a foolproof way of getting your stuff ashore, but you and I both know nothing is foolproof. So you probably have an alternate plan in case something happens to plan one. Maybe you have a dozen plans, but it never hurts to have one more, does it?"

"I'm listening."

"Now you know I know every deserted cove, bay, inlet, every deserted stretch of beach in the Islands. You know that, because you had me checked out completely before you started. Now my deal is this, if none of your other plans work out, then I guarantee to land you undetected somewhere in Hawaii, and in return you let Myra and me go."

"Like I said, Jamison, you really don't have anything to deal with. But I'll tell you what, if I need you and you really do put us ashore safely, I'll figure you're in with us. After that, this boat belongs to us. Any time we need it for anything, you'll be right there to go anywhere we want to pick up anything we want." He paused and then added, "You'll be paid for those charters, of course. Is it a deal?" He put out his hand and Chris knew he was lying. If he hadn't held out his hand to shake on it, if he hadn't mentioned being paid, Chris might have been inclined to believe him. But George was suddenly acting too friendly and Chris knew he had no intention of keeping his word.

"It's a deal," Chris said shaking hands. "What watch am I supposed to stand?"

"Larry, Max and I will stand the watches. You just keep everything in good running order."

"OK" Chris went on deck knowing he was right. If George didn't trust him with standing watches he certainly wasn't going to trust him with future charters. George was going to kill him. George had no choice. Chris knew too much for George to let him live.

Chris calculated if George stuck to this course it would take him well north of Wake Island and then he would probably head southeast toward the islands. But which of the Hawaiian Islands was George headed for. George was too smart a man to try to take the heroin in aboard the *AHWANAH*. Therefore George must have made some other arrangements for getting the goods ashore. For a while Chris considered a local helicopter, but ruled that out almost immediately. A helicopter would have to be continually going back someplace to refuel. The obvious way to do it was with a shallow draft, high-speed powerboat. Such a boat could sit in the same area several days fishing and no one would think anything of it. The question Chris wanted answered was where George was going to meet this boat.

It was not until after dinner when the other three went on deck with cups of coffee Chris had a chance to talk to Myra alone. "When you were in Honolulu did you and George go to any of the other islands?" he asked sliding across the dinette seat to where he could lean across to where she was doing the dishes.

She turned to look through the hatchway before answering. "George and I went Kauai one time."

He was disappointed. Kauai was the first island they would come to. The north side of the island was almost completely uninhabited. Might be a place to land, but that meant they would not have to go by any other island to get there. "Was it a business trip? I mean did he go there to meet with anyone in particular?"

"I don't think so. He asked me where I wanted to go and I chose Kauai. He took me there to sort of repay me for leaving me behind when he and Steve went to Maui."

"Maui? Are you sure?"

She looked out the hatchway again. "Yes. I told you about it. That was the day I came down and tried to warn you, but you had gone out sailing."

He leaned back in the seat and sat staring at the overhead. He remembered her telling him she had come down to warn him when the others were gone, but he didn't remember her mentioning Maui. Maui! That had to be it. Everything fitted. There were all kinds of fishing boats operating out of Kahului and Lahaina, or even from little harbors and bays on Molokai with all kinds of places they could land undetected. That was it. George was planning to rendezvous with another boat somewhere off of Molokai or Maui. He was absolutely sure of it. He felt more confident now that he knew what George's plan was, and best of all was they would have to pass Kauai and Oahu before they got to the rendezvous point. George would have to keep him on board until they were past Oahu. If the Coast Guard had been alerted because no one had heard from the *AHWANAH* for two months, then that was the area where they were most likely to be spotted and contacted. And if George had to keep him alive and well until the very end, then he would also have to keep Myra alive and well, because if he didn't, Chris would jump over the side when he knew the Coast Guard had seen them.

But with each passing day he began to feel more desperate. There seemed to be no escape. Nor was Myra very encouraging. They had plenty of opportunities to talk and make plans. The other three left them alone much of the time and Chris understood George wanted them to become attached and even dependent on each other. But every time they talked they became more aware of just how futile any plans they devised were. There was no way to get the guns away from the three of them. There was just no way of taking back control of the boat.

It was after they had passed north of Midway and were on a southeasterly course toward the Islands that Chris suggested, “Maybe when we are as close to Kauai as I think we are going to get, we could jump over the side some night. We might make it to shore if we’re lucky. It’s the only chance we’ve got.”

“It’s no chance at all, really,” she said. “Even if we did manage to make it to land, he’d be standing on the beach waiting for us when we walked ashore. The only way out is for us to kill them before they kill us. I’ve even tried sometimes to think of some way to poison their food, but you don’t have anything on board I can use. Besides, if we were to come back without George, his father would be after us. Any way you look at it, Chris, we’ve had it.” She said the last sentence in the same sad, resigned voice she always used when she pointed out why one of his plans wouldn’t work. “Oh, God,” she moaned, “if only there were some way to sink this boat so the three of them drown while you and I could stay alive. But everyone, including his father, thought we had all drowned, then we might have a chance.”

Sink the boat? He was horrified. His first reaction was to be hurt and angry with her for even suggesting it. Many times in his life he had contemplated how he would handle the boat if he lost an arm or a leg, but he had never once considered how he would get along without the boat. But after the initial shock had passed, the idea became a little more acceptable. Within a week or two he would probably be dead and in all probability the boat would be sunk too. Well, he wasn’t going to lose by default. If he was going to die, it might as well happen while he tried to save the two of them. They had nothing to lose. And if his boat was to sink, then he decided he was the only one who had a right to sink her. He had handled every plank of wood, every screw, every bolt, every nail, every piece of cloth, and put them all together. While he was going through adolescence the woods were curing in sheds. He had always assumed he and his boat would end their lives together. He had it planned that way. When the time was right—and he would know when it was time—they would set sail for a deep ocean trench, and there, with all sails set, he would open the seacocks and they would go down together. That was the way it was supposed to have been.

"Myra," he said leaning a little toward where she was drying the last of the dishes, "We have two weeks left. If this wind holds and we make as good time as we have been we may only have nine or ten days. From now on, when you have free time, I want you to go up to the foredeck. If I'm already there, come sit with me. And sometimes when you are up there, I'll come and join you. Especially at night. If you wake up in the night for some reason, put on some warm clothes and go sit on the deck for an hour or so. Not in the cockpit, but on the foredeck. If I see you get up in the night, I'll come and join you. I want them to get used to the idea of us being up there all the time."

"You got an idea about how to get us out of this?"

"I'm not sure yet. I'm working on one."

He didn't want to tell her what he was thinking, partly because he was afraid the two of them might inadvertently talk about it sometime when the others might overhear them. Too, he didn't want her to tell him why the plan couldn't work. She would be right, but he didn't need her to confirm one, or more, of the hundred reasons why it wouldn't work. It was a last resort, a plan he would only use if nothing else came up, a plan that depended too much on luck, but right now it was the only plan he had.

Each day after that Chris found projects on the foredeck that needed taking care of. Fittings that hadn't been polished in years suddenly gleamed with a new brightness. Boxes of spare parts were sorted through and rearranged. Sails he knew would never be used again were taken out of their bags and checked to make sure the hanks were all on securely and there were no seams or tears that needed sewing. He knew George was watching him, and that was exactly what he wanted. He wanted George to get used to the idea of his puttering around fixing things. One time he didn't see George come up behind him when he was working on the deck box forward of the cabin. "What are you doing now?" George asked and for a panicked moment Chris had the frightening feeling he had been discovered. Then he realized there was nothing in that box yet that could give away his plan.

"Just fixing this hinge. It's been wearing loose for weeks. The holes needed plugging and the screws reset," he said when in fact he was loosening the snug fit of the lid so it wouldn't make any noise when it was opened or closed.

"I would think you would let that go until you got back in port."

"With you doing all the navigating and me not even standing watches, I got nothing else to do. Have to do something with my time or I'll go buggy."

"The problem with you, Jamison, is you can't just sit back and enjoy a completely relaxing cruise," he said laughing and started back toward the cockpit.

Chris watched him walk aft wondering if he suspected anything. Why did George choose this time to look closely at what he was doing instead of when he was changing the fuel filters? There was nothing there yet that could give the plan away, but he couldn't help worrying.

He finished working on the lid, closing and opening it a couple of times to make sure it didn't squeak or stick anywhere, and then went aft. He left the mooring lines that had been stored in the box lying on deck as though he had forgotten to put them back. That night, when he was sitting alone on the foredeck, he let the mooring lines and fenders, which had almost completely filled the box, slip silently over the side.

During the next five nights, when he went forward to sit on the deck, he carried up something for the deck box, packets of raisins, dried fruit, candy bars, tin-foil wrapped packets of peanuts, all packaged in zip-lock plastic bags. The hardest things to smuggle up there were the plastic bottles of water and two life jackets. He got the life jackets up there one at a time by putting them in pillow cases as though he were carrying a pillow forward to sit on. Although he felt an excited sense of accomplishment each night when he smuggled something more into the box, his days were filled with anxiety someone might find the things hidden there. Every time Max or Larry started forward along the deck, he became tense with fear until they stopped to sit down on the cabin top. Once Larry had gone all the way forward and sat down on the box and Chris had watched anxiously until he finally came back.

Day or night, no matter what he was doing, Chris was studying the enemy. It got so he could almost predict to the minute when George would reach for a cigar, or Larry would get himself a beer.

Max didn't smoke at all and Larry was a chain smoker. The first thing Larry reached for when he woke up, even while still lying in the bunk, was a cigarette. And most important of all was that both Larry and Max tended to doze off when they had the midnight watch. It was understandable. The boat was well balanced and when correctly trimmed the boat pretty much sailed herself. The movement of the waves in the dark, combined with the red glow of the binnacle light shining on the floating compass card, could be hypnotically lulling. From time to time Chris and Myra would leave their place on the foredeck and go aft, and even below, just to see how far they could get before the man on watch woke up. Chris himself had fallen asleep many times at night holding the wheel. But as far as he could tell, George never dozed when on watch.

When he had the mid watch Larry always fell asleep twenty to thirty minutes after he came on watch. His head would sink to his chest, stay that way for ten or fifteen minutes and then jerk up as he woke up. He would reach into his pocket for his pack of cigarettes. Max, on the other hand, didn't fall asleep until he had been on watch an hour or more. Then his head would fall to one side and often roll back and forth with the gentle rolling of the boat. When he woke up he would raise his head slowly, look around, stretch, and then stand up behind the wheel for a while.

Chris made it a point of going on deck for thirty or forty minutes every night at one or two in the morning. Many times he woke up Myra and she would join him up there. Sometimes he would sit in the cockpit for a few minutes and talk trivia with whoever was on watch before going forward. But his surveillance of the others was mostly done from below. By hanging onto the grab rail, he could lean out of his bunk and look through the hatch to the man on watch. He spent hours hanging there by one hand until his arms ached and he had to lie back down for a few minutes to rest. But as tiring as it was, it was a safe place to watch the others. If he saw one of them headed forward along the cockpit, or heard someone turn the handle to the forward compartment, or heard Larry turn over in his bunk, Chris could just let go and be lying in his bunk without their ever being able to catch him spying on them.

Chris knew Larry's habits best. George and Max slept behind the door to the forward compartment and it was hard to know how soundly they slept in there. Larry on the other hand bunked in the main salon across from Myra and Chris knew his every sleeping habit, which side he usually started out on, the sounds he made when he was turning over in his sleep, and the difference in the sound of his snoring when he was on his side and when he was on his back.

The habit that irritated Chris the most was his smoking in bed: the one last cigarette before he fell asleep, the glowing tip making an arc through the darkness when he raised his hand from where it dangled over the edge of the bunk up to his mouth, and then back again. The first thing he did after being called to go on watch, or when waking up in the morning, was to prop himself up in the bunk, and with his eyes still closed, feel along the shelf till he found his cigarette and matches. After one deep drag he would throw the match on the floor. As often as not, the match was still burning when it landed on the floor.

Chris had complained about it once, but Larry's response had been, "Drop dead, Jamison." But it was Larry's smoking in bed that became a key to Chris' plan.

CHAPTER EIGHTEEN

Chris lay in his bunk, wide-awake, wondering and planning. Without being able to do any of the navigation, or even to see George's plotting sheets, he had no way of knowing exactly where they were, but he guessed they must be one or two days northwest of Kauai. If George was thinking of landing on Kauai, Chris' plan had no chance of working. Even if he and Myra were able to get over the side, the currents, and the winds to the north of the island would carry them past and away from it. The only way they had any chance at all was to go over when they were north of the channel between Oahu and Molokai. Those islands were only fifteen miles apart and the winds and currents that funneled between them would be the most likely to wash them ashore.

At other times he wondered if all his thinking and planning would do any good. He and Myra were both still alive and since Steve had been killed, George had not made one threat against either Myra or himself. Sometimes he tried to convince himself George was really going to let them go and yet he knew that could not be.

Lying now in his bunk he tried to understand George's story about needing him in case they were stopped. At the beginning he had accepted it but the more he thought about it, the less plausible it seemed. Now he imagined them all being arrested and landing in Jail. Then it dawned on him. He was the fall guy. If things went wrong George and his friends would say they knew nothing about the heroin being on board. It would be his word against theirs, and the law was more likely to believe an upright, pillar of the community than the operator of an illegal charter business. George's hotshot lawyers would have him and his friends out in no time, while he sat in Jail. With him alive to take the rap, George was really running no risk at all. He wondered how they would handle Myra. Probably the safest way would be to bail her out at the same time and then have her killed later. He decided he could not take any chances of the Coast Guard, or anyone else, picking them up, and nor could he let George make his rendezvous.

He leaned up on his elbow and looked out of the hatch. Max was sitting sideways to the wheel on the windward side of the cockpit facing down wind. From the settee berth directly in front of him Chris could hear Larry snoring. He didn't know if George was awake in the forward compartment or not. Probably not. He had the next watch. There was no light showing through the vent slats of the door nor was there any sound of snoring coming from the forward cabin. He thought for a moment of waking Myra and going to the foredeck to tell her his plan and then decided maybe right there in the galley would be the safest place. Max couldn't see them from where he was. If Larry stopped snoring they would stop whispering until they heard him start again and they would always hear George turning the doorknob.

He got out of his bunk, carefully crossing over to the dinette side where Myra was sleeping in the converted berth. He looked over at Larry's bunk and was pleased to see he was lying on his side with his back to them. He looked through the hatchway again to check on Max and then bent over Myra's bunk touching her on the shoulder. She woke with a start and he put a finger to his lips.

"Anything wrong?" she whispered.

"No." He sat down on the edge of her bunk where he could look through the hatchway as he talked. "Tomorrow when you're fixing breakfast I want you to complain about the stove not working right. Do it where George can hear you. Not too much, but enough to give me reason to check the tanks. At lunchtime really bitch about it. I'll have it fixed so it really isn't working right by then."

"O.K. But why?"

"Please. I can't explain it all now." He started to get up and then sat down again, looked up toward where Max was at the wheel, turned to see Larry was still sleeping and asked, "Do you know how to swim?"

"Yes. A little bit."

"Good. We're going to have a long swim ahead of us. I have a couple of life jackets and some food and water stored in the forward deck box. When the time comes, we're going over the side."

"What are you going to do about them?"

"After we get off the boat is going to blow up," he said and went back to his bunk.

She lay there wide-awake. *How is he planning to blow up the boat? How well do I really know how to swim?* Everything raised questions. *How can we go over the side without being seen? If we're seen they are sure to shoot us. How far will we have to swim? What if we're attacked by sharks?* She visualized floating in the water, with no land to be seen anywhere, hungry and thirsty, with sharks circling them. If she had to die, it would be a lot easier to be shot. At least it would be quick and painless.

She got up and poured herself a drink from the ever-present gallon jug and then crossed over to the other side glancing through the hatchway as she passed. She stood by Chris' bunk wondering for a moment if he was awake. She didn't really know what she wanted to ask him.

He leaned up toward her and asked, "Does the idea scare you?"

"A little, I guess."

"It scares me a lot."

Knowing he was frightened didn't make her feel any better. "What do you think our chances are?" she asked not sure she wanted to hear the answer.

"I don't know. Twenty-five percent. Maybe fifty-fifty."

"Those aren't very good odds, are they? But I guess it's a lot better than staying here."

"The odds of dying if we stay here are a hundred percent. Yes, I would say it is a hell of a lot better than staying here."

* * *

At seven o'clock the morning sun shimmered off the undulating blue of the ocean surface. A few whitecaps crowned selected waves and a swarm of flying fish exploded out of the sea less than fifty feet off the starboard beam. Larry sat at the wheel and Max, with a stopwatch in his hand, stood next to George who had the sextant to his eye. George was unaware of the blue of the water, the flying fish, or the warming rays of the sun. He was a little irritated that there had been clouds overhead earlier so he had been unable to get a star sight. Now he would have to be satisfied with an inexact position obtained by advancing his morning sun sight to his noon sight. He would have to wait until evening to get an exact position from star sights. His dead reckoned position put him about a hundred miles from Kauai. When he was getting that close he wanted to know exactly where he was.

He went below where Myra was fixing breakfast and Chris was sitting at the dinette reading a paperback. George was sure Chris was just sitting there hoping to see where they were when George figured the morning sight. He wrote down the time from the stopwatch, the angle on the sextant and put everything away. He sat down across from Chris. "How about a cup of coffee, Myra," he said taking out a cigar.

"It's not ready yet."

"Why ever not? What have you been doing all morning?"

"The stove's not working right. If I turn on more than one burner the other one goes out. I've only got one burner to work with."

"Damn it, Jamison. You got nothing else to do. If you didn't spend so much time reading that stupid book, you might be able to keep the stove working."

"I'll check on it right after breakfast."

"No! You'll check on it now!" George shouted.

Chris closed the book and put it back on the bookshelf. He went to stand next to Myra in front of the stove. He winked at her and said, "Well, it may just be the Propane bottle is low, but it looks to me like the burners are dirty," he said and went on deck. From the lazarette he got the last full bottle of propane. There were two bottles in the tank box, one of them had run out a month ago, and he replaced it with the spare, full bottle. He would switch over to the fresh tank closer to the time they went over the side. He wondered how many cubic feet of gas there was in a five-gallon tank of liquid propane. How fast would it escape through the valve he was planning to install? How much gas would it take to blow up a forty foot boat?

He took the empty tank back to the lazarette. "I don't suppose that helped any did it?" he asked when he was back in the cabin.

She hesitated for an instant, trying to decide what he wanted her answer to be. "No. Not really."

"Yeah, just as I thought. It couldn't be that easy. I'll clean the burners after breakfast."

"Why can't you do it now?" George asked.

"I can, but I have to take the stove all apart. Do you want to wait a couple of hours before you have your breakfast?"

George just glared at him and Chris got his book and went on deck.

Chris waited to start working on the stove until George and Max were sitting at the dinette playing gin rummy. He wanted them there, where he could keep track of them all the time. He didn't want one of them coming unexpectedly down the ladder behind him. Also they were less likely to pay attention to what he was doing if he did it right in front of them.

He took the stove apart, putting all the parts, knobs, grates, burners, stovetop, and even the oven door on the floor behind him. It would take extra effort for anyone to step over that fence of junk to get next to him to take a really good look at what he was doing. Through the hatchway he could see Myra sitting at the forward end of the cockpit ready to warn him if Larry left the wheel to go below for something. Leaning back from his work he could see Larry sitting at the wheel wearing a straw hat with a cigarette dangling from his lips. At the dinette George laid down a hand of cards saying, "The name of the game is gin. What did I catch you with?"

"Seven."

"Everything doubled for spades give me another seventy-four points."

"Man, but you are lucky today."

"Don't worry about it, Max. It's only money," George said adding the score to the pad.

Chris reached down behind the stove and with the metal snips cut the wire casing of the flexible hose. It took several minutes to cut that protective casing. His back started to ache from the awkward position of leaning over the stove to reach down behind it to cut the line while at the same time bracing against the pitching of the boat. With the sweat running into his eyes he wondered if all this would really work. To start with he wasn't sure the Y-valve he had found a couple days ago would fit the hose.

He finally cut through the casing and then the hose and stood up straight, leaning backward with his hands pressed against his waist to relieve the strain on his back. Through the hatchway he could see Larry still behind the wheel. Max and George were still playing cards. "How's it going?" George asked slipping a card into the fan in his hand before discarding one.

"It's all messed up. I had to take the main line apart. Some water got into it," he said.

"Water has a way of getting into things on a boat," Max said without looking up from his cards.

It took Chris almost half an hour to put the Y-valve into the line. The sweat poured off him and into his eyes as he bent over the stove trying to force the metal valve into the small opening of the unyielding rubber hose. It was supposed to fit. He had bought it a long time ago when he had considered putting in a gas heater. After all that time of looking through his parts boxes for a valve he knew he had and now the thing didn't fit.

He finally got the valve into the line with the clamps turned tightly down. He attached the piece of clear plastic hose to the other leg of the Y-valve and strung it behind the stove and under the floor to the bilge. When they were ready to leave all he had to do was turn the valve and the gas would go and accumulate in the bilge. He was counting on Larry lighting a cigarette first thing when he was called to go on watch. When he did, the gas would explode.

He put the stove back together, turned on the overhead valve to the tanks and tried to light one of the burners. The match burned down almost to his fingertips and he guessed the gas was going to the bilge instead of to the stove. He reached behind and pushed the little handle on the valve in the opposite direction. This time the burner lighted. He reached up and turned off the overhead valve, turned off the burner, and turned on the engine room exhaust fan to remove whatever gas had escaped into the bilge. He left the fan running while he put his tools away, stuck his head into the engine compartment to see if he could smell any gas, turned off the fan and went on deck. "It should work all right now," he said to Myra and walked forward and sat down on the deck leaning against the deck box with the escape supplies.

He had just taken the first steps toward killing three people. He told himself it was either them or Myra and he. He knew George was capable of killing someone, yet at the same time he found it hard to believe George was going to kill them. He made himself think of Steve, remembering him floating face down in the water with his back blown away. But that was different. Steve had tried to double-cross George. *But I haven't done anything to hurt George*, he thought. *Neither did the guy on the other boat. I don't know that anyone killed that guy. I just assumed he had been killed. Maybe they just stole the boat. And leave someone to report it stolen? Maybe they bought it. Then why didn't they buy a boat for this part of the operation?*

Myra came forward and sat down next to him. “Do you know where we are?” she asked.

“Not exactly, but from the birds I guess we are getting close to an island, probably Kauai. Why do you ask?”

“We’re getting close to something happening.”

“How do you know?”

“George is getting up tight.”

“I hadn’t noticed anything.”

“One indication is his playing cards. Have you ever seen him play cards before?” she asked without waiting for an answer. “He hardly ever plays cards except when he’s getting nervous. Does it to calm himself down.”

“Well then maybe we’re closer than I thought we were. There’s no way for me to know for sure. He won’t let me anywhere near the chart table. I wish I knew for sure where he was planning to transfer. Damn! I wish I knew what was going on.”

“Don’t worry about it. Everything will go all right.”

Her remark irritated him. He hated it when people who had no idea of just how serious things were threw out some blithe remark. He turned to snap at her and caught her looking at him so intently he realized she was not being naive. She was as aware of the situation as he was, and just as frightened and worried, but she believed they would make it, and her assurance bolstered him. “You know you really are a very beautiful woman,” he said. It was not exactly what he had meant, but he didn’t know quite how to tell her she had him feeling confident again.

She smiled, surprised. “Oh, you’ve just been at sea too long,” she said, “but thank you, anyway.”

“I don’t suppose you have a heavy wool sweater with you.”

She shook her head.

“I have an extra one. I’ll throw it on your bunk sometime today. Even soaking wet wool will help keep you warm. You have a pair of tennis shoes, or something like that, don’t you?” She nodded. “Wear them too. We may have to wade over coral reefs getting ashore. And wear that jacket with all the pockets in it. I have a pair of parachute style pants that has zippered pockets everywhere. You don’t have something like that too, do you?”

“Just the jacket. Anything else?”

“I don’t think so. Everything else is in here,” he said touching the side of the box they were leaning against. "Oh, yeah, be sure to put any personal papers, you know, wallet, driver's license, anything like that you want to take in plastic bags."

* * *

From where he was lying in his bunk, Chris saw Larry's feet, then his legs, and finally his whole body as a shadow in the darkness come down the ladder. He made his way through the main salon and knocked on the forward compartment door. "Hey, Max, it's me."

The door opened and Larry handed Max his gun. Chris wondered sometimes if Larry resented having to sleep in the same compartment with Myra and him without the protection of a gun. Whether he resented it or not, Larry always turned in his gun before going to bed.

At four AM he heard Larry getting ready for bed, the glow of the cigarette moving from the ashtray to his mouth, the face visible when he dragged on the cigarette. Larry lay down with a sigh, took the last few puffs on his cigarette and then snubbed it out. A few minutes later Chris felt the difference in the motion of the boat as it changed course. He rose up in his bunk to look at the compass that had always been next to his bunk, forgetting for a moment George had moved that compass to the forward compartment. He pulled himself forward until he was leaning on the chart table and could look out the porthole above it. He saw the stars changing position in the circle of the porthole as the boat changed course. He pressed his face against the glass and off to one side saw the dim flash of light over the horizon. My, God, he thought. That must be Kilauea Light. He didn't know off hand what the flashing sequence of Kilauea Light was, but that had to be it. He couldn't see the beam itself, only a dim glow in the night sky, which meant they must be over twenty miles away, but less than fifty.

He lay back. It had to be Kilauea. If it were any other light, he would have seen an island during the day. If George did not reduce sails and kept generally to this same course, they would be north of Oahu in twenty-four to thirty-six hours. He started figuring the watches. George was on now, from four to eight. Then Max would have the eight to noon, Larry the noon to four, George the first dog-watch from four to six, Max the second dog from six to eight, Larry the eight to midnight. He kept counting off the watches for the next twenty-four hour period. He had lucked out. Everything depended on Larry having either the midnight or the four to eight in the morning watch. He counted the watches again, turning down his fingers, making sure he had counted correctly. He had. Less than twenty-four hours from now, when Max was on watch, he and Myra would be going over the side. Larry would be called to go on watch at four in the morning and when he struck the match for his first cigarette it would ignite the escaped gas. Three to four hours after they had gone over the side George, Max and Larry would all be blown up with the boat.

CHAPTER NINETEEN

It had been a picture perfect day. Billowy clouds moved in ever-changing shapes across the azure sky. The boat kept up a soothing rocking. A school of porpoises had bounded gracefully around the bow for almost half an hour. In the middle of the afternoon a school of flying fish had winged their way in and out of the waves with mahi-mahi breaking water in hungry pursuit.

Chris was aware of those things, once thinking it might be the last time he would see them, but mostly too preoccupied to really appreciate them. Most of the time he was mentally rehearsing how they would go over the side, trying to anticipate anything that might go wrong. The most crucial moment would be right after they were in the water. They would have to go over the side at the bow and Max would be at the wheel at the stern. He might easily see them as the boat went by. The thing they had to do was go over the high side. If Max was not directly behind the wheel, he would be sitting on the high side, one leg braced against the other side of the cockpit. That was how he usually sat. Going over the high side meant a longer drop to the water and maybe the sound of a splash as they entered, but with the boat heeled over they would have four or five feet of hull to hide behind. On the low side there might only be a foot or so and he might see. Even if he did see them he probably wouldn't get off a good shot before they were safely behind the boat. Even in daylight it was almost impossible to hit a bobbing object in the water when the boat was also rising and falling. At night there was almost no chance of being shot. His concern was in not being seen. They had to leave the boat with the others not knowing about it or the plan wouldn't work. It wasn't a foolproof plan anyway: Larry might not have that wake-up cigarette, or Max might decide in the middle of his watch he wanted a drink of water instead of coffee from the thermos in the cockpit. But it certainly wouldn't work if Max spotted them as they went over the side.

He lay in his bunk thinking he should have told her to wear a bikini under everything else. That way if they came ashore at a beach where there were people, they could get rid of their life jackets and clothes and blend in with the crowd.

The ship's clock struck eight bells and a couple of minutes later George came below. He stood for a few moments at the chart table, moving a pair of dividers across a chart of the islands, then turned off the dim red light and went back on deck. Chris had the sinking feeling he had guessed wrong about the rendezvous point. Maybe they were rendezvousing that night. If they weren't what was George doing staying up? He had been up since early in the morning and he should be getting some sleep before he went on watch again.

George came back down and walked through to the forward compartment and Chris breathed a sigh of relief. He leaned up on one elbow, staring at the closed door, until he saw the light go out through the ventilation slats. He lay back down and raised an arm to look at the luminous dial on his watch. Eleven after twelve. *How long would it take George to fall asleep? Was George lying there worrying about something?* Larry groaned and turned over in his sleep. Chris looked at his watch again. Twelve fourteen. Could that be right? Only three minutes since the last time he looked at his watch? Wait until twelve-thirty. George should be asleep by then and Max should be dozing off at the wheel. He heard Myra get up. She stopped by his bunk and whispered, "See you in a few minutes."

The minutes dragged by. He lay in his bunk, looking at his watch every few minutes until twelve twenty-five and could wait no longer. He looked through the hatchway and was pleased to see Max was sitting in his usual position and he was beginning to look sleepy. He pulled his trousers on over his swimming trunks and felt along the shelf for the plastic bag with his wallet and the papers to the boat. He sat down on the edge of his bunk to pull on his tennis shoes and tied the laces. His feet felt awkward in them. He pulled on a T-shirt and then hesitated before pulling on the heavy, turtleneck wool sweater, dreading its itchiness against his bare neck and arms. He forced himself into it and immediately felt stiflingly hot. He grabbed the windbreaker, planning to put it on when he got on deck, then thought better of it. It was cool enough up there for a light jacket, but not for a heavy sweater. Max might start wondering if he saw a sweater. He pulled on the jacket to hide the sweater. He zipped it up and then looked around the cabin wondering if he had forgotten anything. He walked over to the stove, leaned out to check on Max and then reached up to turn on the overhead valve. It squeaked. He had never known it to do that before. He leaned back to look through the hatchway to see if Max had heard it. No, he couldn't hear a little noise like that through the sound of the wind. He turned the handle the rest of the way quickly. He then reached down to turn the Y-valve that would send the gas to the bilge. There was no sound of escaping gas. He had to know. He knelt down and gently lifted one of the floorboards, put his face to the opening and sniffed the distinct smell of butane. He put the floorboard back quietly and climbed the ladder.

"You couldn't sleep either, huh?" Max asked as he came on deck.

"No way. That Larry snores loud enough to shake a screw loose."

Max chuckled. "Another day or so and his snoring won't bother you."

The remark could have meant anything, but Chris took it to mean only one thing and consoled himself with the thought that if everything worked out correctly, Larry's snoring wouldn't bother anyone ever again.

He went forward and saw the glow of the red running light reflected off the deck. For weeks George had been sailing without running lights and now, tonight of all nights, he had suddenly turned them on. Chris had forgotten about the lights. He should have loosened a bulb, or disconnected a wire. He tried to remember whether or not you could see that glow from the cockpit. You could always see the light reflected off the sails. Right now the lower area of the sail reflected the green of the starboard light, but could you see it on deck? He imagined himself back in the cockpit and tried to remember exactly what he could see when he was behind the wheel. There was the deckhouse with the dinghy on top of it which cut off the view of the bow. That's why had been sure they could go over the side at the bow without being seen. He imagined himself leaning to one side in the cockpit and looking forward. He didn't remember ever seeing a glow on the deck. The bow curved in too fast. He thought that only by standing on the seat of the cockpit could one see the glow on the deck and where they were going over the side, but was he remembering it correctly?

He sat down next to Myra. In the warmth of the night she had the sleeves of the bulky sweater and windbreaker pushed above her elbows trying to keep cool. He, leaning against the deck-box, adjusted the floatation cushion behind his back. They had sat that same way so often before in preparation for this night. He was aware, as he had never been before, that four feet right below them George was lying in one of the forward bunks. Was he asleep, or was something keeping him awake? In the past they had whispered about their plans, encouraged each other it would work. Tonight they sat silently, holding hands. From time to time Chris would lean to one side and rise up a little to look past the dinghy to where Max was. Chris was relieved that each time Max was looking at the compass, or up at the sails, or up at the stars. Not once was he looking their direction.

At two minutes after one Chris looked back and saw Max leaning back in the cockpit, his head rolling from side to side with the motion of the ship. Just as Chris had observed so often in the past, Max was asleep. "I'll go over the side first. Watch carefully how I do it and what I hold on to. As soon as my head disappears you come. I'll be right below you. I'll guide your foot down to the bobstay to step on as you come down. We've got to get into the water without making a splash." He had explained all this before, but she listened and nodded. "Now if Max sees you as you're going over, just drop into the water. I'll be right there to catch you. And if for some reason you think he saw me, just dive over the side. Are you ready?"

She nodded and he turned around on his knees and opened the deck box. He took out the two life jackets with the bottles of water tied up inside them and tied a line from them to around his waist. They took the plastic bags of food and stuffed them in their pockets. After filling the pockets of his parachute pants with the food, he tied the diving knife to his lower leg. Occasionally he would rise to look at Max. He closed the deck box cover and just then Max woke up, looked around at the sails and compass and then stood up and stretched. They knelt on the foredeck motionless waiting for him to sit down again. He stood behind the wheel, swaying a little, his legs spread against the rocking of the boat. *Sit down! Sit down! Sit down, damn you, sit down!*

It was at least fifteen minutes before Max finally leaned over, picked up the cushion, and then sat down adjusting the cushion behind his back. Stretching his legs in front of him he braced his feet against the opposite side of the cockpit. Chris breathed a sigh of relief. Max was again facing sideways and would now have to turn his head to see anything going on up forward. There was no hope of his dozing off again, but they were out of his line of sight.

They waited another five minutes and then Chris started forward, crawling backward on his belly, pulling the life jackets with him. His foot touched the toe rail and he looked back to see if he was starting over the side where he wanted to. He was relieved that his view of the cockpit was completely cut off by the deckhouse. If he couldn't see Max, then Max couldn't see him. For some reason the sign he'd seen on the back of trucks, "If you can't see my mirror, I can't see you," came to mind. Myra had started crawling back too, her feet almost to his head. She was up on her elbows dragging the two cushions behind her. It was not something he had suggested and he admired her now for having thought of it. He kept pushing himself backward until his legs were hanging over the side and then he lowered the life jackets and water jugs over. He felt the line tug at his waist as the jackets bounced alongside the boat. Holding onto a cleat with his left hand, and onto the toerail with his right, he lowered himself over the side, sliding his left foot along the curve of the bow, until he felt it land on the bobstay. He hung there for a moment, his left foot on the bobstay, his right knee braced against the side of the boat, the line attached to the life jackets tugging at his waist, his chin even with the toerail. He heard the dull thudding of the water bottle filled life jacket hitting the hull with the wave action. Three feet away from him Myra was lying on her belly looking back at him. He let go with his left hand, motioned for her to follow, and then reaching down to grab hold of the bobstay dropped into the water.

The five knot current of the boat moving through the water almost made him loose his grip, but he hung on tightly with both hands, pulling himself against the curl of the bow water until he could hook his arm over the bobstay. When he looked up after getting himself in position to help her down, her feet were just starting over the side.

* * *

Myra kept inching backwards till her stomach was at the toerail and her legs hanging over the side. She thought she felt Chris reach up and take her ankle to guide her foot to the bobstay, but just then she felt a hot, burning sensation in her arm followed by the worst pain she had ever experienced and then she heard the sound of the shot. She looked up and to her left and saw Max coming toward her along the deck. She felt paralyzed, partly by the pain of the shot and also by the thought that being shot was what she expected to happen to her and there was nothing she could do about it. She looked down at her arm and in the dim light of the running light saw the stain of blood spreading out along the deck. She heard another shot and felt the wind of it rushing by her head and at the same time Chris pulling on her leg. She gave one great push with her arms, almost like doing a sudden push-up, her torso rising a little off the deck, the wounded arm sending a shock of pain up her shoulder, Chris pulling heavily on her leg, and she slipped between the lower life-line and the toerail into the water. She started floating away from him. He reached for her, grabbing a handful of clothing, pulling her toward him. "I'm hit, Chris. Oh, god, it hurts so much."

"Where? Where are you hit?"

"My arm. My right arm. Oh, god, it hurts." He moved around her until he could put an arm around her waist and felt her good arm tighten around his neck.

He saw the shadow of Max leaning over the side as he ran forward along the deck looking for them. Chris fought his way around the bow to the other side. The boat slipped by, the boom and main sail passing over their heads. He saw someone come out of the hatch as the cockpit slipped by. He didn't know if it was George or Larry. He and Myra were even with the transom and for a moment they were caught in the glow of the stern light and then it moved away from them and they were in the darkness of the water. He floated there, holding on to her, her arm around his neck, watching the small light moving away from them and in that dim light of the white oval stern with the faint letters *AHWANAH* barely discernible. "Well, I guess we made it," he said and relaxed his hold on her; aware now of how tightly he had been holding her to him.

She didn't answer him, but rolled over a little, her arm slipping from around his neck. Her head rolled over to the other side when he let go of her. He reached for her again, pulling her to him, and with his other hand he lifted her face out of the water and felt along her arm till he felt the spot that was still sticky and warm from oozing blood. He couldn't tell how bad it was, but it was bad enough she had passed out. He was treading water trying to keep both of them afloat. He felt for a pulse at her neck and was relieved when he found one. He thought it was a little weak, but it was there. The first thing to do was to get the lifejackets onto the two of them. It was all he could do with food-filled, water-soaked clothes to stay afloat.

"Myra. Myra. Don't quit on me. We can make it," he said hugging her to him, her head resting on his shoulder. It was hard trying to keep her head above water and get the jackets loose at the same time without losing the bottles of water tied inside them. He finally got a jacket on her and let her float free while he put his on. He reached for her again, pulling her toward him, holding on to her arm, trying to locate the wound. She had been shot in the fleshiest part of the arm between the elbow and the shoulder. The loss of blood had to be stopped. He turned her on her side, holding her so her head rested on his shoulder, and clamped a hand over where the blood was coming from. He wished she would say something. He wondered if the blood would attract sharks. He had heard three shots and wondered if she had been hit anywhere else. He tried to feel along her body thinking if she had been shot the blood in that area would be warmer than the water. He was angry with himself for not bringing medical supplies. In the medical chest he had all kinds of bandages, compresses, antibiotic and all kinds of painkillers including morphine. *How could I have planned something like this and not considered we might have needed medical attention of one kind or another?* At the same time he wondered what medical supplies he would have selected.

When he didn't find any other wounds he released his hand and quickly folded the windbreaker and sweater up and took off his belt and pulled it tight around the wound as a compress.

They floated with her head on his shoulder, one arm around her and the other arm reaching across to keep the wounded arm out of the water. He wished it were daylight. Not until then would he know how bad her wound was. He wished he could be certain she was all right. It was his fault she was hurt. Maybe if he had sent her over the side first they would both be all right now.

The hours passed slowly. Every half hour he would loosen the belt on the compress, let the blood flow for a couple of seconds and then tighten the belt down again. Once he thought she opened her eyes and tried to say something, but when he put his face close to her, her eyes were still closed. He was continually feeling her pulse, and whereas he would be filled with terror as his hand moved toward her throat, he had a great sense of relief when he felt the pulse and knew she was still alive. Morning would come and he would know then what he had to do.

CHAPTER TWENTY

With the sound of the first shot George woke up completely and reached for his gun. With the second shot he had the gun in his hand and his feet on the floor. By the third shot he was standing in front of the door sliding back the hasp. Then he slowed down and opened the door cautiously, standing to one side in case it was Chris doing the shooting. In the darkness of the main salon he saw Larry sitting in his bunk groping for his cigarettes. "What's happening?" Larry called.

George ignored the questions, reached for Larry's gun and handed it to him as he passed. "Come with me," George barked and Larry followed with his gun in his right hand, a book of matches in his left hand and an unlit cigarette in the corner of his mouth.

At the bottom of the ladder George stopped and looked cautiously over the sill of the hatchway. There was no one at the wheel or in the cockpit area. He climbed the first two steps of the ladder slowly; his left hand on the hold rail, his right hand holding the gun in front of his face as he cautiously raised his head high enough to see over the cabin top. He saw Max moving quickly along the port side, his left hand holding onto the lifeline, his right hand holding the gun. George quickly climbed the rest of the way up the ladder. "Take the wheel, Larry," he called over his shoulder and ran to where Max was standing on the foredeck. "What happened, Max?"

"They tried to get away."

"I don't see them on board so it looks like they made it, doesn't it?" George said with icy anger.

"Not alive they didn't."

"Do you guarantee that?"

Max turned to where he had seen Myra go over the side and found what he was looking for. "Look, here's Jamison's blood," he said pointing to the spot. He was glad to see it was a fairly large spot. "She was already starting over the side when I got her. I put one shot in her head, the next two went into Jamison."

"So there's some blood on the deck. What I want to know is if you guarantee they are both dead."

"Yes," Max said thinking if they weren't they soon would be. He was certain there was no way Chris could make it and he was certain from the way Myra dropped when he shot her that she was, if not dead, not long for this world.

George stared at him for a minute and then said, “What did they do, just come up here and jump over the side?”

“No, they sat up here for a while like they always do and then tried to sneak over. They were trying to crawl out here when I saw them,” he said pointing to where he had last seen Myra. “If they had just jumped over I probably wouldn’t have been able to hit them.”

“Did they have life jackets?”

“No.”

George strode to the cockpit and sat down. He did not consider Chris impulsive, and yet it was foolish to try and escape without life jackets. With life jackets they had a reasonable chance of being seen by boat or a small plane. Without jackets they would wear themselves out just trying to keep afloat. Nor did he fully believe Max’s story. If it hadn’t been for the blood, he would have suspected Max of having found them gone and firing the shots to cover up for his negligence.

Myra should have known they could not really get away. She knew him well enough for that. As soon as he had that thought he became suspicious. Don’t either of you eat or drink anything that isn’t in cans. Especially the water. If you’re thirsty have a beer or a soda or something.”

“There isn’t any beer or pop left,” Larry said.

“We should be off this thing by tomorrow night. If things get desperate we can drink the juice from canned fruit or vegetables. If they were planning to poison us, the water supply would be the easiest and surest way to do it.”

“Poison us?” Larry asked both puzzled and frightened.

George ignored his question. “Max come with me.” He went below and turned on every light. “Look through his junk, Max, and see if you can find a picture of him. There should be a passport or something, unless he took it with him.”

Max started looking through the compartments and shelves closest to Chris’ bunk, throwing clothing on the bunk and riffling through notebooks and papers while George went forward to the head. He opened the small door below the sink and checked all the hoses. They were still connected to their through-hull fittings. If

Chris had been planning on scuttling the boat, this was not where he was going to let the water in. He headed for the galley sink. Max held out a couple snapshots. “This is all I could find,” he said, “what do you want them for anyway.”

“I’m going to put out an open contract on the two of them.”

“They’re both dead, I tell you.”

“Then you don’t have anything to worry about, do you?”

Max turned away and went back to looking through Chris’ things in order to be doing something and not have to answer George. He had the awful feeling George knew he was lying, but he would be in real trouble if he admitted Chris and Myra had gotten away. He wondered what the odds were of their making it. He had been lucky to hit Myra. He wondered how seriously he had wounded her. It must have been pretty serious or there wouldn’t have been time for blood to get all over the deck before she went over. He saw the scene again, her legs over the side, her body lying on the deck, her arms stretched away from her as though trying to hold onto the deck. When he saw her he had fired, not having time to take careful aim, his body swaying to keep balance as he moved forward along the rolling deck. He wondered if there were any bullet holes in the deck. If there was only one, he could say the other two went into Chris and Myra. If there were two bullets in the deck, George would know he was lying. He was aware of how lucky he was to have hit her at all, especially in a place that left that much of a smear of blood along the deck. He would have to try, without being obvious about it, to keep George from going up there in the daylight.

George opened the door below the galley sink, peered into the darkness and then went across to the chart table to get a flashlight. He crossed back and getting down on his hands and knees, shone the beam of light into the darkness under the sink. He had to stick his head into the opening to see the through-hull fitting. When he saw there was no water coming in there he went to check in the engine compartment. He shone the light back to the through-hull fitting and then just as he was about to pull out the beam of light reflected off the end of a clear, plastic hose. He sat looking at it for a moment. It was not connected to anything. Why was it there? He tugged on it and heard something rattle behind the stove. He got up and looked behind the stove and saw the Y-valve. He looked up and saw the overhead valve was open and turned it off, shouting through the hatchway, "Don't smoke, Larry." He checked the burner valves. They were all off. He started pulling on the hose and the stove rocked back and forth on its gimbals with his yanking. He pulled up the clear plastic hose and stood there for a moment looking at the end of it. Jamison had planned this for a long time. He had rigged this up when he was supposed to be cleaning the stove. Myra had been in on it from the beginning. She was the one who had complained about the stove not working correctly. He reached over and threw the switch for the bilge exhaust fan. He stood there becoming increasingly furious, but there was with it a tinge of admiration. It wasn't a bad plan. If the boat didn't catch on fire, a couple of them would probably have been asphyxiated in their sleep.

He wondered why he didn't smell any gas. It had been fifteen or twenty minutes and in that time there would have been at least some smell of gas in the bilge. He opened the engine compartment door again and put his head inside and smelled the gas. He left the exhaust fan running and went on deck.

Max came on deck a few minutes later. "I didn't find any more pictures, but here's some kind of address book."

George took it without saying anything. He was getting cold sitting there just in his shorts. He stood up. "Max, you still have the watch. We'll talk about this in the morning." He went below, stopped by the chart table for a moment to look through the book and then went forward, turning off the lights as he went.

Larry followed George below and Max sat behind the wheel worried Chris and Myra might make it. It was unlikely, but if they did he was in trouble. He had been friends with George for a long time, but friendship wouldn't mean anything if those two made it to shore. If they made it George would have two counts against him, first he had let them get away and then he had lied about it. He had wounded Myra. Of that he was sure. If they survived they would have to get medical attention. Doctor's offices and hospitals were the place to look for them first and he would have to get to them before George learned they had not been killed.

In the forward compartment George was disturbed by the way things had happened. He sat in the darkness of the forward compartment, back resting against the bulkhead, his legs stretched out in front of him considering possibilities. He was not particularly worried, but he didn't like it when things didn't go precisely as planned. Changes required rethinking and replanning. He had not really underestimated Chris; instead things had been going so well he had become lax. If they had both been killed, then there was nothing to worry about. But if they had not been killed they might just make it. Anyone capable of planning and carrying out the rigging of the stove without attracting attention would also be able to provide, food, water and floatation. In the morning he would take a count of the life jackets.

The important question now was when would they get to land or be rescued? He wondered if Chris had taken one of the emergency distress transmitters. He would have to check that too. He thought there had been three of them, two in the chart table and one in the dinghy. If Chris used that they could be rescued at first light. He should have confiscated the emergency beacons when he destroyed the radio transmitter. He had not taken them because in the back of his mind had been the thought that if some unexpected emergency sank the boat the beacons would be useful. He knew now he had been wrong in not searching the boat when he took it over, but that was water under the hull. The important thing now was to get off this boat and sink it as soon as possible.

CHAPTER TWENTY-ONE

Stars faded into morning gray and rays of sunlight shafted through horizon clouds. Daylight only made more apparent the enormity of the ocean on which they floated. In the troughs walls of water surrounded them and on the crests he could see mountains of water extending away from him in all directions. He could not see the islands. All through the night he had sustained himself with the knowledge they were there, that when daylight came he would be able to see the ragged cliffs rising behind lush, green flatlands, but there was none of that. Where the island should have been there was only the pile-up of clouds and he remembered the old Hawaiian myth that if the clouds disappeared from the tops of the mountains the islands would sink into the sea.

Oahu was there underneath that pile-up of clouds. Or was it? Maybe the island really had sunk into the sea. That's why the birds flew around in circles above them. They had lost their nesting places. Or perhaps the clouds were a portent of a coming storm. A storm that would wash them away to eternal oblivion.

A frigate bird glided toward him, skimming the steep surface of a wave. He could see its beak and eyes, its legs and claws were extended, its forked tail spread. At the last minute it veered off, tucked in its legs and flapped away. It had tried to land on them. He followed it with his eyes, turning his head to look up into the sky.

He looked at Myra. Her eyes were closed and her body limp, and he was afraid for a moment she had died. He had held her all night, lying on her side with her head on his shoulder. He had finally found a way to arrange the life jacket in such a way it propped the wounded arm out of the water. He felt her neck again and was relieved to feel a pulse. As far as he could tell she had been unconscious all through the night and he thought that was probably best since that way she didn't feel any pain.

He looked at the arm that was propped out of the water. He had done his best all through the night to keep it as dry as possible. In the darkness all he had been able to do was pull the sleeve of her sweater and jacket down over the bleeding area as a compress using his belt to keep it in place. After that there was not much he could do except loosen his belt every hour or so and wait till morning. Now that the morning was here he didn't know what, in the darkness of night, he had expected to do with daylight. The pile of material held in place by his belt seemed to be doing the job. The area was a little damp, but not wet as it would have been if she were bleeding badly. He wondered for a while if he should try and revive her and decided that for the present it was probably better to leave her unconscious. He wondered if keeping the wound out of the water was really important, except that being under water would probably encourage bleeding. He wanted to look at the wound to see how really bad it was, but decided it would be a lot easier to do that when she was awake and could hold the wounded arm out of the water herself.

He wondered how far they had drifted. *Have we moved at all in the past six hours? How fast is the current?* He couldn't count much on the wind. There wasn't enough of them above the water for the wind to have any effect so he was entirely at the mercy of the currents. He moved her over to the left side with her head on his shoulder and her back toward him. With his arm across her chest it was easier to hold onto her and keep both her face and wounded arm out of the water. In that position he started kicking his legs and doing the backstroke with his right arm.

He tried to estimate how much progress he was making. Swimming along Waikiki he did about two miles an hour, but that was swimming freestyle without clothes, life jacket and dragging another person. Back then he was in practice and in condition and probably could have done a twenty mile swim. Now he hadn't been swimming for weeks. If he wasn't careful and tried to do too much he could develop cramps and that wouldn't help anyone. He told himself he would swim for three minutes and then rest for a while, gradually building up the time until his swimming muscles got used to working again.

He had only been swimming a minute or so when he heard her say, "Do you really think we'll make it, Chris?"

Because her back was to him he didn't see her open her eyes and so the first indication she was awake was when she asked the question. Through the sound of his swimming he wasn't even sure he had heard her. For a moment he thought he was imagining it because that was exactly what he was wondering.

"No doubt about it," he said stopping his swimming and hoping he sounded convincing. He turned her to face him and said, "Now that you're conscious we'll take a look at that wound. How does it feel?"

"It hurts. Not as bad as it did at first, but the whole arm feels kind of numb."

"Hold on to me. Put your hand on my head. That will keep the wound out of the water. I want to take a look at it."

"I can keep it out of the water O.K.," she said using her left hand to hold her right arm out of the water. "But it is beginning to hurt again."

He started taking off his life jacket and she said, "What are you doing?"

"I'm going use my T-shirt for bandages. It will work better than the wool sweater." He clipped his life jacket to hers, struggled to get out of the wet sweater, unbuttoned his shirt taking it off and then pulled the T-shirt off over his head. He put his shirt and life jacket back on and then with the right hand he reached down, while at the same time bringing his right leg up and putting his hand through the loop of the handle of the knife, undid the snaps that held it in its sheath. Carefully he cut through her jacket and sweater at the elbow. He took his T-shirt and cut the neckband front and back and ripped it in half and then put the knife back in its sheath on his leg. One half the T-shirt he stuffed inside his life jacket and folded the other half until he had a pad three by four inches. Even wet it had a good thickness to it. He gave it to her to hold while he undid the belt around her arm. "This is probably going to hurt," he said.

"Every time a doctor has said that to me I have wanted to say, 'then don't do it.' I guess I can't say it to you either."

"I'm sorry," he said as he slipped off the thin, waterproof material of the windbreaker. He slipped both his hands under the sweater and spread his fingers pulling the material away from the wound and sliding the sleeve of the sweater off her arm. The wound, about two inches long and as wide and deep as the thickness of his little finger, bled with a steady flow, but with no pulsing. There did not seem to be any particular swelling, and except for right around the wound there was no redness. "Well, it doesn't look too bad," he said.

"Well, I'm sure glad to hear that," she said, "because it sure doesn't feel too good. And what about all the blood? Man, it hurts."

"That's not bad. In fact it's good. It's cleaning out the wound. Here, take this and hold it over it," he said squeezing out half of the T-shirt and handing it to her. He took the other half and wrung it out as best he could and folded into a second pad. "O.K. We'll use this one," he said removing her hand and replacing the cloth she was holding with the one he had neatly folded. "Hold that tightly against it." He took the sweater he had cut away, rinsed it out and then folded it and placed it on top of the T-shirt. "Just adding a little padding," he said. He took his belt and tightened it around the wound.

The belt was an eight-strand sennit plait of seine twine he had made himself by following the instructions in ***Ashley's Book of Knots***. Because it was just a braid of cord he could put the tongue of the belt buckle through the braid anywhere he wanted. After tightening the belt around the compress he cut the cords six inches from the buckle, unbraided them a short distance and then knotted off each strand so the short belt around her arm would not come unraveled. He started unbraiding the long section he had cut off. He cut off two of them and then sliding the cut off sleeve of the windbreaker up her arm slipped it back over the wound with its compress. With the twine he tied the sleeve off at the elbow and above the wound and said, "Well, that will protect it from getting wet from splashes and a quick dip, but not from being under water, so you still have to do your best to hold it out of water... Are you hungry?"

"I can wait a while if you think we should."

"We'll have a drink of water and then something to eat," he said breaking the seal and taking the cap off a water bottle. He handed it to her and she took several swallows and handed it back to him. He took one swallow and then capped the bottle making sure the string was secure around the neck. It floated alongside them as he reached down and pulled out a bag of raisins. He had to use his knife to make a break in the tough, plastic bag. They each had two handfuls and then he rolled the top down tightly and tied it shut with string from his belt.

He rolled over on his side, his left hand holding on to the collar of her life jacket and started the sidestroke, his right arm pulling through the water, his legs kicking under her. She was on her back, her left arm holding her right arm out of the water. She started kicking, her feet splashing behind them. "Try not to let your feet break the surface," he said. "The sound of splashing can attract sharks. And don't kick too fast, you'll tire yourself out."

Her legs grew tired and she stopped kicking. His legs got tired too. He was out of practice and his shoes were an added weight to his kicking. He let go of her, telling her to bring her feet up to him and he took her sneakers off. They would not need them till they walked out of the water. With the laces he tied them to the front of her life jacket. On top of the shoes she could rest her wounded arm comfortably out of the water. He took his shoes off and tied them to the front of his life jacket. He looked at his watch. He had only been swimming for half an hour. It seemed a lot longer than that.

He started kicking again. It was easier this time without his shoes on. He did it for twenty minutes and when he stopped he was a lot more tired than he thought he should bc and then remembered he had not slept for more than twenty-four hours. "How's your arm feel, Myra?"

"O.K. I guess. Doesn't seem to be hurting as much as it was before, but it still hurts."

"I have got to get some sleep. Will you stay awake and see we don't separate, or should I tie us together."

"You can tie us together if you want to, but I'm going to hang on to you for dear life."

He smiled a little. "O.K. Keep your eyes open. If you see or hear anything wake me right away," he said. He was afraid that as soon as he was asleep his head would fall to one side or the other waking him up. He finally found a way of tucking his shoes between the high, wide collar of the life jacket and his jaw that prevented his head from falling forward or to either side. Resting in the water, with his arms stretched out on either side of him, he closed his eyes.

* * *

She felt suddenly alone. He was there, and yet he wasn't there, he was someplace else unaware of her and she was suddenly aware of the enormity of the ocean in which she floated. The water rose and fell unceasingly. She had her hand caught in a strap of his life jacket holding on to him. He lay so still it was hard to know if the rising and falling of his flesh was his breathing or just the action of the waves on his body. She was suddenly afraid he was dead, and she tugged on his arm. “Huh?” He opened his eyes.

“I’m sorry. I didn’t mean to wake you.”

He smiled a little and for some reason she resented his smile. It was as though he was content with where he was, sleeping there like there was nothing wrong, and then she remembered how long she had been asleep. She had not felt the pain in her arm when she was asleep, nor had she been able to think of where she was. When he was awake, she had been able to believe they would make it, because he was always so confident they would make it, but now she was aware only of the boundless and endless sea stretching away forever with no sign of deliverance in any direction. The sea itself seemed to be wanting to drag her down. It was only the yellow life jacket that kept the sea from fulfilling its desire. And even if the life jacket was able to keep them afloat for all eternity, how long would the food and water last? She became terrified at the knowledge of how pitifully small their food and water supply was. If they didn’t drown they would starve to death. She tried to tell herself it wasn’t that far to land. The reason they couldn’t see it was because they were so low in the water. Chris had explained to her one time that for every three feet of elevation you could see a mile further.

* * *

He woke up about noon, disoriented, with the overhead sun shining in his eyes and his stomach growling with hunger.

“Hi,” she said when he opened his eyes.

“You’re still here,” he said.

“Of course I’m here. There’s not a whole lot a places I can go,” she said hoping it sounded like a joke.

He untied the laces that had kept the shoes tucked under his chin and rubbed his neck. “I dreamt I was out here all alone. That you had stayed on the boat.”

“Nope, I’m still here. I’m not letting you get away from me. I think we should tie ourselves together just in case we both fall asleep at the same time.”

He nodded while turning slowly in the water. The bank of clouds was still there, but he couldn’t see the island. He reached down and brought out the bag of raisins. Through the clear part of the plastic he could see the bag was almost a quarter full of water. He untied the twine he had hoped would keep it closed and offered her the bag. She reached in and grabbed a handful of the raisins. “They’re all slippery,” she said carefully lifting out the few raisins she was able to get and putting them in her mouth. It was awkward having to hold the bag up out of the water and try to reach inside for the slippery raisins. He held out a hand, tipping the bag toward it, letting the amber liquid drain between his fingers and then quickly tipped the bag back when a clump of raisins landed in his hand, closing his fist over the precious food. A raisin dropped from his hand as he was carrying them to his mouth and he quickly jammed the remaining raisins in his mouth and tried to get the one that had gotten away. It kept swirling out of reach. He kept staring at the spot where the raisin last disappeared; waiting for it to reappear, ready to grab it. The fact it had gotten away from him both angered him and for some reason perplexed him. It was as though that little raisin had a mind of its own.

Pinching the opening together he was able to pour off most the water. With the water gone he poured the slippery raisins into both their hands. They each had three handfuls and then he closed the bag again, pressing all the air out of it before folding the top down tightly. He tied it with the string again and this time tucked it under a strap on his life jacket. From another pocket he got the bag that had the candy bars. He handed her one and took one himself and then closed the watertight bag leaving it puffy with air inside. He tied a piece of twine around it letting it float alongside them. It was less likely to get water inside floating than stuffed in his pocket. He held his in his teeth while he unwrapped hers for her. He slid off the paper cover and let it fall into the water. He folded back the tinfoil wrapping and handed it to her. She smiled, took one small bite, and said, “I shouldn’t eat this. It will spoil my appetite for dinner.”

He smiled and thought he was glad she was there. It would be awfully lonely out there all by himself. “How does your arm feel?” he asked.

“The same.”

“I’ll look at it again when we finish eating.”

“My goodness, with all we have to eat that may be hours from now.”

They ate their candy bar slowly, nibble by nibble, he folding back the tinfoil as he went, she grabbing it with her teeth and pulling it out of the tinfoil sleeve a little before she bit it off. When he was through he wadded the tinfoil into a little ball and threw it from him. He wondered if a fish would be curious about it as it sank. When she was through he reached for one of the bottles of water. "Are you thirsty?" he asked.

"The food has made me want water, but I'm not really thirsty."

"Good. Let's each take only three or four swallows," he said handing her the bottle. She took her ration of water and then handed the bottle back to him. He took his swallows, capped the bottle and said, "Let's take a look at that arm." He undid the twine at the upper end of the cut off sleeve and looked inside. "Doesn't look bad. No sign of infection and not too much blood." He tied the sleeve closed again and said, "Well, I guess it's back to work. Don't kick your feet too hard. I don't want the exercise to start your blood flowing again." He tied a piece of twine to the front of his life jacket and tied the other end to the back of hers. Lying on his back he started swimming using a steady backstroke.

CHAPTER TWENTY-TWO

George stepped on deck not real happy with the lunch of canned beans and pear halves Larry had prepared for them. The fact that they were all moving around for the first time in a month without shoulder holsters and guns was a constant reminder Chris and Myra had gotten away. He thought that if Chris could rig the gas to kill them he could also have a backup plan. Since the seacocks were all right then maybe Chris had poisoned the water or what little food they had left that wasn't in sealed cans.

His thoughts alternated between wondering what Chris had done to the boat he hadn't discovered and worrying Chris and Myra might be rescued. He would be glad to get off this boat. At the speed they were going they would be at the rendezvous area between three and three-thirty in the afternoon. He ordered the sails reduced. He didn't want to run the risk of being seen meeting the other boat and making the transfer in broad daylight.

He was just about to go below again when he heard the small plane. It was just a speck of tinsel in the sky reflecting the sunlight. Through the binoculars George watched the twin-engine Beechcraft heading north from Oahu. Must be going to Kauai. Even as he thought that he saw it bank into a turn and come toward them. *What was going on?*

The plane passed almost directly above them. It banked, turning and descending. It passed less than a hundred feet from them, just above the surface of the waves, close enough for them to see the pilot and a passenger inside. "Wave and smile at them," George ordered raising his hand to wave as the plane went by. It climbed away from them, turned, and headed in a southeasterly direction. "Just some guy flying around," George said, but he couldn't help being disturbed by the plane. It meant someone had seen them.

* * *

After leaving the *AHWANAH*, Frenchie flew fifteen miles out along the coast of Molokai looking for Johnny Bigelow's boat. There was one sampan with lines out moving westward along the coast, but nothing that resembled Johnny's boat. He hadn't really expected to see it. He headed toward Kahului, still looking for Johnny's boat, and then headed for the airport. On the ground he headed for the nearest telephone. He had been ordered not to use his radio or cell-phone. "This is Frenchie. Let me talk to Mr. Kalama," he said into the phone.

Kalama came on the line. "Yeah, Frenchie, did you see them?"

"I think I found them Mr. Kalama, about fifty miles away."

"That close, huh? How come you didn't spot them yesterday?"

"I don't know, Sir, but I've only been flying out a hundred miles, just like you told me. Overnight they came into my search range."

"You're sure it's him?"

"I think so, Sir. I went real low by the boat. Only saw three guys on board. One of them fits the description you gave me of Mr. Costellos."

"O.K. I'll get back to you. Where are you?"

"A public phone at Kahului Airport."

"What's the phone number there?" Frenchie gave it to him. "Stay right there. I'll call you back," Kalama said and hung up and dialed Johnny Bigelow's number.

"Yeah?" Johnny answered.

"This is Kalama, Johnny. Frenchie thinks he saw them about fifty miles out. How long will it take to get to where you're supposed to meet them?"

"I tink maybe dey slow down. Mr. Costellos not like meet in daytime."

"Kalama hesitated. Up until that moment he planned to be on the boat when Johnny picked up George Costellos. He had felt he should be there. For that reason he had kept Johnny in port and sent the plane out every day looking for them. Now suddenly he thought better of it. If anything went wrong, he didn't want to be there. Furthermore, the boat was not the place to give George the news about his father. "Well, things have changed Johnny, you go meet them. I'll send Frenchie to Molokai to bring them here as soon as you get there. You call me as soon as Frenchie takes off and I'll send a car to pick them up at the airport."

"Yes, Sir," Johnny said and waited until he heard the phone go dead before hanging up.

* * *

On board the *AHWANAH* they sat around the cockpit each upset with the inconvenience caused by Chris and Myra escaping. Larry considered Max responsible, and Max was not really sure that George believed him. After searching the storage compartments they had found a large can of grapefruit juice and one of tomato juice. George had rationed out the two juices. "Sure wish we could drink the water," Larry said.

George glared at him. "Go ahead and drink the water for all I care."

"The emergency water underneath the dinghy should be all right," Max said. "He couldn't have gotten to that without lifting up the dinghy and we'd have seen him do that."

George nodded angry he had not thought of that himself.

"Might as well break it out, Larry," Max said and Larry went forward and started untying the lines that held the dinghy. That also irritated George. He didn't like the way Max was giving orders. He thought for a moment of countermanding Max's suggestion but knew he had no good reason for it. It would only make him look petty. He went below angry, irritated and worried. He went to the forward compartment, closing the door behind him. Things were just not going right. First Myra and Chris had gotten away, then the plane had flown over them and now Max was finding ways to get around his orders. And yet it was not really those things that were bothering him. Instead it was a premonition that after all the time, effort, planning, and distance, something was going to go wrong with the operation. He lay on the bunk with his hands folded behind his head, staring at the overhead beams.

He tried to figure out why he had the strange worry. He was not a worrier. He made his plans, considered all eventualities and then went ahead. He had to admit Chris and Myra getting away was an eventuality he had not planned on. He wondered if there were other eventualities he had not planned on. Only a fool would have tried going over the side. He tried to put himself in Jamison's place. Only if he were reasonably sure he was going to make it would he have tried something like that. Obviously Jamison had thought they could make it. In some ways Jamison had seemed so wishy-washy, had never put up any kind of a real fight, and George had been lulled into thinking Jamison would go along with anything. He had underestimated Jamison. Myra too, for that matter. That's what bothered him. Myra. Myra knew too much. All Jamison could tell them about was this trip, but Myra went way back. Their escape colored everything. He had expected to see boats and planes in this area, but now every time he saw one he wondered again if Chris and Myra had been rescued. If anyone that looked like the Coast Guard came alongside and wanted to board the boat, the boat would have to go to the bottom. He couldn't let them find anything. He would have to sink the boat eventually anyway, so he might just as well get ready for it now.

He got up from the bunk with the idea of telling Max to disconnect the hoses from the through-hull fittings, and then decided to do it himself. At least then he would know it had really been done. He started in the head and thought for a moment of leaving those connected in case someone wanted to use the toilet. Forget it. If they have to go they can go over the side. He went through the boat closing all the seacocks and disconnecting the hoses. He went on deck satisfied with himself. If the Coast Guard so much as headed their direction, he could open the seacocks quickly and the Coast Guard could take the credit for rescuing them from a sinking boat.

It was four in the afternoon when George spotted Bigelow's boat. He had been examining every boat or plane that came in sight through the binoculars, basically looking for the Coast Guard markings. He was sure it was Bigelow's boat, and it was headed straight for them. It was coming slowly with all the fishing lines out. He continued to watch him through the binoculars, irritated that Bigelow continued toward them. He knew he had told Bigelow he didn't want to make the transfer in daylight. He changed course a little so as to miss Bigelow and a few minutes later the powerboat changed course so as to remain on an intersecting course.

Three hundred yards away Bigelow started taking in his fishing lines and putting out fenders. George scanned the horizon in all directions through the binoculars. For the moment there were no other boats to be seen, but he would have felt better if Bigelow had done as he said and waited until dusk. He considered ordering Bigelow away, but things might be worse later. There might be boats in the area, or the wind might pick up and the seas get rough. Right now there were no other boats around and the seas were relatively smooth. He ordered the sails down and the *AHWANAH* rocked gently, dead in the water.

Bigelow maneuvered his boat carefully alongside. By controlling the speed and direction of one or the other of the two engines he was able to keep right alongside without any trouble. George was the only one he knew and the first to step aboard. Johnny hoped he would not have to get into a long conversation with him. Bigelow felt uncomfortable with him on board, afraid he might say something wrong. He didn't want to be the one to tell George about his father, or even be around when George learned about it.

He stayed on the flying bridge keeping his boat alongside the AHWANAH, watching as they handed the luggage across. He guessed the four black cases must contain the heroin. The last to be handed over was the duffel bags. As soon as the black cases were on board George carried them to the main cabin and then climbed to the bridge, leaving the other two to handle the last things.

"Welcome aboard, Mr. Costellos. Drinks and pupus in da 'frigerator," Johnny said and went back to concentrating on keeping his position alongside the other boat.

"Any other boats around?" George asked.

Johnny turned and pointed to a spot on the radarscope. "Dat dere da closest. 'Bout twenty miles. One kine fishing sampan. No have radar on."

George stood looking at the scope for a moment. The outline of Molokai glowed a pale yellow mass on the side of the scope, becoming bright as the sweeping line went by and fading out by the time the line swept by again. Max came up to the bridge and said, "Everything's taken care of George. She's on her way down."

"Any radar along here that might have us on their scope?" George asked pointing to the yellow blotch that was Molokai.

"Naw. Nuttin' dere."

"Very well. Stand off a little bit, but I want to stay here until I see her go down.

Johnny nodded, pushing forward on both throttles a little and moved twenty yards away. He eased back on the throttles, took it out of gear and slid into the helmsman's chair. Larry came up with a bottle of beer in his hand and said, "Man, that is good. I haven't had a cold bottle of beer for three months."

"Plenty beer an' food. You like I get you somethin'?" Johnny asked George.

George shook his head and stood with his hands on the rail looking at the *AHWANAH.* Larry sat down in one of the side seats and Max leaned back against the control console. Larry finished the beer, threw the bottle over the side and went down to get himself another one.

George stood, tightly clutching the rail. He wanted desperately to see that boat disappear. It seemed to take forever for the boat to go down. "Did you open all of the cocks?" he asked without turning his head.

"All of them: cockpit, engine, galley and head," Max answered. He resented George questioning him. He looked past George's head to the *AHWANAH.* It was settling at the stern, the bow rising slowly as the stern settled. The water came even with the transom top, the bow high showing the brown bottom paint with spots of barnacles and coral growth. It kept tilting slowly, the water even with the cockpit combing, showing the forward edge of the keel.

Suddenly it tipped on end with the sound of rushing water and the crashing of pots and dishes falling out of cupboards. It slid steadily backward into the water, past the main hatch, past each porthole, past the forward hatch, past the Sampson post, and then the water closed over the angry face of the figurehead. The point of the bowsprit disappeared below the water and George's hands relaxed on the rail. He turned away with a great feeling of relief, smiled contentedly and said, "I'm sure Mr. Kalama has told you how much I appreciate your letting us know about Steve Margolis trying to double-cross me, but I just wanted to tell you myself, that if there is anything you want, you just let me know."

"Ey no beeg ting, Bruddah."

"Oh, yes it was, and I'm not going to forget it." Johnny shrugged amiably and George said, "Do you have a shower on board?"

"Shua ting. Down laddah on da port side. Plenty hot wattah. Da towels in da—" but George was on his way down the ladder before Johnny could tell him where the towels were. He turned back to the controls, put the engines in gear, pushed both throttles forward and headed for Pukoo Bay.

* * *

Max stood looking over the bow of the boat, disappointed and frustrated. He didn't know what Steve's double-cross had been, but if this Bigelow had told George about it then he was not the one to be trusted with information about Chris and Myra. Max would have to wait until he got back to Los Angeles and could arrange it through someone he knew he could trust not to tell George. He went below and flopped into an easy chair in the main salon. "Anything to drink beside beer," he asked.

"Almost anything you want," Larry said pointing toward the galley. "In the cupboard over the sink."

Max got up to fix himself a drink. From the head he could hear the shower running and above the sound of the running water was George's voice singing. He wished George would hurry up. There were others wanting to take showers.

For twenty minutes George luxuriated in the hot, fresh-water shower. He felt relaxed and confident. It was good to be rid of that boat and on the way to civilization. He had always considered himself above powerboats. To him people who owned powerboats were not real sailors, but right now, even the faint hum of the engine was a soothing sound. He stepped out of the shower and dried himself with a heavy, blue-and-green, striped towel. When he was dry he wrapped the towel around his waist and went into the main salon to his duffel bag. He took out his shaving kit, some clean underwear, a blue, floral, aloha shirt and white slacks, and carried them all down below. He laid his clothes out on the bunk in the forward stateroom and went back to the head to shave.

He went back to the main salon wearing the clean clothes. His shirt and trouser were wrinkled and smelled musty from being in the duffel bag so long, but his after-shave lotion covered most of the musty smell. He sat down in a chair next to the duffel bag and took out a pair of blue socks and white shoes. The shoes and socks felt firmly tight on feet that had not worn any shoes for almost three months. He went into the galley, sliced two limes in half, squeezed them into a glass, threw in the ice cubes and poured in the Coke. He took a sip of his drink. It was marvelous. He went back to his chair, setting his drink in the gimbaled drink holder and reached into his bag for the last package of cigars. He had been saving them. Now there was no need to conserve. In a few hours he would be where he could buy all the cigars he wanted. It surprised him a little that he was no longer concerned about Myra and Chris. If they had been rescued in any condition to talk he wouldn't be sitting here right now with a cigar and a drink. Maybe Max really did kill them. If not, they weren't going to be found now with night coming on.

More out of curiosity than fear he turned on the radio. He turned the dial until he found a news station and listened until the announcer started repeating the news stories. He turned off the radio. There was no mention of bodies being found or survivors being picked up. He looked over at Larry and Max and said, "You two look terrible. Why don't you go get cleaned up?"

CHAPTER TWENTY-THREE

Frenchie landed the plane at Honolulu International Airport and maneuvered along the taxiways to the private hanger area where the black limousine was waiting. George got out of the plane cautiously. He was always a little uncomfortable when he wasn't in complete control of things. He had been nervous ever since leaving Johnny's boat. Someone else had planned this part of the trip and he didn't trust it completely. At least they had landed at Honolulu and that was something of a relief. Ever since he had gotten on the plane he had thought of how easy it would be for Frenchie to land at some remote airfield, kill them and make off with the shipment. He could not forget Steve had tried to double-cross him.

He had talked with Kalama before he had boarded Frenchie's plane, but he would not feel entirely safe until he was face to face with Kalama. There was something going on he didn't understand. He stood by the plane while Frenchie unloaded the luggage and handed it to the driver. George and Max took the black cases and then waited by the trunk of the car until the lid was closed before getting into the back the car. He felt a little better now that they were on the ground. The driver seemed to be going the right direction and as long as he stayed on main streets there wasn't much the driver could do against the three of them. But at each intersection George thought of how easy it would be for the driver to get to some deserted area where others, with more men and guns than the three of them, were waiting. George was not used to being vulnerable.

He had a great sense of relief when the driver pulled into the Kalama's driveway. The steward opened the front door of the house as the car pulled up. When the car came to a stop he opened the door for them to get out. George was back on familiar ground and nothing had gone wrong. He had succeeded. The first thing to do was call his father and say they were back. He stood by the car while the luggage was unloaded and let Max and Larry carry the black cases, while he followed behind.

The steward went ahead of them leading them to a room where he knocked on the door and then opened it for them without waiting for an answer. Larry and Max went in setting the cases down against the wall near the door. Kalama came from behind his desk, holding out his hand. "Welcome back, George. Your trip was apparently successful," he said smiling. He shook hands all around as George made introductions and then said, "If you Gentlemen will excuse us, I have some business to discuss with Mr. Costellos," He said opening the door. "The steward will show you to the dining room where there is food and drinks waiting." He closed the door behind them and then walked to behind the desk saying, "I'm glad everything went well."

"Thank you. Johnny and Frenchie did a good job at this end. Let them know I appreciate it and won't forget it. I wonder if I could use your phone. I'd like to call my father right away."

"Won't you please sit down? There are some things you should know before you make your phone calls," Kalama said sitting down behind his desk.

George sat down in the same ornately carved Oriental chair he had sat in the last time he was in this room. He was irritated. He didn't like being put off. Who did this Lester Kalama think he was refusing to let him use the phone? He sat glowering at Kalama. The other man folded his hands on top of his desk, stared at them for a moment, and then finally looked up. "I wish I were not the one to have to tell you this, George, but your father died of a heart attack, cardiac arrest, ten days after you left here.

"You're lying," George shouted jumping up.

Kalama looked down at his folded hands and slowly shook his head. "I sincerely wish I were," he said and then looked up and added, "There was no way for me to get to you at the time. I didn't even know where to start looking. Neither did anyone else. I didn't hear of it until someone told me about the funeral. I started making inquiries and what little I found out I have just told you. I'm genuinely sorry, George. I didn't know your father extremely well, but what personal contacts we had, and all our business contacts were most amicable."

George nodded.

"I'll leave you now to make your phone calls," Kalama said, taking the phone out of a drawer and setting it on top of the desk before leaving the room.

George Costellos sat with his elbows resting on the carved arms of the chair, his chin in the palms of his hands, tears seeping out from between the tightly closed eyelids. He could not believe the high, wing-backed chair at the cottage would never again frame his father's silver-haired, old head, or his arm would never again be placed confidentially around George's shoulders. Never again would they joke and laugh together. He felt empty and was invaded with a fear he had never known before. He also felt guilty for not having been there. There were so many things he would have wanted to hear and to say. There was no chance of that now.

He sat there for half an hour, his eyes tightly closed, his teeth clenched, his fingers digging into his cheeks. When he finally relaxed he felt very tired. He took several deep breaths and then forced himself to get up and move to the chair behind the desk. He reached for the phone, sliding it closer to him across the desk, and then sat staring at it. *Who am I going to call? Papa? No. Can't talk to Papa anymore. Who then? Margaret? Yes, Margaret.* He started to dial the number and then remembered it was long distance, pushed down the receiver button, holding on to the button while trying to remember the procedure. It finally came to him and he slowly dialed one, then the area code and the number. The phone rang six times before it was answered. "Costellos residence."

"This is Mr. Costellos. Let me speak to my wife."

"Oh!" He could not miss the surprise in the maid's voice. "Yes, Mr. Costellos. One moment please. I'll call her."

It was several minutes before he heard Margaret's voice, sleepy and irritated. "Hello, George." There were no questions about where he was, or how he was, just the abrupt greeting.

"I'm in Honolulu. I just learned about Papa—" He started to get choked up and couldn't say the rest.

"Yes, Papa died February second. He's buried at Forest Lawn," she said coldly, accusingly.

He sat there with the phone to his ear knowing she was expecting him to say something, but he couldn't think of anything to say. He couldn't let her hear his choked voice or confide in her. The long silence was finally broken by her angry voice. "Over two months since Papa died and not one word from you. Where the hell have you been that you couldn't make it back for your own father's funeral?"

She had no right to talk to him like that. "I was on a business trip," he said angrily.

"Then why is it not one person knew where you were? We sent

telegrams to every office in every country. Not one person had seen you, or was expecting you. Not a soul knew anything."

"Papa knew where I was," he said defensively and then wondered why he was making excuses to her.

"Unfortunately he couldn't tell us where to find you," she said sarcastically.

"I'll be home tomorrow," he growled.

"I'm sure the boys will be glad to see you," she said and hung up.

He sat there for a moment the dead phone against his ear unable to believe she had hung up on him. He hung up the receiver, got up from behind the desk and went to find Kalama.

The three of them got up from where they were sitting when he walked into the living room. Max came toward him. "I'm sorry, George, really sorry. Your old man was one of the best," he said putting a hand on George's shoulder.

"Thank you," George said. He hesitated and then said, "I have to get home right away."

"I'll have reservation made right now," Kalama said. "Are all three of you going?"

"All of us."

"You want commercial or private charter? I have friends at ExecuJet. We can probably get you out tonight. But considering the way the DEA is checking private flights coming into LA from the Islands, I wouldn't recommend you taking your cargo with you. But then you couldn't take it on commercial anyway."

"Thank you. Let's go with the private charter. Do you have a safe place we can store it until I can get it to the mainland?"

"Certainly. That's no problem at all. Excuse me a moment while I make a phone call. He returned a short time later. "I told him I'd have you at the plane by eleven. You should be in LA by five in the morning."

Thank you. The next thing I want to know is who's taken over since my father died."

Kalama thought for a moment and then said, "I don't know for sure. From all I can tell, your operation there is currently being run by Mark Heathly. I don't know who he is, but that is the word I have from my sources."

"I see," George said. He was pleased Kalama had said, "your

operation." It meant Kalama still considered him the boss. But if Mark was really in control then it wasn't his operation any more. He would have to go to war to get Mark out. He could do it, but there would be a lot of people who would go down with Mark, a lot of blood spilled, and worst of all was operations would be disrupted for a long time to come, but it would have to be done. "Has Mark Heathly been in contact with you," George asked.

"Oh, no. He probably doesn't even know we have a working agreement. As you know, my arrangements were always, and only, directly with your father."

George nodded and sat down, staring at the floor. He wondered just how strongly Mark had consolidated the Organization behind him since Appy's death. Mark was one of the reasons George had made this trip, not to convince Mark, but to sway those who were on the fence about Mark. There were undoubtedly many who would have been loyal to the Costellos name, and these might all return once he was back on the scene, but with Appy dead, and he nowhere to be found, they would have had no choice but to follow Mark. Well, Mark might temporarily have control of the Organization, but he didn't have the international contacts. Just as important, Mark didn't have the safe-deposit box full of dossiers Appy had so meticulously compiled over the years. Only he and his father knew they existed and to whom the codes referred. Any one of the folders would have thrilled a district attorney. Not one folder had ever been turned over to anybody, though from time to time a folder might be removed and destroyed when someone died, and sometimes details of the dead entered in someone else's folder. The dossiers had been one of many insurance policies, a lever Appy had never needed to use, but which had been available if it were ever needed. George did not even consider sending out Mark Heathly's dossier. Mark was too close to the top and if intensely investigated, could expose George. But he did consider exposing lesser people; people who could only implicate others to one or two levels below Mark himself. The dossiers would eat away at the roots of Mark's empire. George realized he might even have to eliminate some of his own people in order to protect himself, but he would do whatever was needed to get his Organization back.

Kalama excused himself and George said, "Things don't look too good, do they, Max?"

"There's no way of knowing until we get back to LA," Max said. "Things probably look a lot worse to you because there's no way of knowing what is really going on, and the news about your father makes everything look worse."

George nodded and asked, "If Mark has taken over, Max, who are you with, him or me?" He intended it as a surprise question. Under the circumstances he expected Max to say he would support him, but maybe from the way Max answered he would be able to tell whether or not Max was lying.

"You," Max said simply, looking him right in the eye.

George nodded. He couldn't be sure, but he thought Max was probably telling the truth. "And you, Larry?"

"I never did like Mark Heathly."

"What I have to know is how strong he is. Who will, and who will not support me. Who, if anybody, was against Mark's taking over? That's what you two are going to have to find out for me."

"We may have to get inside to do that."

"I know," George said and Max thought, *You're finished, George. You haven't got anything going for you but a couple hundred pounds or so of China White and some things about the organization no one else knows. By this time Mark has found out all he needs to know. Maybe not everything, but enough to be effective.*

If George was finished, Max, on the other hand, felt he did have something to bargain with. If Mark didn't already know about Kalama and Pakash, and the chances were good he didn't, then Max certainly had something Mark would like to know. And Mark certainly didn't know about the four black cases sitting in the other room filled with China White. Yes, he could work with Mark. And Max had the advantage that for the time being George needed him; needed him to do things he couldn't do himself.

Kalama came back into the room. "You have two hours before we leave for the airport. Would you like to take a nap, or freshen up? We have plenty of guest rooms."

"No, thank you." George said. "I'll sleep on the plane and I took a shower on the boat."

"Well, if there's anything you want, please let me know."

George nodded absent-mindedly and Kalama left the room.

* * *

Lester Kalama sat in the back seat of the limousine on the return trip from the airport. He had put George, Max and Larry on the plane and hung around long enough to see it take off. Riding back along the almost deserted Nimitz Highway he thought about Costellos' chances. From all he had been able to learn, Mark Heathly was pretty well in control. He had seen no point in relaying that information to Costellos. No sense making things worse for the poor boy than they were. The news of Appy's death was enough for one evening. All the indications were that George Costellos was through and would probably never be in any position to claim the property he had left behind in Honolulu. Lester was eager to get home and take a look inside those black cases. They were his now. Mark Heathly had no claim to it. Yes, Lester Kalama's final business arrangement with the Costellos Organization had been most profitable.

CHAPTER TWENTY-FOUR

A handful of water splashed over the collar of his life jacket hitting him in the face and waking him from his semi-sleep. It happened often during the night, sometimes startling him, sometimes frightening him and sometimes playfully. He opened his eyes. In all directions the water sloped up to the crest of the waves around him, a deeper darkness against the star-studded darkness of the sky. Not far from him the form of Myra rested on the water. She was so still that for a moment he had the sudden fear she was dead. He pulled the seine twine that held them together until she was close enough for him to touch her cheek. His hand hesitated over her face for fear touching her would wake her and with the waking would be the pain of the arm. He put the back of his fingers delicately against the cheek and the warmth of it reassured him she was still alive.

He wondered where they were and how far they had gone. He had spent most of the afternoon on his back swinging his arms and kicking his legs. He couldn't really think of it as swimming. Now, as then, he wondered if he was really making the half-mile an hour he hoped for. He saw a spot of light, brighter than many of the stars, moving across the sky and he wondered who was in that plane and wished he had a flare he could send up. *Would they see it? Would they report what they had seen so that by morning the Coast Guard helicopter would be out looking for them?* But he didn't have a flare. Even if he had a flare he couldn't use it because there would be a story in the paper about their rescue and George would know exactly where to find them.

He wondered if he had brought the two of them to their death. If so than a flare would at least buy them time until George had them killed. The thoughts of drowning and the foolishness of his action were more acute this night than they had been the night before. He had been a lot more confident they would make it then than he was now.

He rolled over on his back and started swimming, his arms moving in a windmill fashion, his legs kicking behind him. He felt one of his feet kick her and heard her say, "Chris?"

He stopped his swimming. “I’m sorry. I didn’t mean to wake you.”

“I wasn’t really sleeping. Not really. My arm won’t let me sleep. It hurts more than it did before.”

He pulled on the cord bringing them close together. “Is it throbbing—at your elbow, or at your shoulder?”

“Only a little right where I was hit.” He reached over to lift her arm a little so he could reposition the shoe under it. “Owah! That hurt.”

“I’m sorry. Move your arm bending it at the elbow.”

“I can’t. It hurts too much.”

“You can’t let it get stiff.” He took hold of her elbow with one hand and took hold of her hand with the other. He slowly started to bend her arm at the elbow.

“Oh, Please, Chris, that hurts too much,” she said and though she was trying to control her voice he knew she was crying from the pain.

“We’ve got to keep it limber. Got to keep the circulation in it. I can’t look at it now, but we can’t let it get stiff. I’ll keep working it. When the pain gets too bad squeeze may hand.”

“I can’t squeeze your hand. It hurts too much,” she sobbed.

“O.K. Then scream if I go too far.” He moved her arm with slow, gentle strokes that went just a little bit further each time. He did it for a count of sixty. She cried out a couple times and then he said. “O.K. now you try it. Move it yourself. Just a little bit, that’s all you have to do.”

She was able to move it a little. He adjusted the shoes on her life jacket and placed the arm back on top of them.

“You hungry?”

“I’ve been hungry since we left the boat.”

“Yeah. I know what you mean.” He reached into one of the pouch pockets and pulled out a packet. “Don’t know what we have here,” he said using his teeth to help open the strong plastic bag. “Ah, dried apples.”

They finished the seven-ounce bag of dried apples and followed it with a granola bar and five swallows of water. “Well, since I’m awake and fed I guess I’ll try swimming for a little while. Don’t forget to move that arm from time to time.”

He lay back in the water, found a star to keep focused on and started stroking and kicking. He knew Myra was kicking too because the drag on the line connecting them was less. He could tell when she stopped kicking from time to time to rest. He kept it up for what he guessed was an hour and then stopped to rest. She turned to face him as they rose to the crest of the wave and then she pointed over his head and shouted. "A light, Chris. A light." By the time he had turned they were in the trough of the waves again. "It was there Chris. Really it was." she said excitedly.

"I believe you."

They rose on the next wave and he too saw the little speck of light, not a star, and not moving like the light on an airplane, but fixed in one place. Against the darkness of the star filled sky he was sure he could see the outline of mountains. "That's it, Myra. That's Oahu," he shouted even more excitedly than she was. Suddenly the mountain was gone as they slid down the side of a wave and banks of water surrounding them cut off their view. A wave raised them again and the light was still there. It wasn't his imagination. He didn't know where the light was located, maybe a tower on some old sugar plantation, or a missal tracking station, but it didn't matter, the island was there, and they had been going the right direction.

He swam for another half hour and then was too fatigued to go on. They had not gotten any real sleep and he knew that was beginning to get to him. "I'm going to try and get some sleep," he said, but he was not sure she had heard him. She had stopped her kicking a long time ago. It would be light in a few more hours and if he could get some sleep now he could make the most of the daylight hours.

The wind had died down some and whereas there had been whitecaps on the tops of waves since they had first gone into the water, the whitecaps were gone and when they rose to the top of a wave the water was as smooth as in the troughs. He reached over and took her left hand. "We'll be all right," he said.

He woke up as the black of night was changing to gray and the stars were retiring for the day. The waves rose and fell gently and smoothly. Through his salt encrusted eyelashes he did not really see the island. He splashed water on his face to wash away the accumulated salt and when he looked again the island was clearly defined and he could distinguish the different hues of green in its valleys and ridges. "Do you see the island?" he asked.

"Yes. I've been watching it. How far away do you think we are?"

"Ten miles or so. I'm going to start swimming. Are you real hungry?"

She shook her head and he knew she was every bit as hungry as he was, but he wanted to get started. "We'll eat something at eight o'clock," he said leaning back and starting to swim.

She kicked along with him, sometimes using her good arm. They swam looking into the rising sun, headed away from it, going toward their island.

It was almost nine o'clock when he stopped and turned to look at the island. It seemed no closer than it had been when he started swimming three hours ago. *We're not going to make it. Swimming doesn't do any good. The currents are taking us away from the island. Nonsense. Everything; logs, dead fish, bottles, every-thing eventually gets washed up on the beach.*

"You hungry?" he asked reaching and unzipping another of the pouch pockets. "Well, look what we have for breakfast. Corn nuts."

With his soft, wrinkled, water soaked hands he had trouble opening the tightly sealed package. Again he used his teeth to rip open the package. The package suddenly gave way, snapping away from his teeth, scattering a third of the bag into the water. They both scrambled for them, catching them before they floated away and throwing them into their mouth. They finished off the corn nuts. It was a large ten-ounce package and their jaws were tired from the chewing. They waited a few minutes before they each had a small bag of dried pears followed by all the water they wanted. They still had three bottles of water left.

At noon they stopped swimming, turned around and just floated there looking at the island. In one place they could see the stone geometric of what had once been a building. They couldn't see buildings along the shore yet, but just the fact they could see a man-made structure gave them the sense they were not alone in the world. They rested for a while, her with her one good arm around his neck, he with an arm around her waist below her life jacket. There was a certain security in holding on to each other, a security that made them reluctant to let each other go when Chris suggested they have something to eat.

They finished eating and lingered in the water just looking at the island. It was as though there was no hurry. They had done so well there was no doubt now they would make it. In both their minds was the question of what they would do after they had made it. "I'm sorry about your boat. Did you see the explosion when it blew up?"

"No. I guess maybe they discovered it," he said. "I'm sorry, I guess George and all of them are still alive. What are we going to do? Will George really hunt us down like you said he would?"

"He will if he thinks we are still alive. And my guess is Max is in deep trouble for letting us get away. So Max may be looking for us too."

"I remember once you said George would be waiting on the beach when we went ashore. Maybe we're safer staying right here."

She smiled a little. "Well we will probably be able to get away from George one way or another, but if we stay here we are never going to be able to get away from this water, and frankly, I'm getting a little tired of it."

"Well then I guess we better start swimming again."

Late in the afternoon they were able to make out buildings: a house, a roadside store, or a service station along the shore. They waited impatiently for the crest of the larger waves that could raise them above the other waves around them so for a moment they could catch a brief glimpse of the buildings. If he could make out buildings, then they couldn't be more than five miles away. Just five miles, that's all they had to go. He rolled over on his back and started swinging his arms more forcefully. Myra started stroking faster with her one good arm and kicking harder and he reminded her not to kick so her feet broke the surface, the sound might attract sharks.

For the first time since he went into the water he began to worry about sharks. He had thought of them before, but had not been really concerned. Now he could not get them out of his mind. Sharks were everywhere, but they were most prevalent along the shore line, just outside the reef where they could prey on the reef fish, having easy picking of injured fish that had gotten away from fishermen and eating refuse carried along the shores by the currents. What if they were below, watching them from below? *Don't move. Don't make any noise. Your arms are splashing. Movement attracts them. Noise attracts them. But if we don't move we can't get away from them. Sharks can hear a rain drop falling on the foam of a whitecap. Who told me that? Harry Kam probably.*

He couldn't help but think of what he knew of sharks, prehistoric monsters whose only purpose was to kill and eat. One of the earliest forms of life, they had survived since the beginning of time because they could see and hear for miles and smell a single drop of blood in a hundred gallons of water. *They're all around. They see us, hear us, smell us. Why didn't they attack? Were they well fed and lazy?*

He knew thinking about sharks was bringing him to the edge of panic and yet he couldn't seem to stop. He tried to think of other things, but his thoughts always came back to sharks. He thought of stopping and talking to Myra, but that would just leave them, sitting in the water for the sharks to come to. He kept looking all around them expecting any minute to see a fin slicing through the water. He remembered Harry Kam telling him the only way to handle a shark was to punch it real hard on the nose. Shooting it with a spear gun would only wound it and anger it and the blood from it might attract other sharks. Harry had always carried a billy club with him whenever Chris had gone spear fishing with him. Although Harry swore the only way to get rid of a shark was to hit it in the nose with a billy club, or to punch it, Chris had never seen it done. Night was coming on and when it was dark he wouldn't be able to see a shark, not clearly enough to punch it. "Don't you come near me," he growled. He had not spoken loud enough for Myra to hear him and he kept talking to himself. He felt better when he heard his own voice. He wondered if Myra had talked to herself since they entered the water. "You get close to me and you'll be sorry. I'll tear you apart. I'll rip the teeth out of your mouth and make them into a necklace."

He thought of the shell necklace hanging over the ship's clock, then of the clock itself and then of the boat. He wondered where they had sunk it. He'd seen the *ROMSEY* go down and he knew his boat was at the bottom and he was no longer scared of the sharks but angry with George and Max and Larry. They were the ones who had forced him into this situation. They were the ones who had tried to kill Myra. One way or another he would get even with them.

When night came they were able to see lights. From time to time they would stop swimming and turn and look at the lights. There were the steady glowing lights from a few houses higher up on the slopes, and when they were on the top of a swell they could see the lights from the houses along the shore and headlights of cars moving along Kamehameha Highway. In some places they could see the pin pricks of light from the lanterns of fishermen walking along the reef. One by one the lights began to disappear as the night progressed. Cars along the highway became less frequent, the fishermen went home, the lights in the houses went out and all that was left was spots of light from the streetlights along Kamehameha Highway.

From the stars he guessed it was midnight when he sensed a change in the motion of the water and thought he heard the sound of waves breaking. He stopped swimming and pulled Myra over to him. "What's wrong?" she asked knowing he was not stopping to eat.

"Listen. What do you hear?"

"Waves. Waves breaking on the shore," she said excitedly. "We made it. We made it."

He untied the shoes from around her neck and then had her lay back and raise her legs while he put her shoes on her feet. He untied his own shoes from around his neck and lifting each leg up, his knee to his chest, put his shoes on. "Let me go ahead," he said.

He floated in his life jacket, keeping his legs beneath him, using just his arms to move him forward. A wave came behind them, moving them forward and dropping them down and he felt the sharp pain as the coral cut through his trouser leg and he started to fall. He swung his arms to right himself, felt the reef under his feet, and stood in waist-high water. He reached for her, grabbing her life jacket, pulling her up beside him. Another wave came, knocking them over and carrying them forward. They stood up, this time inside the breaking point.

They walked across the reef, hanging on to each other when they lost their footing and stumbled. They fell into deep water. They were inside the reef. He started swimming, hampered by his life jacket and bottles of water tied to his waist, the bottles of water seeming to tangle in his stroking arms. He stopped, untied the bottles of water and threw them away. Myra, still tied to him with the six-foot length of seine twine was laughing, giggling.

In a frenzy he yanked at the straps of the life jacket and threw it from him. He started swimming again, furiously, free style, with only his shoes and baggy trousers as encumbrances. He found himself suddenly out of breath and had to stop, gasping for air. "Take it easy," Myra said, "or you'll make me feel guilty for slowing you down."

He nodded a little shocked at his sudden desperation. He started swimming again, slowly, steadily, as though he were swimming along Waikiki Beach, Myra floating behind him, doing all she could by kicking strongly and swinging her one good arm. "Maybe I should take off my life jacket," she called but he didn't hear her.

The shore was there, he could see it now, just a few yards ahead of him. His left hand touched bottom. He stopped swimming, let his feet sink to the bottom and stood up. Myra was standing beside him. He took her hand and they tried to run for the shore, but the water wanted to hold on to them, tripping them. They kept stumbling and getting up again.

He fell down on the beach where the reef-broken waves lapped at the shore and lay face down on the damp sand. He sensed more than felt Myra sit down next to him. She was taking off the life jacket and then she was untying the seine twine that had held them together. A wavelet washed ashore up to his waist and beside him he heard Myra laughing again. A deep chuckle escaped him, and then a second and a third. He broke out laughing, rolling back and forth, half in and half out of the water, Myra laughing with him. On his back he threw his arms wide and then hugged himself. He sat up and reached over and hugged her, being careful of her sore arm, and then fell back in the sand, his arms around her, her left arm under him and her right arm resting on his chest. "We made it. You brought us through. You saved my life."

"We did it together."

"No. Not just here, but getting me away from George. You saved my life."

They lay there for a while in each other's arms and then crawled up to the dry warm sand. He dropped over on his back and fell asleep and she sat there for a while just looking at him and then she too lay down next to him and fell asleep.

CHAPTER TWENTY-FIVE

The death of Apistolos Costellos caught everyone except him unprepared. The first reaction of almost everyone was disbelief. It was incomprehensible that Appy would ever die, and the person who considered him the most invincible, and was the least prepared for his death, was Susanne.

For three days before he died she had him exclusively to herself. It was three days away from business. It was three days when Appy didn't make any important decisions. He had said it was time he had a vacation, and business could just wait for a while.

The first day they drove in her car along the coast to San Simeon and the Hearst Castle. It was something both of them had always wanted to do, intended to do, but had never gotten around to doing. They lingered over dinner because there was no place they had to hurry off to, or telephone calls that had to be made. It was pleasant to order another drink before dinner enjoying the warmth of the fireplace on one side and the view of the ocean on the other.

They spent the day taking tours the whole day, walking endlessly and climbing innumerable steps. He was impressed with the art treasure, and the money spent, but considered the castle ostentatious and lacking in unity despite the fact that an architect had been employed for her entire life incorporating the accumulation of statuary, pillars, walls and entire rooms into the construction of the castle. There was no envy in his silent criticism. He had no desire to erect a shrine to himself. He had a son and two grandsons, all of whom were more than well provided for. He was content.

That evening Appy complained of being tired. It did not surprise Susanne. She was tired too. It had been a full day. But tired or not, she thought he should have something to eat. She offered to go out and get something, or call room service, but he said he wasn't hungry. When he poured himself some of the brandy they had brought with them and lit his cigar, she knew he wasn't going to eat anything. He finished his brandy and cigar and was in bed and asleep by seven-thirty. Through the night she heard him turning fitfully in his bed and she worried about his not having eaten anything.

It rained on and off all the next day, and Appy dozed much of the time while Susanne drove back down the coast. She was worried about Appy. She had never seen him acting so tired and so she assumed he was sick. Maybe he was coming down with a cold, or the flu, but whenever she asked him if he hurt at all he said, “I’m fine, Girlie. Never felt better. Just tired.” Still she was anxious to get him home. Ten miles from the Cottage he was his normal self again and began talking about where they should go to dinner. And there was a play he wanted to see.

“Maybe we should stay home and relax tonight. I’ll fix something for dinner.”

“No. No. We’re going out tonight, Girlie.” That settled the matter.

It was almost midnight when they left the theater. “Now that’s what a show should be,” Appy said walking to the car, “something to laugh at and tunes a guy can remember.” He started quietly humming some of the music. As soon as they were on the freeway he sang at the top of his voice, pounding out the tempo on the armrest of the car door. Occasionally he would stop in the middle of a tune and laugh and say, “Remember the part where...” and would go back to singing.

When they got back to the Cottage, she helped him off with his suit coat, took the things out of its pockets putting them on the dresser, and hung the coat in his closet while he went and sat down in the bedroom armchair. She brought him his brandy and cigar and then knelt down in front of him taking off his shoes while he lit his cigar. She left him there wiggling his toes, sipping his brandy and smoking his cigar while she went into her bedroom to undress.

She was sitting in front of the vanity brushing her hair when she heard him call her. His voice sounded strained. Even stranger was that he called her by name, something he seldom did. She ran the few steps from her vanity to his room and saw him sitting straight in the chair, his arms lying flat along the arms of the chair, his hands clutching the ends of the arms. He looked as though he were straining at something. A thin wisp of smoke was rising from the cigar in the ashtray. The brandy snifter was lying on its side on the thick carpet with a dark track spreading out from the brandy snifter’s lips. All these details reached her in a flash as she rushed to the dresser to get his pills. She put the pill in his mouth, standing over him until she was sure he had swallowed it and then rushed to pick up the phone.

“Dr. Gisler,” he said in a strained whisper.”

“Yes, I know. Don’t talk,” she said as she dialed the private number that was given to only a few special and affluent patients.

In answer to Dr. Gisler’s questions she explained what they had done that evening and how Appy looked at the moment. She gave him the address slowly, repeating it to make sure he had it correctly. “Very well, get him lying down and I’ll call the hospital and have an ambulance there right away,” he said and hung up. She had the feeling, despite his words; he considered Appy’s attack bothersome and unimportant.

Holding his left arm around her neck, and placing her right arm around his back, she managed to lift him from the chair and move him the short distance to the bed. Still supporting him she sat down on the edge of the bed and lowered his body to a lying position. “The safe-deposit box—” his voice was a strained whisper.

“Yes?” She knew the one he was talking about. She was always being sent to put an envelope in it, or take one out.

“If I die—”

“You’re going to be all right. Don’t talk. Save your strength.”

“Take everything out. Keep the money. Burn the papers. Burn all the papers.” Even in a whisper his last sentence was an emphatic command.

“All right. Now be quiet. You’re not going to die.”

“Promise!” he gasped.

“I promise,” she said. For the first time she had the fearful realization he might die. She went to the front door, turned on the outside light, and looked down the empty street for the ambulance. She left the door open behind her so they would not have to wait when they arrived.

She went back into his room. “Sonny?” he whispered, then opened his eyes and asked, “Where’s Sonny?”

“He’s coming. He’ll be here in a few minutes,” she lied desperately.

She thought she heard the ambulance and she went to the front door to check but it was just a passing car. She stood in the doorway for a few moments waiting impatiently, wondering if they would arrive sounding their sirens. *Where were they? Maybe they couldn’t find the place. Should have called 911. They would have had someone here by now.*

She went back to the bedroom. He must have heard her, or sensed someone was there, because she heard him trying to talk. She stopped at the bed, taking one of his hands. In a forced whisper he gasped, “Burn the records— Sonny. Get out of it—”

She didn’t answer him, but walked around the bed to the phone. She picked up the receiver and as she did she knew it would do no good to call 911, there was nothing anyone could do. She sat down on the bed, still holding the receiver in her left hand, and reached over with her right hand to feel his pulse. She leaned over and put her ear to his chest. There was no breathing and no heartbeat. She sat up, tears streaming from her eyes and stared at the receiver in her left hand. What was it doing there? She put the receiver back and sat on the edge of the bed crying. She heard the ambulance arrive, but did not go to the door to show the attendants in. There was nothing they could do now. She heard them come into the room and when she turned to look at them they were just three, tear-distorted figures in blue.

Two of them left the rolling stretcher they were pulling and rushed to the bedside, undoing his shirt. They knelt on the bed beside him, working furiously with blue boxes and red boxes while another came around and putting an arm around her led her from the room. He set her in the corner of the couch crying and left her there. She heard their voices saying strange things she couldn’t comprehend and finally one of them came out and said, “Are you related to him?”

She nodded. There was no reason to tell him the truth. He was just a stranger who had come out of the night too late.

“I’m sorry,” he said. “You shouldn’t stay here all by yourself. Is there someone I can call for you?”

She shook her head. “I called my husband. He should be here soon.” *Get out of here. Just get out of here.* She heard the other two wheeling out the stretcher behind her and then he turned and left, following them, closing the front door behind him.

She sat there for almost an hour, glad they were gone, glad she was alone and didn’t have to control her tears. She sat bowed over with her arms crossed on the arm of the couch, her forehead resting on her arms. She had loved Appy and knew he loved her. He was the kindest man she had ever known. Now he was gone.

She finally forced herself to stop crying. Appy would not be pleased with either her crying, or his being the cause of it. She stood up feeling completely tired, her body and head aching. She went into the bathroom and splashed cold water on her face. It relieved the burning of the eyes behind the eyelids a little bit, but did nothing for her headache. She took three aspirin and a tranquilizer, set the clock radio alarm for five o'clock and flopped back on the bed and cried herself to sleep.

She woke up just before the alarm went off, with eyes that didn't want to open and body that did not want to get out of the bed. For a moment she had the overpowering urge to start crying again, but she controlled herself. There were things she had to do, things Appy wanted her to do.

She showered and dressed quickly and started carrying her things to her car. They had accumulated slowly, one at a time over the past years. She packed her cosmetics and contents of her dresser into the suitcases she and Appy had used to go to San Simeon. Her dresses and suits were carried to the car draped over her arm, taken off the rack with the hangers still in them. When she had cleaned out her closet, dresser, vanity and night stand, she checked the other closets and rooms in the house, coats from the foyer closet, jackets from hooks by the back door. She was doing it to protect Appy, but also to be out of the place before someone came along and made her leave. The last thing she did before she left was to go to Appy's desk and get the key to the safe-deposit box. She checked the back and front doors to make sure they were locked, backed out of the garage, and then pressed the remote closing the door behind her, making sure it closed all the way before she left.

When she got to her apartment building there was someone parked in the stall assigned to her and she had to drive around until she found a visitors stall. She carried the first of the two suitcases up with her on her first trip and looked around when she entered. She had been there so seldom recently that she had to look around and adjust her thinking. Her first thoughts were where she was going to put all the stuff that was piled in her car. She would also have to find out to whom she paid the rent. For the past several years the rent had been paid by one of the Costellos companies and she didn't think that would continue. By the time she had the car unloaded, had made up the bed and generally straightened the place out she felt she needed another shower before heading for the bank.

At two minutes of ten Susanne sat in the parking lot outside the bank waiting for it to open. She wanted to get there before the bank, or anyone else was notified Appy was dead and all his safe-deposit boxes sealed until the IRS and others could inspect them. On the floor on the passenger's side there was a suitcase size attaché case. Although she had to wait only a few minutes it seemed ages before she finally saw somebody unlocking the glass, front doors.

The cashier smiled and greeted her by name as she pushed the button to let Susanne through the counter-high door. She signed the book and was taken to where her key was inserted into the box at the same time as the banks key. The clerk carried the box for her to a cubicle with a chair and a desk in it. He set the large box down on the desk and then left closing the door behind him. There were a lot of file-size envelopes and folders and she had to arrange them carefully to get them all into the case. She called for the attendant to return the safe-deposit box to its place, locked the attaché case and walked out. The case was heavier than she expected it to be and it took all her effort to walk naturally and not give the impression she was carrying a heavy burden. She put the case on the floor on the passenger's side and headed for the Cottage. She had considered just going to her apartment and dropping the papers down the garbage chute, but she knew that was not what Appy meant when he said to destroy the papers.

She drove by the Cottage once to make sure no one else was there. She turned around at the end of the street activating her door opener even before she turned into the drive. She pulled into the space beside Appy's car and went into the house. In the living room she knelt in front of the fireplace, opened the case and took out the first manila folder. She opened it, laying it and some of the papers on the fireplace basket and lit them with her cigarette lighter. She watched cautiously as the flame caught making a black curl of the brown and white papers. The flame burned, creeping along the edges of the papers until it got to the bulk of the papers where it flared a little and then burned out. She felt frustrated and angered by the lazy flame as though it were somehow conspiring against her. She had a sense of urgency. She had to get these papers burned before someone walked in and found her burning them.

She took the papers out, lighting the envelope a second time, holding it by the corner until it was burning well and then dropped it back in the fireplace and started crumpling each sheet of paper into a ball and tossing them into the flame. She crumpled the sheets of paper lightly, dropping them in one at a time, waiting until they were burning well before she dropped the next one in. The flames grew higher and she was soon able to throw the balls of paper in as fast as she could crumple them. At times she was tempted to just throw in a whole envelope, but she restrained herself, emptying the contents of each envelope and feeding the sheet in one by one, sometimes flat, sometimes in a crumpled ball. In some of the envelopes there were packets of money. She was glad the first envelope had not burned easily forcing her to open all the envelopes. She set the money aside and burned only the envelope and any papers that were with it. Appy had said she could keep the money. She did not take time to count it, or speculate as to how much there was. She felt only relief the money was not something she would have to take time to burn.

She dropped the last crumpled sheet of paper on the fire and sat watching it burn while she dropped the money in the case and snapped it shut. She waited until the flames were gone and then she stirred through the ashes with a poker to make sure there were no unburned bits of paper. She hung the poker back in its place, picked up the case while at the same time standing up. She looked around the place one last time regretting she would never be coming back. She went to her car and backed out.

CHAPTER TWENTY-SIX

Margaret Costellos did not hear of her father-in-law's death until eleven-thirty in the morning when she was getting ready to go to a charity luncheon. She did not learn of it earlier because the doctor with the ambulance had told Dr. Gisler a young woman, a relative, had been with Appy when they arrived at the house. Dr. Gisler assumed the woman was Margaret, or one of Appy's daughters and she would notify the rest of the family. He called Margaret because she was George's wife and George was head of the family now.

When the maid announced Dr. Gisler was on the phone, Margaret had a tightening feeling of fear. Something must be wrong with Appy. There could be no other reason for Dr. Gisler to call. She took the phone hesitantly and in a trembling voice said, "Hello?"

"Sorry to intrude at time like this, Margaret, but I did want to personally express my condolences and tell you how really sorry I am about Appy's death. He was not just my patient, but he was also a friend. I shall miss him terribly."

She hesitated a long time before answering. *Appy dead? He was talking as though she already knew about it. When did he die? How did he die? Why hadn't she been told about it immediately?* These were all questions she wanted answered, but she didn't want to appear ignorant since Dr. Gisler seemed to assume she knew all about it. "Thank you," she said finally.

"Was it you, or one of George's sisters, who called me last night?"

It couldn't have been any of the girls or she would have been told about it. "Estella," she said thinking Estella was the one Dr. Gisler was least likely to know.

"I don't suppose George is back yet?"

"Hopefully tonight or tomorrow."

"Appy once told me he had made all the arrangements for his funeral with Hoffman and Hoffman, and in the event of his death I was to contact them. I'm sure George was aware of that. When I couldn't get hold of him at the office I went ahead and called them. I hope that meets with your approval?"

"Yes. Yes. Doctor. Thank you."

"If there is anything else I can do please don't hesitate to call."

"Thank you, Doctor, I will." She set the cellular phone on the table and sat for a while wondering who it was that had called Dr. Gisler. *It must have been Appy's current mistress, but who was she? And where had the two of them been when he had died, at the Malibu house, or somewhere else?* These were all unimportant questions, really, that she could get the answers to later. What was important now was to contact the rest of the family. She dialed George's office and got hold of Appy's oldest son-in-law. "Harry, this is Margaret. Papa Costellos died last night—"

"No!"

"Yes. Where is George?"

"Well, ah—I don't know exactly."

"Find him! Someone in his office, or in the company, has to know where he is. Last time he talked to me he said he was in London. Call every branch and foreign office until he is located. You tell Jack and Frank about it and then the three of you meet me here at one o'clock. The four of us will go to the funeral parlor to make the arrangements." She didn't want to be questioned, so she hung up before he could ask them.

She sat there for a moment wondering if there was anything else that should be taken care of. Hoffman and Hoffman. They should be called. It would just be a formality. Knowing Appy everything was certainly taken care of from selection of the casket to the flower arrangements. She listened patiently to Ronald Hoffman's condolences all the time wondering what percentage of Hoffman and Hoffman was owned by the Costellos' empire. When he was through she told him the four of them would be there at two.

She hung up the phone and leaned back in the chair. Now that things were put in order she had time to indulge in personal feelings. She genuinely regretted Appy was dead. She was fond of the old man, much fonder of him than she was of her husband. Her two sons adored Appy. She would have to be careful how she told them about Appy's death. She wished, without any shame, that it had been George instead of Appy.

When Harry, Jack and Frank arrived at the house, George had still not been located. "You know, of course," Harry said, "that by the time we learned of Appy's death it was night time in Europe and most of our offices in Europe were closed for the day. I've assigned some people to keep calling through the night, but we haven't had any luck so far."

"Somebody must have his itinerary. His secretary must have made phone calls and written letters making appointments and reservations," Margaret said exasperatedly.

"He told his office Appy's office was taking care of all the arrangements, but that office doesn't know where he is either."

By noon the next day every conceivable source of information around the world had been contacted with no results. Presidents of corporations expressed their condolences, but they had not seen him, nor were they expecting him.

Margaret Costellos did not really care her husband could not be found. She didn't care where he was, or what he was doing, except his not being there made things awkward. What would she say to people if George did not get back for the funeral? It was finally decided by the family that if anyone should ask their story would be that George had been under a terrible strain lately and with his father's death he'd had a breakdown and he was in a sanatorium in England. She liked the story. She felt that her serene handling of the death of her father-in-law gave her a certain heroic proportion while implying George had been unable to cope.

At the meetings with the company attorneys in the days following the funeral Margaret became more aware of how vast the Costellos holdings were. She didn't learn all there was to learn about the extent of the empire, but she did learn enough to know the ten million dollar trust fund Appy had set up for each of her sons was minimal compared to the entire fortune that now belonged to her husband. She learned other things, which in the total picture were not really important, but very interesting. She learned of a second house in Palm Springs, two apartments in New York, a hunting lodge in Canada, and the Cottage. She understood the two apartments, the house in Palm Springs and the hunting lodge belonged to the company, but George owned the house at the beach. It had originally been owned by Appy, but had been deeded over to George two years ago. Why another beach house, smaller to be sure, than the one she knew about, so close to the one the family already had? She couldn't help but be curious about the Cottage because it was family owned rather than company owned, and because none of Appy's daughters or their husbands; Harry, Frank and Jack knew about it either.

When she finally found time to satisfy her curiosity and inspect the Cottage, Margaret decided it must have been where Appy stayed when he wasn't at the Bel-Air house. The title may have been in George's name for legal purposes, but this had obviously been Appy's home away from home. There were a few of George's things around such as his sailing trophies, but everything else was Appy's. Once she was satisfied it was Appy's, she was no longer curious. She wouldn't tell George she knew about it, but if she ever needed him in a hurry for some reason this would be one place to look.

As the days grew into weeks Margaret Costellos settled back into a life that was much like it had been before Appy's death. That her husband was not at home was nothing new, but with each passing day she wondered how he could not yet have heard of his father's death. Certainly somewhere, someone he knew must have spoken of it. Thinking he might be on some secret business deal only he and his father knew about she arranged to have all the calls coming into Appy's side of the house transferred to her phone. George might try to call his father without ever trying to get in contact with her. But after a month had passed and there was still no word from him she began to wonder if he had been in an accident or been killed. The thought of his death did not bother her much. More than anything else she just wanted to be certain.

* * *

Within the Organization there were, generally, three opinions of what should be done when Appy died. Nearly half the organization was in favor of waiting until George returned. Had he been there he would have had no trouble taking control of the Organization. As it was, people began to get tired of waiting for a leader who couldn't be found. After three weeks they were all carrying out orders from Mark Heathly.

Another segment opposed to Mark Heathly was made up of those who wanted the control themselves. But they were interested only in themselves and would not support each other and so were never unified in their opposition to Heathly. Heathly, on the other hand, who was in charge of distribution, was supported by all of the regional distributors and district dealers right down to the street peddlers. Many of them didn't care who was on top as long as they were supplied with something to sell. For the first two or three weeks after taking over, Mark had an anxious time trying to learn where all the sources and suppliers were, but by the end of the month the supply was coming in steadily and the organization was doing almost as much business as when Appy was alive. By the end of six weeks Mark knew he was in complete control. Even if George did show up there wouldn't be anything he could do to get the organization back.

* * *

At a little after eight on Monday morning Juan Parelles knocked on General Heathly's door, went in without waiting for an answer and stopped six feet from the foot of the bed. He stood at parade rest, his feet sixteen inches apart, his hands clasped behind his back. Heathly finally put down the morning paper and put down his reading glasses. "Yes, Juan?"

"Briggs just called, Sir. He's still on the line. He spotted Costellos at L.A.X about seven this morning. Came in on a private charter. Maxwell and Anderson were with him. Before we could alert the others the three of them left in separate taxis. Maxwell and Anderson got away. The only one Briggs could tail was Costellos. He went to a house in Malibu. Reynolds is watching the house now."

"So Maxwell and Anderson were with him," Heathly said running a hand over his shaved head. "I figured they were. They all disappeared at the same time. What about Margolis, any sign of him?"

"Briggs didn't mention him, Sir."

"Well, those three don't matter anyway," he said waving his hand. "Call off the surveillance units and set up a duty roster with two men to watch Costellos 'round the clock. I want to know every time that guy moves, where he goes and who he sees," Heathly said reaching for his glasses.

"Yes, Sir," Juan said and left the room.

CHAPTER TWENTY-SEVEN

Consciousness came to Myra slowly, an awareness that both her arms were hurting her. She became aware of her head on his shoulder, her wounded arm resting on his stomach, her left arm pinned between her side and the sand, her right leg thrown across his thighs as he slept on his back. His right arm was around her. She had the amusing thought that they had finally slept together and Chris would be embarrassed if she were to point it out to him as innocent as it was. They really were alive and on dry land.

She rolled away from him, aware of the stiffness throughout her whole body and especially the sudden electric vibration of an arm that had "fallen asleep" coming to life with the blood that rushed into it. In some respects that arm was more painful than the wounded arm. Rolling over she punched his arm which woke him. In the early morning darkness she saw him raise his head a little and look over at her.

"Hi," she said.

"How does your arm feel," he asked.

"Really bad, but I'm so glad to be on dry land I don't care. Do you know where we are?"

He rolled over on his stomach and propped himself up on his elbows. He turned his head to look to the right and to the left and then said, "Well, since there are no houses right in front of us we are on the beach of some park. Lots of trees. I'm familiar with this place. My guess is we are on Pounders Beach."

She had sat up and was looking away from the water. They saw the glow from the lights of a car go by beyond the trees. "This is unbelievable," he said. "We're only a stone's throw from Laie." He rolled over and sat up. "We might as well get rid of all this junk," he said starting to unload the bags of food from his pockets.

"What are we going to do now?" she asked as she started taking her lifejacket off and pulling things out of her pockets as best she could with one hand.

"Are you hungry?"

"Famished."

"Then the first thing we are going to do is get some real food. There's a McDonald's just up the road here a little ways."

"Think it's open yet?"

"If it isn't it will be by the time we get there. Everybody from up this way headed to work in town swings through for their breakfast coffee and Egg McMuffin."

They left the beach, walking through the trees and at the parking lot dropped her life jacket and packets of food in a trashcan. They walked along Kamehameha Highway, he in a shirt and swimming trunks carrying the parachute pants rolled up in a bundle with their wallets and papers in the pockets. She was in cut-offs and wearing his windbreaker to cover the makeshift dressing on her arm.

He wondered as they walked along which of his friends he could trust. He had to be careful. The first place George would be looking for them would be the yacht harbor. The only friends Chris had were in the harbor. Charlie wouldn't do. He liked Charlie and would have trusted Charlie with his life, but Charlie liked to brag and talk story. He ran down the list of people he thought he might be able to count on. Randy Hessler. Randy, in his mid-fifties, had done a lot of sailing in his day, but his days were over. He managed to get by on his military disability. Chris had never really been close to Randy, had never wanted to be friends with him. Everything about Randy: the horribly messy condition of his boat, the fact that he hadn't hauled his boat out to paint the bottom in at least three years, the lumbering way he walked, the sloppy way he ate, all irritated Chris. And yet when he came over with his six-pack of beer, Chris never had the heart to tell him to "shove-off."

More than anything else Chris felt sorry for Randy. Randy had some good sailing stories, but Chris had heard them all more than once. It embarrassed him when others in the harbor sometimes referred to Randy as "your buddy Hessler." He knew that though he didn't like Randy, Randy considered him a good friend. Whenever Randy landed in jail he called on Chris to bail him out. He always paid back the money along with a bottle of Jack Daniels and promised not to do anything that would put him in jail again. But Chris could count on him landing in jail at least twice a year on charges ranging from "drunk and disorderly" to "interfering with a police officer in the performance of his duty." Randy was the kind of guy who would park his wreck of a VW van in a no-parking zone when there was parking space fifty feet away. He bragged he had never paid a parking ticket. He never shouted obscenities in the bars he frequented on Hotel Street until a policeman walked in and then it was always at the cop. There was nothing Randy would like better than to think he was aiding a fugitive. Chris thought of how ironic it was that the only person he could trust to keep his mouth shut was a guy he didn't care for very much.

It was just beginning to get light as they walked through the parking lots of the Polynesian Cultural Center toward McDonald's. Already the cars were lined up at the drive-thru window. He found a phone and called Randy. The phone rang more than twenty times before it was picked up and Chris knew Randy was hung-over. "Knock it off. Call back later—"

"No, Randy, don't hang up. This is Chris. I need your help."

"Chris?" the voice asked perplexed.

"Yeah. Chris Jamison. I need your help."

The voice immediately indicated an increased alertness. "Hey, Man. Where are you, Man? What's happening? Ain't seen you around for a couple of months or more."

"Listen, Randy. I can't tell you over the phone, but I need your help. I'll be in the McDonald's in Laie. Can you come get me?"

"Where's your boat, Man?"

"It's a long story. Where does that paramedic you know live, the one you are always buying special medicine from?"

"In Kaneohe."

"You think he'll be there today."

"Hey, Man, he'll call in sick if he thinks there's something in it for him. You need something?"

"A friend of mine has a wound. We'll need antibiotics mostly, and I'd like someone who knows more about these things than I do to look at it. I can't go to the hospital because they'll report it to the police."

"Hey, Man, I'll check and see if he's gone to work yet. Then I'll be on my way. Should be there in an hour or so," he said and hung up.

By the time the faded and rusty VW van arrived Chris and Myra had their fill of a variety of items from McDonald's breakfast menu. Chris spotted him as he turned off the highway and the two of them were out the door and waiting for him almost before he pulled into the parking lot. Chris introduced Myra to Randy and since Chris had described Randy to her while they were waiting she was not surprised to see a traveling junkyard. There were all kinds of things on the floor between the front and middle seat. Randy had to push plastic bags of things aside to make room for her to sit on the middle seat. Behind that seat it was piled up to the middle of the windows with all kinds of junk; old tires, on and off of the rims, ropes of all kinds, sails wadded in one corner and indented in such a way as to indicate someone had at some time fallen asleep on them. There were gasoline cans, plastic gallon jugs, and cans of oil rolling out of their case.

"The doc is on the night shift so things are cool with him," Randy said as soon as they were in the car. "So how did she get shot, Man?" he asked pulling out into the early morning commuter traffic.

"It's better you don't know, Randy," Chris said. "What you don't know you won't be able to tell anyone."

"What, Man, you running from the cops, or something?" he asked almost gleefully.

"Worse than that, Randy, we're running from the mob," Chris said knowing Randy would be impressed with the word "mob." Randy looked at him wide-eyed for a moment and then went back to looking at the road. "Drive slowly along here, Randy, I've got to find us a place to hide out." He knew Randy would like the idea of "hiding out." From the clutter on the dash Chris found a piece of paper and a ball-point pen and jotted down the telephone numbers from four signs advertising Vacation cottages for rent.

"I'd like to borrow your van for a while this afternoon, Randy."

"Sure, Man. Anything you want."

"After we finish with this paramedic friend of yours I want to drive you where you can catch a bus to town and take your wheels for the afternoon. I'll have it back to you before you're up tomorrow morning. Is that cool with you?"

"Sure, Man. Just leave the key under the floor mat on the passenger side."

Randy's friend was at home alone when they arrived. He wife was at work and the kids were at school. He took them into a brightly lighted room off the garage. He indicated for Myra to sit down and sat down on a stool facing her. Taking off the makeshift dressing he said, "Well, doesn't look too bad." He started to clean the wound a little. "You've been in the ocean with this. Salt water probably helped stop any infection. In a few months a plastic surgeon can remove any trace of a scar."

"Oh, I'm going to keep this scar as long as I live to always remind me of what happened," Myra said.

The paramedic shrugged and started putting on a dressing. "You can get more of these pads at Longs," he said as he put the last piece of adhesive in place. He handed her some extra pads and a tube of antibacterial ointment. "Change the dressing once a day." He gave her a bottle of pills with the instructions they were to be taken three times a day for the next week. "You shouldn't have any problems," he said standing. "That'll be two hundred bucks."

Chris unrolled the bundle that was his pants and from a zippered pocket took out the plastic bag with his wallet. He took out two, $100 bills, two of those George had given him. "Man you should open a practice," Chris said handing him the bills.

They dropped Randy just ahead of a bus headed for Ala Moana Center and then went to Longs in Kaneohe. While Chris was making phone calls making appointments to see the cabins for rent, Myra was buying make-up, shaving gear and other toiletries. From Long's they went across the street to the Windward Shopping Mall. They didn't look much different from anyone else who went to the mall after a day at the beach, sand on their legs and matted hair. They were just there earlier than most beach goers. They separated just so people would not remember seeing them together agreeing to meet back at the van in an hour. At Sears he bought a couple changes of shorts and shirts while she shopped for the same kind of things at Macy's.

They had not planned to get their hair cut at King's Den Haircutters, but they both went there because there were operators just waiting for someone to walk in. Chris was in the chair, his hair and beard cut and his face being lathered for a shave when she walked in. They didn't give any indication they knew each other, and the only reason Myra knew it was him was because she recognized his Topsider canvas shoes. Back at the van she said, "Man we have to get some make-up on you. The bottom half of your face looks like you're wearing a white mask."

"Tell me about it."

"Aside from that, I like you without a beard. You've got a nice face, Mr. Jamison."

"So do you."

They got some groceries at the Safeway across the street from Windward Mall and headed up the coast. At Hauula Beach Park they showered and changed into their new clothes in the bath house and then Chris sat on the step of the van while Myra proceeded to apply makeup that would, as much as possible, cover up the whiteness of his lower face.

A short distance up the road they rented a cabin less than a block from the beach. It was the first one they looked at. It had a bedroom with a clothes closet, a bathroom and what could only be thought of as an "everything" room. It was the area into which they entered with a space that might be considered to be the living room. Off to one side was an old oak table and four chairs, and beyond that clustered in one corner of the room and somewhat separate from everything else was the stove, refrigerator, kitchen sink and cupboards for dishes. The gas stove had to be lit with a match and the refrigerator was well rusted on the outside, which was not unusual for appliances constantly exposed to humidity and salt air. At the other end of the area from the kitchen was a queen size bed and a couch with a floor lamp next to each of them. There was no TV, phone, or radio. The floors were covered with linoleum throughout. If it was old, it was also spotlessly clean and the landlady accepted his two-week's rent in advance without asking for any identification. After she left they stood in the middle of the "everything" room. For the first time in months they felt safe, and for Myra, for the first time in years, she felt free.

CHAPTER TWENTY-EIGHT

George Costellos walked around the Cottage feeling strange in his own house and uncertain of himself for the first time in his life. He wished there were someone he could talk to. He could understand things better sometimes if he could talk them out, but he wasn't ready to face Margaret, nor did he really think he could talk to her, even about Appy, and he certainly couldn't share his feelings with Max. The person her really wanted right now was Myra. He had always been able to talk to her. He wondered if Max really had killed them. He should have told Kalama about them, but he had not been thinking straight right after he heard of his father's death. He was getting neglectful, a sure sign he needed some rest. He hadn't had any sleep to speak of ever since Jamison and Myra had gone over the side.

He wandered into his father's bedroom. Things were exactly the same as they had always been, clothes hanging in the closet, books on the night stand next to the bed, even cuff links, a bottle of pills and some change in the caddy on top of the dresser. It was hard to believe his father was actually dead; the room was so full of Appy. He wondered for a moment if his father was really dead. All he had was Kalama's and Margaret's word for it.

He walked through the bathroom to the adjoining bedroom. Except for the furniture the room was bare, with no bottles of perfume or creams on the vanity, no dresses in the closet, no shoes in the shoe rack. *What had happened to Susanne? When had she left? Yes, his father was really dead. If he were still alive there would be some women's clothes in this room.*

He sat on the edge of the bed and abandoned himself to sobbing. He sat there until he was too exhausted to cry any more. He reached into his pocket for his handkerchief and blew his nose loudly and then fell back on the bed and fell asleep. He woke up at four in the afternoon and except for a headache felt fine. He was ready to face Margaret and to confront Mark Heathly. He went into the bathroom and took a shower, soaping and rinsing automatically, his mind clear knowing the steps that had to be taken. When he had shaved, using his father's razor, he went to his father's closet and found a few of his own clothes. In a drawer of the desk he found a set of keys to his father's Cad. He went to the garage and got in the car and sat for a few minutes before starting it. Even there, there was the smell of his father's cologne.

It was almost six when he walked in the front door of the Bel-Air home. The maid informed him Mrs. Costellos had gone out for dinner at a friend's home. No, she didn't know where, but the children's nanny would probably know. Yes, the children were fine.

"I'll have dinner in the study. Tell the cook anything will be all right," he said climbing the stairs to his parent's side of the house. He walked down the hall to his mother's room. The nurse stood up as he opened the door. She stared at him and he nodded at her. He stood in the doorway for a moment looking toward his mother's bed. There she was just as she had been for the past 10 years with tubes keeping her alive. He left, closing the door behind him and thinking, *Why couldn't it have been her?*

He crossed over to his side of the house to say hello to the boys, but was uncomfortable with them because they acted so reserved with him. He didn't bother to ask the nanny where their mother was. He went into the study and sat down at the desk and dialed Max's number. All he got was a recorded message saying the number was temporarily not in service.

* * *

At eight-thirty Max walked into Tony's Bar and Supper Club. The hostess smiled and greeted him saying, "Where the hell have you been all this time?" He smiled without answering and made his way to the bar. The bartender came over and said, "Hi, Max. Long time no see."

"Hi, Lou. Has Danny been in yet tonight?"

"Not yet, but I'm sure he'll be in later."

"When he gets in, tell him I'd like to see him."

"Sure. Do you want something to drink while you're waiting?"

"Yeah. Give me a scotch and water," he said and watched as Lou reached behind him for a glass and got a bottle from under the bar. Max understood they were being cautious. Danny was probably in his office at that very minute. The hostess had probably notified

Danny the minute Max walked through the door and Danny was probably talking to Mark right then.

It was almost ten-thirty when Lou told Max Danny had arrived and would see him in his office. Max walked down the small hall, past the ladies' and the men's room and knocked on the door at the end of the hall. He was admitted into a small four-by-six-foot hallway with a door in each wall. The door was closed behind him and the man who had opened the door put his hands on Max's chest feeling for a gun. "I'm clean," Max said.

"Have to do it." The man finished frisking him and knocked on the door opposite the one they had entered.

Danny himself opened the second door. "Hello, Max," he greeted him without making any gesture toward shaking hands and walked around the simulated wood desk to sit down in an imitation leather, high back, swivel chair. He waved a hand at the chair across the desk from him. "We missed you around here, Max. Where have you been the last couple of months?"

"Business trip."

"With Junior?"

Max nodded pursing his lips.

"Well, there have been some changes around here while you and Junior were gone."

"I know. I want a meeting with Mark."

"You and Junior?"

"Just me."

"Are you speaking for Junior?"

Max shook his head. "Nope. I'm looking out for myself."

"What do you want to see Mark about?"

"I have some information I think might interest him."

"You can tell me, I'll pass it on to him."

Max smiled a little. It was not really a smile so much as the twisting of one corner of his mouth. "I'd rather tell him myself."

"I'm sure you would, if you can get to see him," Danny said.

Max didn't answer the challenge but sat looking into Danny's eyes. If he couldn't get a meeting with Mark through Danny he could do it through someone else. He knew Danny knew that, and if Mark thought what Max had to say was important; it would be to Danny's advantage to arrange the meeting.

"Who else was on this trip with you?"

That was a question Mark and Danny probably already had the answer to. “George, Larry Anderson and Steve Margolis.”

“You, Junior and Larry all came back together. Where’s Margolis?”

“George shot him.”

Danny could not control his surprise. “Junior shot him?”

Max nodded.

“Did it himself? Didn’t tell you or Larry to do it?”

“Did it himself.”

“Why?”

“Something about a double-cross. George didn’t tell me any of the details.”

“Have the cops found the body?”

“Not yet.”

“Do you know where it is?”

“Oh yeah. I know and Larry knows.”

“O.K. I’ll see what I can do. Drop back tomorrow night. I’ll know by then if Mark will see you.

“Thank you, Danny. See you tomorrow,” Max said standing up and letting himself out.

“Put a tail on him,” Danny ordered when Max left.

Max walked by the bar waving to Lou as he passed. He winked at the hostess as he went out the door and headed for his car. He saw two men headed toward another car at the back of the lot and knew he was going to be followed. It didn’t matter. He was just going home. There was nothing they could find out by following him tonight so he drove slowly making it easy for them to follow him.

* * *

The meeting between Mark and Max was set for noon on Wednesday at Mark’s penthouse apartment. Mark had bought the place for security, not prestige. There was a guard who checked everyone before admitting them to the elevator. Strangers and visitors had to be on the list and even then they were confirmed before they were admitted into the elevator area. Mark was just sitting down to a pastrami sandwich, a dill pickle and a glass of milk when the lobby called to announce Wilfred Maxwell had arrived. “Let him in,” Juan said into the intercom and sent someone to operate the private elevator.

Mark was halfway through his sandwich when Max was shown into the dining room. He motioned to a chair across the table from him with his left hand while raising the glass of milk to his mouth with his right hand. He took two swallows, put the glass down, wiped his mouth with a paper napkin and said, “You wanted to see me. What about?” He did not offer Max anything to eat or drink.

“I’d like to have my old job back. I think I could be of value to you.”

“You’re with Costellos.”

“We all were at one time, but when a company goes out of business, you go with someone else.”

“I was never with Junior. The old man gave me opportunities and for that he had my loyalty. You on the other hand are Junior’s friend.”

“George doesn’t have any friends. He’d sell anybody for a price.”

Mark put the last bit of sandwich in his mouth, chewed and swallowed it before asking, “What makes you think you could be of value to me? Why do I need you?”

“For one thing, I know where George has stashed more than a hundred kilos of China White.”

“O.K. You know where it is, go get it. With that you might even be able to go in business for yourself.”

“I also know where he got it. You could get a whole lot more. A steady source of supply.”

“I probably already know the source. But you can tell me about it if you want to and I’ll tell you if I think it’s worth anything to me.”

Max hesitated for just an instant. If he told everything he knew then he wouldn’t have anything to bargain with later. At the same time if Heathly knew anything about Kalama and Pakash and he didn’t mention them, then Mark would think he was holding back or didn’t know very much. Most of all he had to convince Mark he could be trusted. George was finished. There was no future there. The best thing to do now was tell Mark all he could and hope he would be impressed.

Mark Heathly listened quietly while he smoked his after-lunch cigar and sipped a cup of black coffee. Occasionally he doodled on the tablecloth with the handle of his spoon. “Stealing a couple of boats every time you want to bring in a shipment is very impractical," Mark said when Max was through.

"That's very true. I'm sure George considered this a onetime deal. He wanted to bring a large shipment without anyone knowing how he did it. He figured it would impress people. But a system can be set up for steady, regular shipments. Larry and I have both been there. I know the lay out and the contacts. I could set it up for you. We couldn't use World Trading Company since that is Costellos' operation, but there are other possibilities."

Mark Heathly was not reacting one way or another.

"In the meantime I can keep you informed as to what George is doing."

"I know everything the guy does the minute he does it."

"I'm sure you do, but George trusts me, at least as much as he trusts anyone, and it might be to your advantage to know what he is planning to do before he does it."

"In other words, you'd snitch on Junior."

"Yes."

"And what's to keep you from telling George what you've found out about me?"

"George trusts me. You don't. You're not going to tell me anything that might be of any value to George."

Heathly smiled a little for the first time since Max had arrived. "Very well, you keep me informed about what George is up to. In the meantime I'll think about the Hong Kong deal. If you find out anything important about what George is planning, you can call me direct. Juan will give you the number."

"I'll be in touch," Max said and got up to leave.

* * *

Mark watched him leave the room. He didn't know what to think of Max. Mark didn't really trust any of the people in the Organization who he'd had to convince to join him. Those who had not supported him right from the beginning were suspect. But for the time being he needed some of them. As soon as he could replace them with people he could depend on completely he would phase out those he wasn't sure of. He didn't know about Max. Max hadn't been around at the time of the take-over. Max would have to prove himself. In the meantime, Mark wasn't risking anything yet. If he had reason to suspect Max he would have him phased out before he was even in.

CHAPTER TWENTY-NINE

George Costellos sat in the living room of the Cottage waiting impatiently for Max. Near him was the high backed chair his father used to sit in. George had not sat in that chair once since his return. He almost felt as though his father would walk into the room and sit down next to him. He was not even aware he was avoiding the chair. He sat on the couch staring at the blackened inside of the fireplace, unaware of the setting sun that could be seen through the glass walls of the sliding doors. He was too worried to be aware of anything except Max, who was already fifteen minutes late.

He heard a car pull into the driveway and got up, walking quickly to open the front door. He opened the door before Max got out of his car and stood holding it open impatiently while Max walked toward him. "Well?" George asked as Max stepped inside.

"I saw Mark Heathly today," Max said walking toward the living room.

"You what?" George shouted.

"He wanted to see me. There wasn't time to check with you. I figured the best thing to do was meet with him and find out what he wanted. Incidentally, I found out by accident while I was there that you are being watched. Did you know that?" Max sat down at one end of the couch and reached up to turn on the light.

"No, but it doesn't surprise me. What did you and Mark talk about?" George said sitting down.

"He wanted to know where we'd been the last couple of months. I told him you took Larry and me on a business trip. I told him we went to Marseillaise, then to Istanbul, back to Marseillaise, then to Singapore, Hong Kong, Honolulu and back here."

"Didn't he ask who I met with and where I met them?"

"Of course, he did. I told him the meetings were always at our rooms at the hotel and you never introduced Larry or me to anybody. You always made us stay outside with the other guy's men while you talked privately. I told him I had no idea who you talked to, or what arrangements were made. I think he believed me. You always have had a reputation of keeping everything very secret. Before Heathly took over not one person knew over a dozen other people in our Organization."

"So he doesn't know anything about Kalama, or the shipment, or who we deal with in Hong Kong."

"I'm sure he doesn't. If he does, he didn't learn about it from me."

"I see." He sat for a moment staring at the floor and then asked, "What else did you find out?"

Max hesitated for a moment to give the impression he didn't want to say anything. "I hate to tell you this, George, but right now things do not look too good. From all I could learn Mark has things pretty well locked up. There are some who would come back to you again, but Mark is leaning on them pretty hard. It's going to take a long time to drive Mark out of the business, but we can do it—"

"Drive him out?" George shouted jumping up. He began to pace in front of the fireplace. "I'm not going to just drive him out, I'm going to kill him and take back what is mine. It's my organization, Max. Mine! He's using my outlets, my runners, my Organization. He isn't smart enough to have set up an organization himself he just uses someone else's. Well, he is going to start squirming pretty soon. The organization is going to start falling apart. The DEA is going to start getting tips. Shipments are going to be stopped and confiscated. Runners, dealers, processors are going to start being arrested. People are going to start remembering it was never like that before Mark Heathly took over. They'll start coming back to me and if I have to I'll turn over top people. I have files—" He stopped talking and pacing in mid-sentence and looked at Max. He had said too much. Had Max caught it?

"Do you mean to tell me you'd destroy what your father spent all those years building up?"

"I'll wipe it out completely before I let Mark Heathly have it."

"There are other ways, you know. We can always put a contract out on Heathly. No one has to know where it came from."

"That's not as easy as it sounds. He hardly ever goes out and when he does he has half a dozen bodyguards with him. But more importantly he doesn't suffer except maybe for a few seconds. I want him to be running scared while what he stole from me disintegrates from under him. The one thing he doesn't know is which cops, judges, DAs and feds we have in our pockets. They are still in my pocket because their monthlies came out of a secret fund that can't be traced to the organization."

"You know, George, it wouldn't be a bad idea if you had some bodyguards yourself, at least till this Heathly thing is settled," Max said certain it was not something George would go for.

George sat down and thought about the suggestion for a moment. He didn't like the idea. It implied he was afraid of Heathly. He wasn't in any danger yet and probably wouldn't be until Heathly started having troubles. "I'm all right for a while anyway."

"Well, I still think it would be a good idea if either Larry or I were with you all the time."

"Thank you, Max, but if you're with me how am I going to find out what I need to know."

Max shrugged. "I still think you should have someone with you."

"I'll be all right. What are your plans for tonight."

"Nothing special. Thought I'd hang around Tony's and just keep my eyes and ears open. I might find out something," Max said getting up.

"Fine, and if I'm being watched it might be better if we aren't together. Don't contact me unless it's important," George said walking him to the door. Max hesitated in the doorway for a moment, looking up and down the street before going to his car.

George went back inside and sat down on the couch. He didn't want to go home to Margaret and her dinner party, but neither did he want to stay at the Cottage. What he wanted to do was go and see Myra. He was suddenly angry with her for not being there. That's when things began to go wrong, when she and Chris had been killed trying to get away. He didn't mind Chris being killed. What he did mind was that he had not been in control of the situation. After that there had been the news his father had died and now the fact that Heathly really was in control of the organization.

He thought for just a fleeting instant he could walk away from it all and let Heathly have the Organization. He certainly didn't need it. He had more money from legitimate enterprises than he could ever use. He didn't need the Organization, but it belonged to him. It didn't matter what it was worth, or how big it was, it belonged to him and he wasn't about to let a low-life like Heathly beat him out of it. First thing in the morning he would go to the safe-deposit box and pull a couple files.

* * *

At three minutes after eleven on Thursday morning George sat with his hands folded on the tabletop in the small cubicle waiting for the safe-deposit box to be brought to him. He stood up when the box was brought in, waited for the clerk to leave and then reached over and pushed the button that would lock the door. He reached into his pocket for the key, turned it in the lid, opened it and stood looking dumbfounded and unbelievingly at the empty interior. *They must have brought him the wrong box, but then his key wouldn't have fit, would it?* He closed the lid to look at the number stamped on the top of it. D-121. He opened it again still not believing it was really empty, let the lid fall shut and sat down heavily in the chair. There were only two other people who had access to that box, his father and Susanne. Maybe his father had emptied the box, but wouldn't he have left a clue as to where its contents were? Susanne would know, but where was she? He had never known where she lived before she moved into the Cottage, but she had to have lived somewhere and she had to be somewhere now. He considered for a moment checking the register to see who had opened the box last, but that wouldn't really tell him anything. It could have been only one of two people and one of them was dead. He had to find Susanne. He locked the lid, took out his key and walked out. The clerk asked "Are you through, Mr. Costellos?" but he didn't bother to answer her.

He left the bank and headed for the beach. Somewhere at the Cottage there had to be some clue as to where Susanne was. He pulled into the garage, shutting the automatic door behind him and went into the study. He sat down at the desk looking at the top of it. There wasn't much there. A piece of plate glass covered the working area. On it was the telephone, a pen and pencil set in a marble base, and a large ceramic ashtray. He lifted the telephone to look under it, hoping there might be a forgotten scrap of paper that might give him a clue to finding Susanne. He did the same thing with the pen and pencil set. He picked up the receiver and was pleased to hear the dial tone which meant service had been restored. He dialed information, but they had no listing for a Susanne Whitefield.

He took out the telephone secretary, turning each card slowly. He recognized most of the code names, all people in the organization.

He thought for a moment that there would be no reason to have Susanne's number in there even under a code name since she lived at the Cottage, but still he kept looking. There were a few names he didn't recognize and he dialed each of them asking to speak to Susanne, and each time the answer was the same, "There is no Susanne here. You must have a wrong number."

He opened the center top drawer. Along the front of it was a narrow tray with some pencils, ballpoint pens, pennies, paper clips and a small pile of business cards. He looked at the cards carefully; front and back, looking for any notes or anything that might lead him to Susanne. He spent over three hours in the house, studying every scrap of paper in the desk, credenza, dressers, kitchen cabinets, flipping through books and magazines. In the kitchen he found a picture of Susanne and another of his father in a packet of pictures in a drawer filled with recipe cards and grocery lists. In a book in her room he found a Christmas card addressed to Ms. Susanne Whitefield. She had been using it as a bookmark. It was from Jackie Matthews with an address for Houston, Texas. The postmark was from two years before. He went to the phone and called information in Houston, but they did not have a listing for Jackie Matthews. He knew Susanne had not put in a change of address with the Post Office because there was a recent electric and water bill addressed to her at the Cottage.

He called Max's number and got the machine. He called his cellular number and said, "Max, I have something I want you to do for me. Can you meet me at the Golden Anchor Bar in an hour?"

"Sure. The Golden Anchor in an hour. I'll be there."

Max was sitting in a booth nursing a scotch and water when George walked in, looked around, and then slid in across from him with the waitress following right behind him. "Coke with the squeeze of two limes," George said and the waitress left. They sat without saying anything until the waitress brought his Coke and had gone again. "Do your remember Susanne?"

"Sure. Your father's secretary."

"I want her found. From all I can tell from my family she was with Papa when he died. I just want to talk to her and find out what it was like with Papa at the end."

Max nodded understandingly.

"She moved out and I can't find her anywhere. No forwarding

address with the post office and no telephone number, but it may be unlisted. I have this picture of her and this address from of a friend in Houston. Don't know if the friend's still there or not. Also no phone listing for her. Put some good PI on it. I want her found as soon as possible. And I don't want anyone to know I'm looking for her. I don't want there to be anyway for the PI to trace back that I'm the one looking for her."

"O.K., I'll take care of it."

"Thanks, Max," he said taking an envelope out of his jacket pocket and sliding it cross the table. "Get a good PI. He'll probably want some up-front money, so there's five grand in there."

Max took the envelope slipping it into his packet while George got up and left leaving his Coke and lime untouched at the table. Max sat there for a few minutes finishing his scotch and water and thinking about George. There was more to it than just wanting to know about his father's death. George had been too desperate and too secretive. There was something the broad had that George wanted. He pulled out his cell phone and called Mark Heathly.

"Fine," Mark said after Max told him what had happened. "Do like he says, only when they find her tell me where she is before you tell him."

CHAPTER THIRTY

At two o'clock on Monday afternoon, two weeks after George Costellos had arrived in Los Angeles, Chris Jamison and Myra Jennings passed through the glass doors of the airport to the hot, smoggy air of Los Angeles. They'd had a little trouble with the security check when boarding the flight because they did not match their driver's license picture. Myra's blond hair, which had never been very long, had been cut even shorter and dyed dark brown. Myra had been scrutinized carefully and when she explained she had cut and dyed her hair was given her boarding pass and permitted into the secured area. As soon as she boarded the plane she had gone to the rest room to complete her disguise. Having been an actress she knew how to use make-up. When she was finished she looked twenty years older and not very pretty. She topped it off with a shoulder-length dark brown wig. She wore loose fitting clothes with a baggy, long-sleeved sweatshirt that effectively hid her figure. The combination of make-up, clothes and wig created the impression of a forty-something matron. She was so successful that for just an instant Chris did not recognize her when she walked by to take her seat two rows ahead of him. The change in Chris with no beard or long hair also caused considerable questioning when he tried to pass through security.

Neither of them was particularly happy to be in Los Angeles. The past two weeks had been almost like an idyllic vacation with each of them discovering each other and their feelings for each other. The first three days they had hardly left the cabin except to go to the beach for a half hour in the early morning and late afternoon until Chris' face had gradually tanned to a uniform color and they could spend all day in the sun if they wanted to.

During those two weeks they had done everything together which was very different from having to get along on the boat. They learned what each other liked and didn't like. They walked the half-mile to get groceries. They played board games they had found on a shelf in the top of the closet and took turns cooking. They swam, lay on the beach and walked hand in hand along the beach in the brightness of the day and the starlit softness of the night.

During those two weeks her arm had healed and to an extent their fear and anger at George had also healed, but they had still had to talk and plan. They had thought of going to the authorities, but they were not comfortable with that. That would probably involve long hours of interrogation and maybe even having to be a witness. Nor were they sure of how much protection they could count on until the authorities had dealt with George. She had told him about the diary she had kept, not a personal diary, but the record of everything she had heard about from George. It was then they had decided they would have to go to LA and turn that information over to the authorities.

Now they were in the land of the enemy and although they were reasonably sure no one would recognize them, they still had a tendency to look nervously over their shoulders from time to time and scanned everyone that was headed their direction. Chris stood holding both their carry-on bags, which was all they had, while Myra tried to flag down a taxi. In the taxi she gave the driver the address of a local auto rental agency a few miles from the airport. If George had someone watching for them it would probably be at the well know, nation-wide agencies, but he didn't have the manpower to watch every local car rental agency in the city.

After checking into a motel they drove to Marina Del Rey where she had her apartment. Since she knew the area she did the driving. She drove slowly around her complex. "Mine's that one there. Up the stairs," she said pointing as they drove slowly by. "I have a car in that garage, but I guess I won't be able to use it. George is sure to be suspicious if it is moved." They headed back to Highway One and she asked, "Do you think you can find my place again?"

"Shouldn't be too hard," he said. They thought it was probably safe for Chris to go to get what they needed from her apartment. If there was someone watching the place they were pretty sure it wouldn't be George, Max or Larry. A henchman would be on the lookout for a woman, but no one in LA had ever seen Chris.

Sitting in the passenger's seat looking across at Myra as they were headed back to the motel Chris was a little surprised to realize he was unhappy with the thought their time together would soon be coming to an end. They had been through a lot together and had come to LA to finish up what had started when he had seen her walking toward the *AHWANAH* between George and Larry. It was George who had brought them together, George who had forced them to depend on each other, and even now they were together in LA because of him. Chris guessed when this was all over they would go their separate ways, and for the first time in his life he was displeased with the idea of being separated from someone. But he couldn't really think about it now. It would have to wait until after they had finished what they had come to Los Angeles to do; when their lives were back to normal, though for him a normal life was having a boat.

His normal life had not been what most other people considered normal. He did not go to a "regular" job, have mortgage payments, though he did have slip fees. He did not own a television set, seldom read a paper and couldn't remember when he had last been to a movie. If he ever had a date it had been to take the lady for an evening cruise on the *AHWANAH.* Normal people knew something about computers. To him computers were something stores used to keep track of what they bought or sold. He knew they were crucial for space travel, but he really had no idea how ordinary people used computers and laptops. Now they had come to LA because all the information she had that would free them completely from George was on disks in a safe-deposit box.

Back at the motel she sat down at the small desk and taking a piece of motel paper and their ballpoint pen said, "This is the way the apartment is laid out." She was not very good at drawing floor plans, but he got the idea of where the living room, kitchen, bedroom and closets were in general relationship to each other. Her main computer was in the bedroom next to the window. From there he was to bring the printer with all the cords that were attached to it. Her laptop was on the right hand side of the top shelf in the bedroom closet. It would be in a black carrying case.

"Now," she said, "sort of hidden way at the back on the right hand side of the bottom dresser drawer is a small teak box with keys and other little junk in it. The key to my safe-deposit box is in there. It's sort of silver looking and shaped—" she started to try and draw a key and put down the pen, "oh, just bring the whole box."

He parked just a little beyond the walkway that led between the redwood fences to the entrances. There was no one in the street and the only car was the same one that had been there when they had been there earlier. Walking between the walls he was satisfied that the only way someone could see him entering her apartment was if they were directly across from the stairwells. He thought it was possible someone might be watching him from an apartment across the way, but he didn't see anyone peeking from behind drapes. He got the printer, the laptop and the box she wanted and was on his way back to the motel in less than five minutes. He kept glancing at his rear view mirror, but it didn't appear anyone was following him.

CHAPTER THIRTY-ONE

George Costellos sat at the desk in the Cottage waiting for the phone to ring. He couldn't understand how it could take a professional detective so long to find someone who wasn't trying to hide. He had spent all morning and early afternoon at the office dutifully initialing reports he did not fully comprehend because all he could think of was that maybe Max was trying to call him at the Cottage. The phone finally rang. He reached for it quickly and then paused when his hand touched the receiver letting it ring a second time. He picked up the receiver, "Yes?"

"George? Is that you?"

"Of course it's me," George snapped.

"Your voice sounded funny. I didn't recognize it," Max said.

"Must be something wrong with the connection," George said forcing himself to sound calm. "Did you find her?"

"Yes."

George breathed a sigh of relief and wrote down the address and telephone number. He hung up and forced himself to wait a full minute before dialing the number. The phone rang four times before it was answered. He knew it was Susanne. "Is John there?" he asked disguising his voice.

"John? No, there's no John here. You must have a wrong number."

"Sorry." He hung up feeling relieved and excited. He had found her and with her, the files. There was no reason to wait. She was at her apartment now. He could be there in twenty minutes.

He drove away from the Cottage feeling confident. Things were beginning to go his way again. He would get the files from her and then maybe he would take her out for the evening. The idea pleased him. She was someone to take Myra's place. Susanne was ideal. Because she had been with his father for so long there would not be any reason for him to be cautious about what he said. She would be someone with whom he could talk, someone in whom he could confide. She could replace Myra in every way. As he approached the apartment building he was thinking of her more as a woman than as a source for the files.

She opened the door as soon as he knocked. "Oh! Mr. Costellos. What a surprise!"

"Hello, Susanne. May I come in?"

"Yes. Sure." she said stepping back and opening the door wider. "Care for a drink?" she asked as he entered. "I have some coke, but I don't have any limes." She closed the door behind him. "I have some bottled lemon juice. Do you want that or something else?"

"That'll be fine. How have you been?" he asked watching her heading for the small kitchen.

"Fine. I have a job with the telephone company now."

"Do you like it?"

"It's all right," she said when she came back into the room with his drink. She handed him the Coke and sat down at the opposite end of the couch. "It keeps me busy."

He picked up his glass and took a couple swallows of his drink while looking at her over the rim of his glass. She was sitting a little turned with an arm resting on the back of the couch looking particularly attractive. "I'm very sorry about your father," she said.

He nodded while setting the glass down on the table. He leaned forward a little, his elbows resting on his knees, his hands folded in front of him. "From all I could learn none of my family had seen my father for two or three days before he died. Were you with him those last days?"

"Yes," she said very quietly looking down at the floor.

"How was he? I mean, did he suffer much? Was he—?"

"No. No," she said shaking her head and looking up. He could see tears welling up behind the blinking eyelids. He liked that. Tears were emotion and emotion was always good where sex was concerned. "We went up to San Simeon for a day just before he died. He seemed to enjoy the trip."

The tears were flowing down her cheeks now. She took her arm down from the back of the couch and clasped her hands around her knees. He moved over next to her and put an arm around her. "That's all right," he said. "Go ahead and cry if you want to. He pulled her closer to him, gently pushing her head to rest on his shoulder. He turned his head and kissed her on the forehead and she raised her head from his shoulder. At the same time she pulled a little away from him. She was snubbing him. The idea angered him. Who did she think she was, anyway? How dare she refuse him anything?

He released his arm and she got up and walked across the room to get a Kleenex. She stood with her back to him as she wiped her eyes and nose. She turned back to look at him and he stood up and asked, "What did you do with the papers that were in the safe deposit box?"

She walked over to drop the wadded tissues in the wastebasket and said, "Your father told me to burn them."

"What!" He jumped up and slapped her violently, her head jerking to one side with the blow. "You what?"

She stood staring at him, stunned and frightened, her left hand rising to the pain swelling in her face. "Your father told me to," she whispered.

He hit her again, with his left hand this time, then the right. He kept hitting her, beating her, beating down in her all the things that had gone wrong in the past couple of weeks, striking out madly at Heathly and Chris and at death for taking his father. Through his anger he heard her screaming his name and begging him to stop. He had to quiet her. The neighbors might call the police. His hands closed around her throat until the screaming stopped. He felt her fingers clawing at his cheeks and face and still he kept squeezing until he finally realized she was no longer clawing at him and it was taking as much strength to hold her up as to squeeze. There was no resistance left in her.

He relaxed his grip and watched as she crumpled to the floor in front of him, blood flowing out of her mouth and nose. He stood staring down at her, not caring whether she was dead or alive. Then he saw her mouth open and heard her gasp for breath and he hated her for being alive. "You bitch," he growled and kicked her in the stomach. He felt calmer then.

He looked around the room carefully, in control of himself now. No, he hadn't touched the door when he came in. The only thing he could remember touching was the glass. He picked it up and took it to the kitchen sink, poured out the Coke, washed and rinsed the glass and then wiped it carefully with the dishtowel. He set it back in the cupboard, opening the cupboard door with his knuckles and holding the glass with the towel. He took the towel and wiped off the coffee table just in case he might have touched that. He hung the towel back on its rack in the kitchen and then came out and stood for a moment looking at her wondering if he should finish killing her. A murder always led to a deep investigation. There was no evidence left in her apartment that could show he had been there and she had known him long enough to know she would be killed if she were to accuse him.

He headed for the door, taking a handkerchief out of his pocket. He stood by the door for a moment listening for any noises. There was no sound of voices or footsteps. If the neighbors had heard her screaming, they were not getting involved. He opened the door, careful to keep the handkerchief between his hand and the doorknob. He looked down the hall. There was no one there. He pulled the door shut behind him, walked to his car and drove away. He became aware of the burning stings on his cheeks as he drove away and thought he should have kicked her again for scratching him.

* * *

The first thing Susanne was aware of as she slowly came to was the terrible throbbing pain in her neck, a pain that became increasingly worse as she became more conscious. She wished she could pass out again, but instead the pain forced her that much further toward consciousness and awareness, one pain continuing to get worse while another became evident. Her whole head and face hurt and ached. She tried to swallow, but that slight action hurt so badly she tried to stop in the middle of it, but couldn't. Just swallowing caused a sharp pain that reached all the way down to her upper chest. Closing her mouth to try and swallow sent pains alongside her ears and down the back of her neck.

Her nose was stuffed and her mouth was dry from breathing through it and filled with the taste of blood. She tried to open her eyes, but only one of them would open. She blinked the one good eye and was relieved that the action did not cause her pain. With the one good eye she looked around the room. She had to move her head and body slowly, but she was finally sure he was gone. She didn't know how long she had been out, but it was dim in her room.

She pulled her arms under her to try and get up and the pain was so bad she almost fainted again. She waited for the spell to pass. If she could get to the phone she could dial 911, but she didn't know if she could make it that far; and if she did, what would she tell the police when they came? She couldn't tell them George had done it. She would tell them someone she had never seen before had tried to rape her and when she started screaming he had strangled her.

She dragged herself across the floor slowly, a little bit at a time. Her stomach muscles felt stiff and painful. She didn't remember him hitting her in the stomach. She crawled slowly toward the table where the phone was. Every time she moved one arm in front of the other, shocks of pain shot through her neck and shoulders. She kept crawling unable to believe it could be so far to the little table at the end of the couch that held the phone. When she tried to look up to where the phone was she discovered she couldn't turn her head. All the pain was just too unbearable. She pulled on the cord pulling the phone down beside her. She managed to push 911 and when the operator came on she tried to say, "help me," but all that came out was a horse whisper. The sounds she made didn't sound like words, even to her. She passed out with the receiver close to her face, the sounds of her choked breathing responding to the operator's questions.

She was in the hospital when she regained consciousness. When the police came to see her, the questions were perfunctory. They couldn't understand her hoarse whisper and had to crane their necks to see what she wrote on the pad they had given her. The description of her attacker could have fit any number of people. She said it had happened about six. No, she had never seen her attacker before. She thought she had locked the door behind her when she came in but her arms were full of grocery bags and she may not have turned the bolt all the way. No, she did not hear him come in. She had just changed her clothes after coming home from work. When she came out of the bedroom he was standing in the middle of the living room. No, nobody else had a key to her apartment. No. She had not lost a key recently. She had asked him what he wanted and he had grabbed her. When she started to scream he had started to beat her and then when she wouldn't stop screaming he had started choking her. Before they left they asked that when she got out of the hospital she come down to the station and look at some pictures. They did not come back.

After the police left she had no visitors until the following afternoon. She was propped up in bed with her eyes closed when she sensed someone was standing next to her bed. She opened her one eye and tried to scream, but all that came out was a hissing sound. She reached for the call button, but he already had it. "It's all right. I'm not going to hurt you," the man said. She didn't know his name, but she had seen him at the Cottage a couple of times. She was sure George had sent him. "I'm not going to hurt you," he said again. "I just want to ask you some questions." He looked toward the door to the hallway and asked in a low voice, "Did George do this to you?"

She stared at him with her one open eye, frightened and confused. If George had sent him to kill her, he should know George had done it. "Look," he said, "we've been following George ever since he got back from his trip. We know he hired a private detective to find you and he visited you just three hours before you were brought in here. Now, what did he want?"

It was all very confusing. Why would George's own people be following him? Was it some kind of trick? Had George decided after he left she hadn't burned the files and was trying this way to find out what she had done with them? The man was waiting for an answer. He kept looking at the doorway and was growing impatient. She pointed to the bed table and he rolled it up from the foot of the bed to where she could reach it. She took the pencil and pad and wrote, "I can't talk." Pointed to her throat and then wrote, "Who are you?"

He turned his head to read what she had written and then said, "I'm Juan. I work for Mark Heathly. Mr. Heathly took over after Appy Costellos died. Now what did George want?"

She didn't know if was true or not. It could be. But it was certainly not the kind of story George would have one of his men tell. He would never tell anyone to say someone else was the boss. Juan was waiting. Staring at her demanding an answer.

"Appy's papers," she wrote.

"What papers?"

"Files"

"What were the files about?"

"People."

He looked toward the door again. "People in the organization?"

"Yes"

"Did you ever read those files?"

"No"

"Then how do you know they were about us?"

"Appy told me"

"Was there a file on me?"

"I don't know. I guess so."

"Where are those files now?"

She was terrified all over again. The last time she had told anyone she had burned them she had almost been killed. But she couldn't say she had hidden them someplace. If they couldn't find them, or she couldn't produce them later on she would be in trouble all over again. Her hand trembled as she wrote, "Appy told me to burn them" She wanted to write more, to explain Appy had told her to get them from the safe-deposit box and burn them, but she couldn't write all that because he asked, "Did you burn them?"

"Yes"

"Is that why George beat you up?"

"Yes"

"Do you know what George wanted to do with them?"

"No"

He stood for a moment looking at her, then reached across and ripped the top sheet off the pad. He crumpled the sheet of paper between both hands and then stuffed it in a pocket and left the room. She breathed a sigh of relief and even that caused pain.

CHAPTER THIRTY-TWO

Mark Heathly sat quietly doodling squares and rectangles on a pad of paper while Juan told him about his visit with Susanne. "Do you think she really burned them?" he asked.

"Yes, Sir. She was too scared not to tell the truth."

Heathly grunted an acknowledgment and sat there thinking, forgetting for the moment Juan was still standing there. *So the files were destroyed. But what was so important about them in the first place? There had to have been more in those files than what George could keep in his head. She had said they were about people in the organization. One thing was certain; George was not going to let things be. He had never really expected George would, but he had hoped maybe George would be satisfied with what he had. From any point of view there was only one thing to do.* "Call Maxwell," Heathly said, "and tell him to get over here. I want to see him right away."

"Yes, Sir," Juan said and left the room to use the phone.

Half an hour later Max stepped out of the private elevator and followed Juan through the living room to the roof terrace where Mark Heathly was sitting with his before dinner bourbon. "Maxwell is here, Sir," Juan said stating a fact of which Heathly was well aware.

"Max, do you know anything about some files George has?" Heathly asked without turning to look at him.

"Files? No, I don't know anything about any files."

Heathly took a sip of his drink, set the glass down, and looked out across the railing. "Junior is becoming a threat, Max. I want him taken care of. I want you to do it."

Max hesitated for just a moment. Heathly hadn't mentioned a specific name or said exactly what he wanted done, but Max knew what he meant. "Any time limit?" he asked.

"The sooner the better."

"Yes, sir," Max said and then waited for an instant to see if there was anything else Heathly wanted to say and then followed Juan back through the living room to the elevator.

Riding in his car toward Tony's, Max had no more qualms about killing George than he'd had about killing Jimmy Harris. He had worked with George for a long time, but now he had no choice. It was a simple matter of survival. Mark could have ordered any number of guys to do it, but had given the job to Max to test his loyalty. The only question was where to carry out his orders. George's beach Cottage would be ideal, but George would have to invite him there. The job didn't have to be done that day, but Mark might be impressed with his efficiency if the job were done the same day the order was given. He saw a public phone and pulled over to the curb. There was no answer at the Cottage, so he called George at the office and waited impatiently while the secretary informed Mr. Costellos Bill Maxie was on the phone. He knew George would be smart enough to know who Bill Maxie was. He heard the clicking as the call was transferred and then George's voice saying, "Hello, Bill, how are you?"

"Just fine, sir. As you suspected, there is considerable dissatisfaction with the present manage-ment and there are some other developments I think will interest you. I think it would be good if we could get together sometime soon to discuss them."

"Fine, I'll meet you in an hour."

Max thought he sounded excited and on a sudden inspiration said, "It may take me more than an hour. My car's having some repair work done on it and I'll have to catch a cab."

"Where are you?"

Max figured out quickly that it would take George longer to get to Max's apartment than it would for Max to get there. "I'm at a little bar not far from my place."

"I'll pick you up in front of your place in half an hour or so."

"I don't want to inconvenience you any."

"No inconvenience. It's right on the way. I have to come back tonight anyway. I can bring you back in."

"See you in half an hour, then," Max said and hung up the phone smiling. It had to be his lucky day. Things were working out even better than he had hoped. His car would not be anywhere in the vicinity of the Cottage for anyone to remember having seen it. There would be no cabby to report a fare to George's beach place. He got into his car and drove toward his apartment completely confident. He pulled into the service station where he usually traded and parked near a tire display. He walked into the office and said, "Hey, Marv, fill her up and give her a wash when you have time. The keys are in it."

"Sure, Mr. Maxwell, when will you want it?"

"I won't need it before noon tomorrow."

* * *

Chris didn't know why he was there exactly, except he'd had an overwhelming urge to see them again. In a way he had to confirm to himself that the people who had hi-jacked his boat and killed a man while he and Myra watched, really did exist. It seemed so impossible that sometimes it was as though it was just a bad dream, but he knew it had really happened. But there was still the fact that the *AHWANAH* was no longer in its slip. He wondered if it were possible that the *AHWANAH* might have blown up or the three of them been asphyxiated. He had to see them again. He wasn't going to do anything to them; he just had to see them, to see them moving, and walking freely in society, and know he had not killed them.

He drove by the Costellos house a couple of times and that night in his motel room phonebook he had found a "Maxwell, Wilfred C." He thought at some time he had heard Larry, or maybe George, address Max as "W.C." There were lots of Maxwells, but only one Wilfred C. Maxwell. He didn't know if it would be the Max who shot at Myra or not, but he had to check.

Maxwell's address was a large apartment building with an electronic cardkey required to open the heavy gate to the underground parking. The front door was heavy plate glass with an intercom to one side for those who did not have a key to the place. There was a security guard behind a desk just inside the glass doors. There was a wrought iron bench on each side of the walk just outside the glass doors. The trees, shrubs and lawn in front of the place were well maintained, but there were enough cars parked on the street that no one was going to think twice about his parking there. This was the third day of Chris sitting in his car outside that building hoping to see Max. Myra had not been pleased with his insistence of spying on George and Max, but he had nothing else to do and she was going through every entry on her disks making sure there was nothing there that could implicate her before she printed the information.

He was parked three car-lengths from the front door, but in the rear view mirror he could see cars going in and out of the garage. He sat with the windows down reading a wooden-boat building magazine. Very few people went in the front door. More cars went in and out of the garage than in and out of the front door. He thought he had seen Max go into the garage once, but he couldn't be sure it was him. He got out and walked past the front door to the end of the block a couple of times just to stretch his legs. He was just about to leave when he saw someone walking toward him from the corner. Even before he could make out his face he knew it was Max.

He watched Max enter the building and even as he was watching him wondered why he was there. Seeing Max again had not really answered any questions and he wondered why he had thought it was so important that he see him again. Yet for some reason he stayed there. He didn't know why. Ten minutes later he saw Max come out and sit in one of the wrought iron benches that flanked the walkway to the front door. A short time later a white Jaguar pulled up and Max got up from where he was sitting and went to stand at the curb even before the car came to a stop. Chris started the car and pulled out to follow them. At a stop light two intersections later he was able to pull alongside. Even through the tint of the Jaguar's windows he knew it was George behind the wheel. He was still staring at George when the light changed so he was slow in getting away from the light. Three blocks later he knew he had lost George in the traffic. He headed back to the motel, feeling melancholy more than anything else. He had seen them, but seeing them didn't make him feel any better.

* * *

George turned into the drive and pushed the button to open the garage door. He drove inside, the door closing behind them as he turned off the ignition. He removed his driving gloves, pulling off one finger at a time, and threw the gloves on the dash in front of the steering wheel. He led the way into the house, dropping the ring of keys in his right-hand coat pocket as he held the door for Max. "Do you want a drink?" George asked.

"A beer if you have it," Max said walking across the room and pushing aside the drapes a little to look out the full-length windows, across the redwood deck to the beach beyond. Far down the beach there were five boys throwing a football, but otherwise the beach was empty. He let the drapes fall back into place and went and sat down in one corner of the couch.

George came back in carrying a beer and a Coke. He set the beer in front of Max, took a sip of his Coke, and sat down in the high back chair. "I've been doing a lot of planning Max. What you told me driving over here this afternoon only confirms what I have to do. I'll have Heathly out of there and on a morgue slab within a month."

"If anyone can do it, you can, George," Max said standing up. "Excuse me a minute, George, I have to use the head." He walked into the foyer bathroom carefully pushing the door closed with the back of his hand. He took the gun out of the holster in the small of his back and the silencer from its pouch next to the holster. All during the ride they had been pressing into his back. He screwed the silencer onto the barrel and released the safety catch. He grabbed a hand towel from the rack and keeping the towel between his fingers and the lever flushed the toilet. He opened the door leaving the towel on the doorknob. Max walked through the foyer holding the gun a little behind him in his right hand. George was bent forward, placing a cigar wrapper in the ashtray, when Max stopped in front of him and raised the gun. George leaned back slowly, holding the cigar in mid-air, looking at him unbelievingly. "What is this, Max?"

"Mark's orders."

The look on George's face told Max that George could not believe Max, or Heathly, or anyone else would dare to oppose him. The first bullet slammed into his brain and killed him, but Max rapidly put two more into his chest. George hung there for just a moment, blood flooding the white front of his shirt, and then he toppled over to the right.

Max stood over him, unscrewing the silencer from the gun. He put the gun in his right hand coat pocket and the silencer in the left hand pocket. He walked over to the chair, grabbed the material of the jacket at the shoulder and pulled the body to lean on its left side so he could reach into the right-hand pocket for the keys. He went into the kitchen. With the knuckle of his index finger he switched off the light George had turned on when he went in to get the drinks. Passing the bathroom on his way out he grabbed the towel he had left hanging on the doorknob. With the towel protecting his hand he opened the door to the garage and the car door. He put on George's gloves and then walked around to the passenger side and wiped off the door and the handle.

The street was empty when he backed out of the drive and the garage door closed behind him. Driving along Highway One he regretted a little that there had not been any witnesses to testify to his efficiency. He wondered if George had a cleaning lady who came in regularly. When would she be at the Cottage next? It might be a week, even longer, before the body was found. Somebody had to confirm George was dead when he reported to Heathly. He wondered if the men assigned to tail George were behind him now. It would be hard for them to see it was not George driving the car. But the way George had been driving, cutting in and out of traffic, he had probably lost them. Somebody should be told. The newspapers.

He left the freeway and parked the car at a meter in Watts. He walked away from the car leaving the gloves on the dash and the key in the ignition. If the car was not stolen by the time the police got around to towing it away, at least parts would have been stolen and it would have been covered with a thousand fingerprints of curious children. Two blocks away he went into a convenience store with a public phone and dialed Mark Heathly's number. Juan answered the phone and a moment later Heathly was on. "Yes?"

"It's been taken care of, Mr. Heathly."

"Good. I appreciate the speed with which it was done," Heathly said and hung up. Max stood for a moment with the receiver still to his ear. He was disappointed. He didn't know why, except he wished there had been more of a reaction. Maybe Heathly didn't really believe him. He hadn't even asked where it had happened. He hung up the receiver and pulled out the tattered directory and looked up the number of the newspaper. He dialed the number of the morning paper and finally a bored voice came on and said, "News Desk. Lafferty."

"I'm calling to report a murder."

Lafferty sounded less bored. "A murder. One moment please."

"I haven't got a moment. Do you want to hear about it or not?"

"Yes. Yes. Please go on."

"I'm only going to say this once, so you'd better get it. The guy's name is George Costellos. That's C, O, S, T, E, L, L, O, S. He was killed about an hour ago with one slug to his brain and two more to his heart at his place at ten-twenty-two Coral Reef Road."

"May I have that address again, please, Sir?"

"Ten-twenty-two Coral Reef Road."

"Did you witness this killing?"

"I sure did. I'm the one who killed him," Max said and hung up the phone. He felt better. He didn't know if Lafferty believed him or not, but he would at least have to report it to the police. The story would be in tomorrow's paper. He wondered if the story would include the information about his phone call.

Two blocks from the phone booth he caught a cab and went to his apartment. He cleaned the gun and silencer and put them away. There was no way the police would be able to trace the slugs they found in George to him. He changed his clothes and walked to the service station where he had left his car. As he expected, it was locked up inside. He walked another block to a bar where he found a taxi and gave the cabby the address for Tony's bar. When Lou put his drink in front of him, Max said, "If anyone should ask, Lou, I've been here since five o'clock."

Lou nodded. "I'll pass it around," he said.

CHAPTER THIRTY-THREE

Myra collected the pages, turned off the printer and closed the laptop. For the first time in her life Myra felt a little lost and at loose ends. She was at loose ends in that she had done what she had come to LA to do. Oh, there were a few little things yet to get cleared up, like getting her clothes and personal things out of the apartment, and faxing the pages she had to the DEA. That's where Chris and she had decided they should go. But after that she had no plans. What was she going to do next? She was realistic enough to know it was a little late to try and pursue an acting career. At the same time she was not at all destitute. Over the years George had been generous in the money he gave. It had always been more than the thing she had said she wanted to buy. When he had bought himself the white Jaguar sedan, he had bought her a blue Jaguar convertible. It was not really the car she wanted, but then George had never consulted her about what she wanted, he had just given her things. The Jag, however, was not something she could return. He would have noticed right away if she had taken it back. The jewelry on the other hand was a different story. When he gave it to her and after she had raved over it and shown her deep appreciation for it he would always say something like, "If you don't really like it you can take it back and exchange it. Here's the receipt."

Once he had given it to her he never asked why she never wore it, or what she had done with it. Most of the things, the most expensive ones, anything over a thousand dollars she had returned. She had put the money, almost a hundred and fifty thousand dollars over the years, in CDs and savings accounts in banks all around LA. She had always thought she would start investing it, but savings accounts and CDs were as far as she had gone. But even invested the money it generated would not be enough to live on. The only reason she was thinking of it at all was because she didn't know what she was going to do next, and it was nice to know it was there to fall back on if she ever needed it.

She wondered what Chris was planning to do now that their reason for being in LA was coming to a close. To an extent she had dragged out the compiling of her information because once they had sent it off there was no reason for them to stay together. Sending the information from her diary had been his idea really. He had explained that if the government went after George, maybe they would be free of the fear that he was after them. She had gone along with the idea more because it would be something more for them to do together than she thought it would really stop George. She felt safe with Chris and now that the time to separate was getting close she was uncomfortable with the idea of being on her own.

She wondered if she was in love with him. She knew she trusted him more than she had ever trusted anyone. He had saved her life and maybe she was just feeling grateful. And yet, the idea of being separated from him was causing her real panic. She had been independent enough to leave home and live her own life, but now she didn't like the idea of him sliding out of her life. At the same time she realized they had never really known each other under normal circumstances. Situations had inextricably thrown them together. They'd been forced to get along with each other in order to survive. Nor did she have any idea how Chris might feel about her. He had never said anything about even so much as caring for her. He had taken care of her in a very real way, but he had never given any indication he cared for her, not romantically. Nurses in a hospital took care of patients, but that didn't mean they cared about them romantically. They'd had their passionate moments, but Myra knew that passion was not love. She heard the car pull in and looked through the edge of the drapes before opening the door. He smiled at her as he got out of the car. "Where were you all day?" she asked as he walked by her into her room with a couple of boating magazines in his hand.

"Walked around the Marina for a while then I was driving around different places, what a friend of mine used to call 'splorin round'."

"I finished the report, or whatever you want to call it. We can send it in any time."

"That's great. Let's celebrate. Go eat someplace a little nicer than this motel's coffee shop and then maybe go to a movie."

"Are you asking me out on a date?" she asked teasing.

"Well, we've been living together for so long I guess it's time we had a pre-arranged, pre-agreed to date."

She knew what he meant. There was no closer living together than being stuck on a boat with someone and they had been together, one way or another, for more than three months.

"I'd like that," she said. "Let's go down to Newport Beach. Lots of good restaurants there and they don't care if you're not too dressed up. They are used to boat people."

"Well, I'll just go get showered and shaved and be right with you," he said heading for the bathroom.

She took him to a little restaurant right on the docks surrounded on all sides by boats. It was known for exceptional chowders, four kinds of fresh baked bread, lobsters and clams. The ***Sea Kettle*** did not take reservations. From the parking lot they had to walk down a long dock with boats tied up on either side and then up a ramp to the small barge that had been converted to the restaurant. They stood in line for half an hour sipping their drinks before they were finally seated. All the tables were outside under an awning that stretched from the kitchen at one end of the barge to cover all of the tables.

She was excited as they sat down. "You know I heard about this place more than three years ago and never got to come here. Now on our first date you've fulfilled a little girl's lifelong dream."

He smiled. "You are neither a little girl, and you never heard of this place when you were a little girl. And I'm not the one to fulfill dreams." He paused and looked around. It had not come out the way he meant it. "It's nice. I like it," he said not knowing what else to say.

They shared the famous six-chowder sampler, split a large bucket of clams followed by a lobster tail each. She had a steamed lobster with Kiwi, lime and Macadamia nut sauce and he had grilled lobster with a black bean and pork sauce. It was when they were halfway through the bucket of clams that they found themselves talking without the shadow of George hanging over them. They didn't realize it had happened, but they were talking to each other wanting the other to know who and what they really were. They didn't talk about the past or their childhood as they had at the cabin, but about their secret dreams they knew might not come true.

They talked until they were two of the last four people there. There were no more sounds of pots and pans fulfilling their purposes from the kitchen. In the still water between the boats there was the reflection of dock lights and boat transoms. When they finally left, it was too late to go to a movie, nor did they want to share each other with the other people in the theater. They walked down the ramp and along the dock to the car with their arms around each other having arrived at the place where they were content just to be with each other with no need to talk.

They drove back slowly along the Coast Highway knowing when they got back to the motel the peace they had known for a short time would be pushed aside by the realities of who they were and why they were there. For a while they had been their real selves despite her wig and atrocious make-up.

* * *

It was while they were waiting to be seated for breakfast that Myra looked over at the newspaper rack next to the cash register stand and saw the headline: **LA. Businessman Murdered**. There was a picture next to the story. Because of the fold of the paper she could see only the top of the head and the eyes, but she knew it was George. The hostess came to seat them and Myra grabbed a paper and threw two dollars on the counter and followed behind Chris. The hostess tried to seat them at a table in the center and Myra said, "May we have that booth by the wall?"

Myra slid in motioning for Chris to sit next to her and the hostess smiled as she handed them the menus. Myra waited until the hostess was leaving and then opened the paper in front of them.

They read the story together silently. It included the part about an anonymous person calling the paper and telling where the body was and that he had killed George. The waitress came up once and asked if they were ready to order and both of them shook their heads. The only thing they said to each other was when Myra asked Chris if he was finished reading before she turned to the inside of the paper. It seemed impossible, and yet there it was in print. They were both shocked by what they read, and yet, as they read the disbelief and shock gradually gave way to relief.

She folded the paper when they were done reading and the waitress was right there ready to take their order. They ordered what they had ordered the day before and when the waitress was gone, Chris said. "I know who killed him."

"Who," she asked a puzzled frown showing through the heavy make-up.

"Max."

"What makes you think so?"

"Well, I did go to the marina yesterday like I said, but I also drove around seeing if I could find Max. I got names and addresses from the telephone book. Do you know what Max's middle name was?"

"Chesterfield, I think. I'm not real sure."

"Well I thought I had remembered George or Larry calling him W.C. one time. I drove by a lot of places and I finally found one apartment building where a Wilfred C. Maxwell lived. I waited around watching the place and I saw Max. And a little while later George came by in a white Jaguar and Max got in and went off with him."

The food arrived and they waited until the waitress had left. "What are we going to do now?"

"Well one of the first things you are going to do is get rid of that wig and take off the gross make-up.

"I'm serious, Chris. What are we going to do? Are we still going to send the papers to the DEA?"

"Well, it changes things a little, mostly because we are going to tell the police about seeing Max with George just before he died. Then we'll fax off the papers. That shouldn't take more than a couple of hours. Then what are you going to do?"

"Move out of the apartment I guess. I don't have a whole lot. I guess I'll put what I have in storage until I know where I'm going and what I'm going to do."

"I can help you with that," he said wanting any excuse at all not to have to leave her. "Then what?"

"I don't know," she said. "I was thinking this morning I should go back and see my folks. It's been fifteen years since I saw them. I was going to call them today. Might even go to church with them. Boy, I can just see the faces of some of the old biddies in church. I wasn't quite as mature when I left home as I am now, and I'll just bet the gossip will be I've had implants."

He smiled a little embarrassed. "That's funny. I was thinking that as long as I'm here on the mainland I should go and see my parents."

"You could take my car. It's not far from here to Seattle. You could do it in two days easy." She was talking quickly, excitedly. "I'd rather have you driving it and taking care of it than leave it parked at the airport or in some lot while I'm gone. You could take me to the airport and pick me up when I got back." She paused then and said more slowly, "Unless of course you had other plans. I don't want to impose on you in any way."

"No! No! Sounds great," he said excited at the thought that maybe she didn't want their association to end any more than he did. "How long were you expecting to be with your folks?"

"Maybe three of four days. I love them, but I don't think I could take the town for more than a few days."

"That will work out," he said. "I'll drive up, spend a couple days with my folks and be back in time to meet your plane when you get back." She smiled at him and he reached over and picked up the check, "Well, we'd better get started."

They went to her room to get the papers. She excused herself and went to the bathroom and when she came out she was without the wig and with a minimum of make-up. He smiled at her. "Lordy, but you are beautiful. I mean without the wig and all that junk on your face. I mean—What I mean is that you look more like you. You got the papers?"

She smiled at him and went to the little motel room desk and took a folder of papers from the center drawer. "Since the maids are going to be in while we're gone it might be a good idea to take the laptop and the printer with us."

They went to a shopping center where they could find a phone. It was too early for the center to be crowded and there was only one other person at the bank of five phones. He held the receiver with his handkerchief in case they traced the call and came to check for fingerprints. She stood next to him ready to keep anyone away who might overhear what he was saying. He dialed the number and then took a deep breath to calm himself. When the phone was answered he took another deep breath and said, "I'd like to talk to anyone who is working on the Costellos murder. I know who did it."

"May I have your name please?"

"No, I won't give you my name and I'm not going to stay on the phone very long. So if you want to hear what I have to say you'd better listen now."

"One moment please," and almost immediately another voice came on and said, "This is homicide detective Ross. I understand you have some information that might help in the Costellos investigation."

"Yesterday, about four-thirty or so, I saw Wilfred Maxwell get in George Costellos' car. That was in front of 1780 La Fond. Maxwell lives there. Apartment number 1402..."

"Do you know what kind of car it was?"

"Yes. White Jaguar. I don't know the year. Personal license plates. G something, L. I think the letter in the middle is either an O or a D. I know for a fact Maxwell had a gun. He probably got rid of it by now. I'm hanging up here now. Do you have a direct line? I'll call you back in a few minutes from somewhere else."

Chris wrote down the number Ross gave him and then the two of them left the shopping center and drove to another one. It was twenty minutes later Chris called back. "Ross here."

"Now, the security guard at the apartment building ought to confirm Max got into the car. I got a good look at them and it was George Costellos and Will Maxwell. I know them both very well."

"Why won't you tell us your name? We may have more questions we want to ask you."

"What is you your FAX number there? I have a bunch of information I want to send you. When you see that you'll know why I won't give you my name. I don't want to end up like Costellos. What's the fax number?"

Chris wrote it down and then said. "I trust you will share what I send you with the DEA. That's where I was planning to send it until I saw this morning's paper. Good-bye." he hung up the receiver and said, "Come on, let's get out of here."

"What's the hurry?"

"From all you've told me about computers they may know where we were calling from the moment we connected and have a squad car on its way here right now."

In a strip mall they found a copy & printing shop that also had fax service. They paid out their dollar per sheet and then had the clerk put the originals through the shredder. They walked out and Chris said, "Well, here it is not yet ten thirty and we've put the lid on a can of bad guys. I guess the next thing to do is find you a storage place."

* * *

They sat in the coffee shop of the motel. At ten at night there were not many customers. They were both tired. It had taken longer to pack her things and put them in storage than they had expected. Along with everything they'd had time to get her airline ticket for a flight the next day. "What are you going to do after you get back from visiting your folks?" Myra asked.

"I don't know exactly. I don't know how to do anything except sail and build boats. But I hear-tell Newport Beach, and down that way, produces more small boats than any other place in the country so maybe I can get a job and with the money I got from George and what I make working on other peoples' boats build another boat of my own. What are you going to do?"

"I don't know."

"You'll have no trouble with a college education and all. Maybe you can even get back into acting."

"Maybe. I don't know."

They were silent for a while, both of them thinking that for the first time in three months they were going to be separated from each other. "You know Myra, this has been an interesting few months. I'll bet there are married couples who don't know each other as well as we know each other. You know, you get to know a person real well when you spend a long time with them crowded together on a small boat. It's real easy to get on each other's nerves when you're stuck with somebody for a period of time. No way to get away from them. The furthest you can get away is to go up to the bowsprit. But you know, you and I got along real well."

"Yes, we did."

"You know there are some women who say they wouldn't let anyone see them without make-up. Well I've sure seen you without yours. I know you snore when you sleep on your right side."

"I do not!"

"How would you know? You're not awake to hear yourself." She reached across and slapped him playfully. "But like I said. I think we know each other pretty good. And I want you to know I like you a whole lot. I think I'm in love with you. I know I have never felt like this about anyone else. I know this isn't a very romantic place to say those kind of things," he said waving his hand to indicate the coffee shop, "but I just wanted say that before we went our separate ways." She started to say something, but he waved his hand to stop her and said. "Now when you go off to Minnesota and I go off to Seattle we're going to have time to think without the other one around. I don't really have anything to offer you. I'm not educated and I don't have much money, or a promise of a great future, but I'm just warning you right now, that when you get back, I'm going to ask you to marry me."

She looked at him and smiled a little. "Well, I'll tell you something, Chris, my education hasn't done me all that much good. But I do have a little money, and if when you come back from Seattle and you ask me to marry you, I'm going to say 'Yes.' If you don't ask me to marry you I'm going to ask you to build me a boat. After you get it built I'm going to ask you to skipper it for me. I'm not letting you get away from me."

www.ingramcontent.com/pod-product-compliance
Lightning Source LLC
Chambersburg PA
CBHW060433180626
46817CB00007B/2787
9781630663766